The Blue House Raid

Robert Perron

Published by And Then Press, 2025.

This is a work of fiction.

THE BLUE HOUSE RAID

Second edition. January 21, 2025.
First edition published in 2020 by The Ardent Writer Press.
Copyright © 2019 by Robert Perron.
Second edition © 2025 by Robert Perron.
ISBN: 979-8991833837
Written by Robert Perron.

To Irene

Acknowledgments

In Korea, I am indebted for research and reviews to Roger Shepherd of Hike Korea (hikekorea.com); Kang Euigoo, translator and guide; Woo Seongjae, who survived an engagement with the Blue House raiding party in January 1968; Song Dalyong, former longtime mayor of Paju; Cha Jeongman, former head of the Beobwon-eup county office; Shin Jong-soon of Jangpa-ri; Hong Seonghee of Nullo-ri; Jung Woonchun of Jangpa-ri; and Lee Jinyong of Gumpa-ri.

In New York City, I am indebted for guidance and encouragement to the author Lore Segal and my fellow writers at her Thursday evening workshops: Laura Bass, Ken Sandbank, Dorotea Mendoza, Robert Macdonald, George Bear, Judith Lichtendorf, Elizabeth Denlinger, Martin Hason, Jean Halley, and Marjorie Tesser. I am equally indebted to the author Robert Roth, publisher of *And Then* literary journal, and the poet Michael Graves, coordinator of the Phoenix Reading Series.

For instruction and reviews, I would like to thank Gotham Writers Workshop and the following instructors: Elizabeth Tippens, Hasanthika Sirisena, Arlaina Tibensky, Kate Angus, David Yoo, Thais Miller, and Susan Breen.

Many thanks to Doyle Duke and Steve Gierhart of The Ardent Writer Press for their superb editing and production of the first edition of this book. Prior to that, many thanks to Matthew Sharpe for developmental editing and Richard Kutner for proofreading. And many thanks to my sister Suzanne Peterson for a final proofread.

Foreword

The Korean War ended in 1953 with an armistice that separated North and South Korea along a four-kilometer buffer called the DMZ (demilitarized zone). The US army took responsibility for defense of the westernmost sector of the DMZ, approximately 40 kilometers; the ROK (Republic of Korea) army defended the remainder of the 250-kilometer barrier. The US sector, although short by comparison, lay only 55 kilometers north of the center of Seoul, blocking the traditional route for an invading army. In addition, this sector included Panmunjom and the JSA (joint security area).

Following the signing of the armistice, Korea remained calm for a dozen years. But as the US bogged down in Vietnam in the mid-1960s, the DMZ saw a major uptick in shooting incidents. These low-level clashes between North Korean, South Korean, and US forces became known as the Korean DMZ Conflict.

The two most egregious incidents of this conflict, the Blue House raid and the Pueblo incident, occurred in January 1968—coinciding with the Tet offensive in Vietnam. The Blue House raid (called the January 21 incident in South Korea) was a commando attack aimed at the presidential palace in Seoul. It was arguably the more serious incident—imagine an attack on the White House, but for Americans it was overshadowed by the capture of the USS Pueblo and its crew, as well as by the war in Vietnam.

Today, farmers work north of Seoul, just below the DMZ, in what used to be called Indian Country and was restricted to the US 2nd Infantry Division. The US troops have pulled back, ceding that real estate to the ROK army. To the northwest of the now-deserted Camp Wally, a company-size compound that had two hooches blown up by a North Korean attack in 1967, a small park contains statues of the Blue House raiding party infiltrating through the DMZ. Other sites commemorate where the commandos crossed the

Imjin River, captured South Korean civilians, and battled ROK forces. The raiders have become the stuff of legend.

Most of the combat around the Blue House raid involved Korean forces. However, one US unit, 1st Battalion, 23rd Infantry (2nd Infantry Division), found itself enmeshed in the aftermath of the raid.

This novel, while centered on the Blue House raid, encompasses the whole of the US soldier's experience during the time of the DMZ conflict with glimpses into the lives of the South Korean population and the conduct of the North Korean commandos. Place names, unit names, and historical events are real. However, the story and characters are fictional. In particular, there is no one-to-one correspondence between a character in the story and a real person, except for several well known historical characters.

Prologue: January 1967, Unit 124 Training Camp

Pak Jun-seok had stood at attention for an hour, bidding his body not to shake. A senior lieutenant, a few years older, mid-thirties, stood nearby in silence, ignoring the cold, a rucksack at his feet. The mid-winter air had seeped through every thread of wool in Jun-seok's uniform and clenched every millimeter of his skin. He wore neither mittens nor gloves and dared not pull his hands into his sleeves.

The cold has done its damage, Jun-seok thought. It can do no more. I accept it.

The two lieutenants were on a small parade ground in front of a barracks of cement blocks. Its front door swung open, and a broad-shouldered officer, a captain, approached. He held a brown hardwood spindle in his right hand, tapping it against the open palm of his left. He circled Jun-seok twice, looking him up and down.

"So you're an officer now? A brand new lieutenant, eh?"

"Comrade Captain," said Jun-seok.

"Shut up," said the captain. Jun-seok pulled in his chin and stared forward.

"For the next few months," said the captain, "you're not a big-shot lieutenant. You're scum. If you survive, then you can consider your exalted status."

"Comrade Captain."

"I told you to shut up." The captain's right hand rose. "Can't you obey a simple order?" The captain's bludgeon slammed the side of Jun-seok's face. Stars shattered his vision, and his knees wobbled.

"Do you have anything more to say?"

Jun-seok tightened his lips.

The captain smiled. "You're a fast learner, Comrade Scum. But you look cold." He turned to the other officer. "Comrade Chong, maybe you can help warm him up."

"With pleasure, Comrade Captain." Chong lifted the rucksack resting at his feet and held it out.

"Put it on," Chong said.

Jun-seok grasped the rucksack with two hands and tilted forward from its weight, at least thirty kilograms. He recovered his balance and put one arm through a shoulder strap, then the other.

"On the double," said Chong.

Jun-seok lifted his left knee and advanced his frozen left foot, then his right knee and foot, bouncing into a standard double-time pace.

"Faster," shouted Chong. "Move your ass, Comrade Scum. Do you think this is a joke?"

Chong came along Jun-seok's right ear. "Do you think this is a joke?"

Jun-seok knew enough not to reply. Chong continued the harangue. "Why are you dragging your ass? Why did you come here? Wasting our time."

The camp buildings of gray block disappeared as Jun-seok turned uphill on a narrow path. His legs ached. His lungs ached. His shoulders throbbed where the pack straps dug in.

Minutes felt like hours. The path turned right and the pitch of the uphill lessened. From behind, Chong said, "Slow down. Are you trying to kill us?" His voice sounded good-natured. Thinking it a ploy, Jun-seok maintained his pace.

"Slow down. That's an order. Okay, that's it. Now slow down some more."

For another five minutes, Jun-seok loped at less than a double-time pace.

"Halt," said Chong. Jun-seok stopped in the position of attention, the rucksack almost pulling him over backwards.

Chong advanced to his front. "How do you feel?"

Jun-seok considered his response as he gathered his wind. "My pain is nothing compared to what the Great Leader has endured for us, Comrade Lieutenant."

Chong threw back his head and laughed.

Jun-seok kept his eyes front and lips pursed. Irreverence unnerved him. Was this a test?

With the back of his right mitten, Chong wiped snot from his nose and tears from his eyes. "You're going to like Unit 124," he said. "Here, let's take a break, and I'll explain a few things. Drop that rucksack."

Jun-seok looked around. Nothing but Chong, ground, rocks, and scrub trees. In Chong, Jun-seok saw an oblong face and lean torso, not starving lean, but muscle lean.

Chong lowered himself to a squat and motioned. Jun-seok removed the rucksack, placed it on the ground, and squatted, facing Chong. Chong pulled off a mitten and from under his jacket, extracted a cigarette and lit it. He passed it to Jun-seok.

"My name is Chong Myung-seung. I went through this same shit a while ago. I got mine directly from Captain Ho."

Jun-seok blew smoke and returned the cigarette.

"One reason you'll like it here," said Chong, "is we eat well. White rice with every meal. Meat every day. Sweets. You know why?"

Jun-seok shook his head.

"Because our comrade commanders love us." Chong again threw back his head and laughed. "Comrade Pak—Jun-seok—do I have to order you to laugh at my jokes?"

Jun-seok forced a smile.

"It's because we're their best," said Chong. "That's why they feed us. They want us tough. And they can't toughen us up just with beatings and running. We need food."

Jun-seok nodded.

"What's your *songbun*, wavering?"

Jun-seok nodded again. Forty percent of the population of the Democratic People's Republic of Korea belonged to the central, wavering class. Thirty percent to the top, core class, and thirty to the bottom, hostile class. Jun-seok's family stood in the upper third of the wavering class, but wavering nevertheless.

"I thought so," said Chong. "Me too. And here we are, with commissions, and members of an elite unit. It's worth a few beatings and running with rocks on your back, don't you think?"

"I agree, Comrade," Jun-seok said with hesitation.

"What is it?" said Chong. "If you have a question, ask it. That's what I'm here for."

"Why don't they take all their candidates from the core class? Why do they let us wavering in?"

"That's easy to answer. Because of the beatings and running with rocks. If you were core, where would you want to be, in Pyongyang or out here?"

At the mention of Pyongyang, Jun-seok thought, I would like to visit the capital city once before I die. And Chong's answer didn't quite satisfy him. Wouldn't the core class want to serve at the highest level no matter the sacrifice?

"The captains are from the core class," said Chong raising his eyes as if in deference, or defiance—Jun-seok couldn't tell which. "Captain Ho, he's core, but he's okay once you get by the initiation. Now I want to tell you something. I could run you until you dropped dead. I could keep you going like we started out. You know why I don't?"

Jun-seok remained silent.

"Because I see you're a good fit for this unit. You're strong. You're dedicated. You're a bit too serious—we'll work on that."

Chong extinguished the flame of the cigarette between thumb and forefinger and pushed the remains into his coat pocket.

"Don't get me wrong. I'm not going easy on you. But I'm not in the habit of killing off good candidates. Also, you're from my neighborhood. You're sixty kilometers up from Koksan-up, right?"

"Right, Comrade."

"So I'm forty kilometers up. We have a cannery and some other factories."

Jun-seok knew the area from passing through.

"Not much where you are," said Chong. "Farms, no?"

Jun-seok nodded. "All farms."

"Okay, Comrade Pak, enough chitchat. Get that rucksack on your shoulders."

A half hour later, the block buildings of the camp came into sight. "Pick up the pace," said Chong. "We must look good coming in."

Jun-seok ran until ordered to stop in front of the barracks. As the front door opened, Chong stepped next to Jun-seok and stood at attention. Ho approached and said to Chong, "What do you think?"

"Comrade Captain," said Chong, "he's lazy and weak, but it can be kicked out of him."

Ho looked at Jun-seok. "What do you have to add?"

Jun-seok stood mute.

"Did I say shut up?" Ho raised his bludgeon. "Did you hear me say shut up? I want an answer, Comrade Scum."

"Comrade Captain," said Jun-seok, "I'm not worthy but will strive every moment to become so."

Ho lowered the bludgeon and tapped it against his left palm. A peripheral glance revealed Chong at attention, not smiling, not a trace of sarcasm. He'd said the captain was okay—but still, one never knew. Words had to be weighed and uttered with care, not with the openness Chong had displayed earlier. Nevertheless, Jun-seok felt relieved. For all the running with rocks and the bludgeoning, this was no worse than grammar school self-criticism.

Chapter One: December 1966, Kimpo Air Base

L orne Boyle arrived in Korea with thirteen months remaining on a three-year enlistment. He'd done two months' basic at Fort Polk, two months' advanced infantry at Fort Benning, and a further nineteen months at Benning as an instructor on the machine gun range. He'd advanced to the rank of Specialist E-4, jumping his base pay to $177.90 per month before deductions.

Fort Benning had suited Lorne. Friday nights he left base and crossed the Chattahoochee River from Columbus, Georgia, to Phenix City, Alabama. Two hours later, his ten-year-old Ford Fairlane trailed dust into the yard of his parents' two-cow farm.

Two cows and thousands of chickens. Everyone thought Pop had gone crazy building a half-acre chicken coop and hauling in day-old chicks. But money rained where before there'd been none. Lorne went over the books with Pop—cost of chicks, cost of feed, selling price of broilers, selling price of chicken shit—the old man was a long way from crazy. Maybe chicken farming made sense even if his partner was a man who used to beat his backside with a piece of cordwood yelling, "Keep smiling, will you? You won't be smiling when I'm done with you."

But at this juncture, Lorraine was the primary incentive for Lorne's home visits. They'd been dating off and on since junior year. He loved the sound of their names together, Lorraine and Lorne, Lorne and Lorraine, and wanted to get inside her pants.

On the weekend after Lorne received orders for Korea, he proposed marriage to Lorraine. They were sitting in the Fairlane, backed into a meadow, eleven at night, putting themselves together. Lorraine had let Lorne undo her bra and suck her tits. She'd unzipped his jeans, wrapped her hand around his cock, and whisked until semen filled his shorts. But Lorne wanted more, wanted proper intercourse in a proper bed before shipping out.

"Lorne, honey," said Lorraine, "that don't make no sense, getting married and splitting up for a year. And what kind of wedding would it be all rushed?"

Lorraine finished buttoning her blouse. She twisted her body to look at Lorne straight on. "I think we should take a hiatus. It's a long time."

"A hiatus?" said Lorne.

"When you come back, let's see where we are."

Lorne had a momentary, not quite subliminal, urge to strangle his once-love, but the urge passed and calmness enveloped him. Lorne extended his smile so it pushed his cheeks out.

"I'm looking to find a job in Montgomery," Lorraine said. "Finding an apartment there."

"Montgomery?" said Lorne.

• • • •

TWO WEEKS LATER, LORNE took a commercial flight to Washington state. On a military transport, he flew to Korea. By the time he finished in-processing at Kimpo Air Base and bused north, Lorraine had faded. The chickens had faded. The world had faded.

From Camp Howze, Headquarters, 2nd Infantry Division, Lorne trucked to Camp Walley in the DMZ. He was the only passenger among cartons of C-rations, having been picked up on a supply run. His ton-and-a-quarter bypassed the road to Nullo-ri, turned left at the Half Moon Club in Changpa-ri, and crossed the Imjin River on Libby Bridge. He trucked in daylight, leaving Camp Howze at noon and entering what the 2nd Division soldiers called "Indian country" at fifteen hundred hours.

The truck passed machine gun emplacements and bunkers, turned right, dropped and rattled across a narrow wooden bridge, rose, and turned left. A few minutes later, the truck stopped and the motor quit. Lorne grabbed his duffel, hopped over the tailgate, and looked around at two to three acres of winter-brown dirt with a smattering of Quonset huts and two cinder block buildings. He tossed a borrowed parka into the back of the truck and stood shivering in his dress greens.

A tall colored E-4, same rank as Lorne, appeared alongside, stamping his feet. "Let's go in the supply room, Boss."

Boss, because I'm white? Or maybe he's just in a good mood.

From the other side of the supply counter, the tall soldier pushed across wool fatigues, parka, Mickey Mouse boots, trooper hat, helmet, flak vest, web gear, mess kit, canteen, and sleeping bag. He walked to the arms rack and returned with an M14 rifle. Lorne hefted the rifle and looked at its side, the first time he'd seen an M14 with the semi-to-auto switch in place. "We fire these full automatic?"

"Up to you, Boss. I don't."

"Why's that?"

The soldier shook his arms in front of him as if he were holding an out-of-control hose. "Jumps all over the place. Most of your fire goes in the air." He dropped his arms. "But it's your call."

The soldier placed five magazines of ammunition and four hand grenades on the counter. He lifted one of the magazines in his fingers. "Four of these go in your ammo pouches." As Lorne stuffed his two pouches, the soldier said, "And the fifth, lock it in your rifle."

Lorne looked up from his ammo pouches. "Right now?"

"Lock and load, but keep the safety on."

Lorne's mentor picked up a hand grenade. "Don't fuck around with these. Don't mess with the pins. Okay, Boss?"

Lorne nodded. He wasn't fond of live grenades.

"Best to secure them and leave them there. Do you know how to do that?"

The soldier picked up Lorne's web gear and pointed to four, small, egg-like holders on the belt. He showed Lorne how to push the grenade down so the handle slid into a narrow sleeve, then how to thread a short strap through the pin and snap it so the pin couldn't be pulled.

The soldier pointed toward the door. "I'll show you your bunk. You won't need it for three days, but you'll want to change and stow your shit. Maybe grab a shower."

"Why don't I need it for three days?"

"Because you're on." The soldier looked down at a clipboard. "You got barrier duty next three days."

As they stepped outside, Lorne said, "Not a big compound."

"Holds one company, Company A. We have the distinct honor of being the northernmost US camp in all of Korea."

"This stuff," said Lorne. "How much of it should I put on?"

"All of it."

"I mean, I suppose I should wear the parka instead of my field jacket."

"Put it all on, Boss, unless you want to wake up froze dead. Except the Mickey Mouse boots. Carry them out there."

"Mickey Mouse?"

"Because that's what they look like? Keep your feet warm but can't be walking in them. Get blisters."

An hour later, Lorne, bulked up, rode shotgun in a jeep with the soldier from supply driving. Both soldiers had thrown flak jackets over their parkas, jammed helmets on their hoods, and had loaded rifles by their sides. They turned left out of Camp Walley and drove to a checkpoint with a sign: ALL PERSONNEL MUST BE ARMED BEYOND THIS POINT. A guard in Mickey Mouse boots and parka waved them through.

As the jeep bounced north, the soldier from supply said, "Twelve and a wake-up."

"How's that?" said Lorne.

"I'm short, Boss. Ask me how short I am."

"How short are you?"

"I'm so short I'm surprised I can see over the dashboard." He laughed.

"What's the wake-up business?"

"Got thirteen days left before I go back to the world. But the thirteenth don't count, Boss, 'cause I'm out of here. So it's twelve and a wake-up."

The jeep came up against an east-west road that formed a T, and made a U-turn.

"Skyline Drive," said Lorne's companion. "Everybody out."

Two minutes later, Lorne looked into the dust of the departing jeep, then west at a hazy sun setting where Skyline Drive narrowed into the horizon. On the north side of the road snaked a line of trenches interspersed with sandbag bunkers, everything frozen in place. Four meters north of the trenches stood a fence of spiked stakes, like Fort Apache from the Wild West. *Camp Walley doesn't look so bad after all.*

A soldier stood in the trench next to the nearest bunker. Lorne walked over. The hood of the soldier's parka enclosed his face except for eyes, nose, and a cigarette hanging from his lips. Lorne couldn't tell his rank.

Lorne said, "New man."

"Welcome to the barrier." The soldier removed his right hand from its mitten, the cigarette from his mouth, and exhaled. He replaced the cigarette and the glove. "Where you from?"

"Alabama."

The soldier laughed. From inside the bunker, Lorne heard two more laughs.

The soldier pulled off the mitten again, this time squelching the cigarette flame with his fingers. "Here's the deal, Alabama. They want us to do two on, two off, all night, two men out all the time."

He dropped the butt in his pocket and put his hand back in the mitten. "But it's too cold for that shit. It's stupid anyhow. So the deal is, one on, three off. Are you okay with that?"

Lorne stamped his feet. "Sure."

"But if anyone asks, it's two on, two off."

"Sure."

The soldier motioned toward the bunker with his hood. "You can crap out. You're on in three hours."

"What do we do?" said Lorne.

"It's just like guard duty. Stand here with your rifle."

"What do I do if I see something?"

"Well, what the fuck do you think you do?" The soldier patted a mitten on Lorne's shoulder. "Don't worry. Nothing ever happens."

• • • •

THREE DAYS LATER, LORNE'S team pulled back to Camp Walley, and that night Lorne trucked across Libby Bridge into Changpa-ri for his first liberty. In a crowd of soldiers, he walked up the road from the bridge straight into the Half Moon Club. He ordered an OB beer and watched the action, his back to the bar, his elbows resting on top. A miniskirt—one of a dozen—asked him to dance. Lorne felt his pecker stir, but he wanted to maintain control. He wanted to get the lay of the land.

"Not right off, honeybunch." Lorne's smile never changed.

The other problem was paying for sex. Lorne was no prude but saw fornication as something garnered through dating and emotional attachment. Saw the act of sex rolled in with romance, preceded by kisses, touches, protests, and surrender. *But* back home, he wondered, wasn't paying for a movie and dinner the same thing as buying sex? He mulled it over. No, it just wasn't the same as cash on the barrelhead.

Another miniskirt walked over. She stood in front of Lorne, hair with blond highlights, and round, western eyes. She mimicked Lorne's wide smile. "Whah a matter, GI?" She raised her right hand and gave it a limp shake. "No like a girl?" Lorne judged her to be older, about thirty, nearing the end of her career, edged out by the younger flesh.

"What's your name?" said Lorne.

"Sybil. You rike?"

"Can I buy you a beer, Sybil?"

"Rike real drink. Rike highball."

Lorne turned and ordered. The bartender poured straight ginger ale into a glass and pushed it to Sybil. Lorne noticed Sybil's eyes on his wallet as he extracted a piece of US military scrip.

"So, Sybil, what's a nice girl like you doing in a place like this?"

"Whah you say?"

"I say, do you like it here?"

"*Yeogi?*" said Sybil, pointing where they stood. Lorne had just learned a Korean word, *yeogi*, meaning here. In the coming weeks, he'd learn that *ubsumnida* meant not here anymore. That *cheogi* meant over there, and *cheogi* with a guttural sound meant way the fuck over there.

"Yeah," said Sybil. "This number one club."

Lorne watched the action, girls grinding against GI crotches, heading out back, leaving the remainder of their dances on the floor. The second OB had loosened him up. Sybil moved away, circling the room, a step behind her younger competition. She sat in a chair against the wall with her mouth halfway between a pout and a cry. Lorne decided they had an emotional attachment, he and Sybil. Plus, he'd bought her a drink. He walked over, extended a hand, and said, "May I have the honor of this dance?"

Sybil stood, stepped into Lorne, and jammed her crotch against his. Lorne said, "Cool your jets, honeybunch."

"Say whah?"

Lorne forced an inch of separation as they two-stepped.

"No wanna go hooch?"

"Don't worry, Sybil. First dance, then hooch."

"Three dollah can do."

"Four dollar," said Boyle, "but first we finish our dance. Okay?"

"Okay, you hot stuff."

• • • •

HOURS LATER, LORNE was back at Camp Walley. Next morning, he boarded the back of a ton-and-a-quarter with a dozen other soldiers. "Where we going?" he said.

The soldier next to him, black-rimmed glasses inside the hood of his parka, said, "Outpost Seiler. You're the new guy? Specialist Boyle?"

Lorne nodded.

"Specialist Rothman," said the other soldier.

Lorne thought of making a joke about their first names being the same but decided Rothman was too dense to get the joke. Instead, Lorne fished under his jacket for a cigarette. He offered one to Rothman, who shook his head. "Don't smoke."

At Skyline Drive, the truck turned left. After a few hundred meters, it turned right and sat idling while a barrier soldier dragged back a gate in the wooden fence. The ton-and-a-quarter nudged through the gate and wound along a narrow dirt road for two kilometers, stopping at the base of a hill ensconced by barbed wire and topped by sandbags. The soldiers piled out and climbed a path to entrenchments and sandbagged bunkers at the top of the hill. They passed other soldiers, the old crew, coming down.

Lorne walked to the northernmost section of the trench line and looked down on a worn path with concrete posts every hundred meters. Rothman came alongside and said, "That's the MDL."

"What's MDL mean?"

"Military demarcation line. The border between North and South Korea. That's what those markers say, in Korean and English."

Lorne lifted his gaze. Three hundred meters north of the MDL stood a North Korean outpost on another hilltop. The North Koreans wore padded jackets and carried submachine guns. They didn't seem to mind the cold. They looked older and meaner than the soldiers surrounding Lorne.

Lorne squinted. Two North Koreans were throwing hatchets at a wooden post. Their right hand wound back alongside the ear, sprang forward, and released the weapon. A second later came the thunk of the hit. They were pretty good.

Rothman nudged Lorne's kidney. "We gotta go to the command bunker. The lieutenant wants to chew on us."

As Lorne turned, he saw an unfamiliar weapon lying on top of the sandbags to his right. "What's that?"

"That," said Rothman, "is an M1 Garand with a sniper scope. If you know what you're doing, you can knock down Joe at eight hundred meters."

"Joe?"

"Short for Joe Chink, a pejorative I don't use. And it doesn't make sense, since they're Korean, not Chinese. But everyone calls them Joe."

"We can shoot at them?"

"If they come over. They're fair game on our side."

The command bunker was warm. Sandbag sides, sandbag roof, a small diesel-burning stove. Twelve soldiers squeezed in and sat on the floor, loosening parkas and lighting cigarettes. The lieutenant looked twenty-four or twenty-five, a couple years older than Lorne.

He deployed his barking voice. "Here's the scoop, men. You got two hours on, two off, day and night, night and day. Understood?"

The floor of the bunker emitted head nods and yessirs.

"When you're off, you can do whatever the fuck you want. But when you're on, you're the fuck on. Understood?"

The lieutenant recounted the latest incident. An American patrol, next sector over, to the west, walked into an ambush in daylight. One dead, three wounded. The soldiers already knew, the scuttlebutt having traveled up the barrier the day before. The soldiers looked around or at the floor, flicking ashes, waiting for the lieutenant to finish his stay-alert lecture.

"No fucking off when you're fucking on," said the lieutenant.

Yessir. Yessir. Head nod. Head nod.

• • • •

LIKE THE BARRIER, THE outpost consumed three days and three nights. Day four saw another evening in Changpa-ri. Lorne wandered down the main street to the Lucky Club. He meandered inside, sipped his OB, and looked around for emotional attachment. No problem there as long as he had scrip in his pocket.

The next day, Lorne walked through a narrow foot gate in the barrier fence with nineteen other soldiers. The men carried nine C-rations each. Rothman had shown Lorne how to stow nine meals by first discarding boxes and nonessentials, then dropping the cans into two socks, tying the socks together at the open ends, and draping the tied socks around the neck like a bandolier.

"Where we going?" Lorne had asked.

"On patrol. That's the routine. Three days on barrier, day off, three days on Seiler, day off, three days on patrol, day off, repeat."

The soldiers also carried sleeping bags by tying them to their web gear or draping them over their shoulders. Four men carried PRC-25s, pronounced prick twenty-five, radios strapped to their backs, long antennae sweeping above them. A hundred meters in, the patrol split into four five-man teams, each with a radio. Lorne's team advanced north a few hundred additional meters onto a south-facing slope. The men dropped their sleeping bags and C-rations. Then they dropped their bodies and sat around smoking and talking. Around eleven, P-38 can openers appeared, and lunch commenced.

Early afternoon, Lorne awoke from a nap to the sound of the team leader's voice. He stood and stretched. The rest of the team did the same. They picked up radio and rifles and moved north single file, leaving their bags but carrying the C rations draped under their parkas so they wouldn't freeze. They crossed a brook capped with ice but still flowing. Their surroundings were thin stands of hardwood, bare for the winter, and occasional clumps of evergreen. Lorne couldn't tell if they were following a trail—there seemed to be worn tracks everywhere.

The team stopped at the sound of breaking twigs and rustling brush to their front. The soldier ahead of Lorne put his rifle to his shoulder, but the team leader turned and knocked it down. "Don't be an ass, Hendrick."

Ahead, no more than a hundred meters, two deer bounded left to right. Smaller than deer back in the world, three-quarter size, like a Disneyland version. "Pop, pop," said Hendrick, "I could've got 'em both."

"That's just what we fucking need," said the team leader. He smiled at Lorne. "Then we'd have to explain why shots were fired."

Lorne didn't know what to make of Hendrick, even against a prevailing backdrop of combat nonchalance. He reminded Lorne of a few drunks he'd seen around town back in the world. Also, one kid in high school who laughed at the wrong times and got pissed at the least provocation. Lorne made a note to avoid walking in front of him, and glanced at Hendrick's trigger guard. Well, that's something, at least he has enough brains to keep his safety on.

A while later, the team crossed trampled, rusted barbed wire with triangular metal signs indicating a minefield. Lorne didn't know the last name or rank of his team leader. Everybody called him Hank. "Hey, Hank," said Lorne. "Are we walking in a minefield?"

"They're old, left over from the war. Never heard of one going off."

"Technically—" said Rothman.

"Technically, shit," said Hank. He looked around on the colorless, leaf-encrusted ground, and pointed. "Looky there. What do we have?"

Lorne thought back to advanced infantry mine field training and recognized the three prongs sticking out of the earth. "Looks like a bouncing betty."

"It is," said Hank. "And them prongs been stepped on."

Lorne nodded. Indeed they had.

"And the mine didn't go off," said Hank.

Indeed it hadn't, but Lorne didn't cotton to Hank's logic.

A half hour later, the team arrived at a worn east-west track. The other side of the track was open, like a field. "This is it," said Hank.

"The MDL," said Rothman.

The team stepped onto the track and walked east. Lorne looked across the open area to his north to a tree line. He couldn't see anyone. A few minutes later, the team came upon a rusted metal sign attached to a concrete pillar. It read, MILITARY DEMARCATION LINE, with Korean characters below, saying the same thing, Lorne guessed.

Hank turned to Lorne and said, "Go on, put a foot across."

What the fuck?

"Go on," said Hank and put his own foot on the north side of the track. The other three team members, Rothman, Hendrick, and the guy carrying the radio, laughed. Lorne put his left foot on the north side of the track, and—following Hank's lead—withdrew it. "There," said Hank. "Now you can say you been in North Korea."

By five, the team had returned to their sleeping bags. They ate another can of C rations and smoked more cigarettes. The woods grew dark.

Hank checked the tuning on the prick twenty-five and picked up its handset. He squeezed and said, "Charlie zero, this is foxtrot three, over."

The radio squawked back, "This is charlie zero, over."

"All quiet, over."

"Copy, out."

Hank put down the handset. "Boys," he said, "I'll see you in the morning."

"Say, Hank," said Lorne.

"What's that, Lorne? Where you from, anyhow?"

"Alabama."

Hank laughed. "Well, you ain't in Alabama no more, are you?"

"I guess not. But what I was wondering—shouldn't we take turns keeping watch?"

Hank smiled, showing his nicotine-stained teeth. "Lorne, it's too fucking cold for that shit."

Lorne settled in next to Rothman, who moved his face close and said in a whisper, "I agree with you."

"About what?"

"About keeping a watch. Me, I sleep with my glasses on and one eye open."

"What's the deal with Hendrick?" said Lorne.

"He's fucked up."

"How's that?"

There came a pause in the night air, like the matter being turned over. "Just born that way."

Chapter Two: February 1967, Skyline Drive

January turned to February, three days on the barrier, an evening in Chang, three days on the outpost, an evening in Chang, three days on patrol, an evening in Chang. The days grew longer and warmer. One day, middle of the month, Lorne stood in the barrier trench, rifle slung on his right shoulder, the rest of his team in the bunker. He heard the tick of a jeep motor and turned to Skyline Drive. The jeep stopped, and its passenger stepped out, six feet tall, colored, his long face framed by the olive hood of his parka. Early thirties, too old for a lieutenant, or even a captain these days, and there were few colored officers anyhow. Must be a senior NCO, an E-7, Lorne guessed.

He walked over and peered. "Are you Lorne Boyle?"

Lorne nodded.

"I'm Abel Priestly."

Lorne had never heard the name.

"Your new platoon sergeant."

Lorne straightened his shoulders, "Sergeant."

Priestly looked up and down the entrenchments, with Lorne following his gaze. Fifty meters west, two soldiers sat on sandbags smoking. To the east, emptiness. Priestly jutted his chin toward the barrier fence. "Do you know our sector?"

"As well as anyone."

"A team didn't report in this morning. Nobody can raise them."

Lorne looked at the stockade fence wanting to see through it. The week before, down the line, five Americans had died in their sleeping bags, hacked to death with hatchets. Lorne had little detail, there being no official report, but scuttlebutt said they were a five man patrol like this one. Sleeping bags had been outlawed but were still carried.

"Maybe their batteries went dead," said Lorne.

"Maybe. You know where they might be?"

"There's some places we can look."

Lorne and Priestly walked up and down the entrenchments, rousing Rothman and five additional soldiers for an impromptu patrol. The men filtered into the DMZ through a narrow foot gate. Lorne took the point position, walking north a hundred meters to an abandoned road with a metal drop gate rusted in the up position. Priestly trailed at six meters, the others behind at equal intervals. All held their rifles at port arms, trigger fingers in place, eyes darting—not a casual patrol. Lorne crossed a small open area of overgrown, frozen rice paddies from another era and entered a stand of bare hardwoods, splotches of frost and snow here and there, but brown frozen ground for the most part. Fifty meters from the south-facing slope the patrols liked for bivouac, Lorne spotted a lump of sleeping bag. He turned and pointed. Priestly brought the six trailing soldiers into a skirmish line, then motioned for Lorne to go in.

Lorne approached with half steps, scanning through the trees as far as possible. He could hear the others' half steps behind him. He counted five sleeping bags close together on the south slope. He saw no radio or rifles. Everything lay still, except for the rustling of wind in the treetops. His half steps brought him to the first sleeping bag, and Lorne dropped to one knee. It was a lanky kid named Will Jenkins. Lorne knew his name because he'd called out his nineteenth birthday the previous week. He'd also called out his shortness—eighty-four and a wake-up. Jenkins lay face up, eyes closed. Lorne was no novice to violence, having slaughtered pigs and chickens and the occasional cow, as well as having seen fingers lost to a cutter bar and what was left of a head when a tractor rolled on it. He looked for hatchet or other marks but found none.

Then Jenkins's lips fluttered and he emitted a short snore. Before Lorne could react, Jenkins's eyes opened to the sound of Priestly, standing over the second sleeping bag, saying, "Get up. Get up now!"

The soldier in the second bag was Hank. Behind him were the team's rifles, stacked against a tree, and their radio. Hank sat up and addressed Priestly with pleading eyes, "Can I take a piss?"

"By all means." Priestly raised his voice to the entire waking patrol. "As soon as you men relieve yourselves, I want you back here standing at attention, and I do mean attention, in a single rank."

Boyle couldn't help but feel bad for Hank, Jenkins, and the others, sloppy as they were. Pulled from middle America as teenagers, sent to patrol the other side of the planet, they just wanted to stay warm and get some sleep. Now they were staring at the full brunt of military justice. As they formed their rank and put their heels together, Priestly said to Lorne in a low voice, "What would you do with them?"

Lorne didn't know—neither what he'd do nor what his answer should be. "Tough one," he said.

Priestly turned to the five rigid soldiers and said, "If this gets reported, it's likely to go to a general court-martial, to set an example if nothing else. That means stockade time and a dishonorable discharge."

"Sergeant," said Hank, "I take full—"

"Shut up," said Priestly. He glanced around at Lorne, Rothman, and the rest of the makeshift patrol that had found the sleeping patrol before again addressing the men standing at attention. "If this goes unreported, it's with the understanding it won't ever happen again."

"It won't ever happen again," said Hank.

"Is that radio working?" asked Priestly.

"Yes, Sergeant."

"Don't you think you should call the command post?" Priestly turned to Lorne. "Let's get out of here."

. . . .

TOWARD THE END OF FEBRUARY, mid-afternoon, Lorne threw his duffel over the tailgate of a deuce-and-a-half and hoisted himself aboard with the rest of his platoon. The truck chugged south, turned east, and rolled across Libby Bridge. It labored up the short strip to the Half Moon Club and turned right. Lorne heard shouts from working girls. Where you go, GI? Come back soon. This your home. A soldier in the back of Lorne's truck balanced himself upright, knees against the tailgate, and blew a two-mittened kiss.

The truck ran south along the river a few kilometers, turned east again, bounced into Nullo-ri, and turned south for the last kilometer. Lorne hopped out, pulling his duffel after him, and looked around. A big compound, Blue Lancer Valley. Three rifle companies, battalion headquarters and headquarters company, plus brigade headquarters and headquarters company. Lorne's company owned a narrow piece of level ground to the left of the main gate. It held a supply room, a command post, a cinder block mess, a hut for the senior sergeants, and a cinder block latrine. Lorne shouldered his duffel and followed his platoon up a slope to the left of the level strip, to a line of four huts that housed the enlisted men.

Next morning, after breakfast, Priestly invited Lorne into the senior NCO hooch. They sat side by side on his bed—a bed, not a bunk, Lorne noticed. In addition, he had a night table plus a wooden wardrobe instead of a tin wall locker. Priestly opened a palm to the narrow partition of a room. "You stay in long enough, Specialist Boyle, all this could be yours." Priestly sounded serious and Lorne feared for a second he was getting a re-up talk. Then the platoon sergeant smiled and chuckled.

Priestly wore a Combat Infantryman Badge over his left pocket. Lorne said, "I'm guessing you been here before, Sergeant Priestly."

"Toward the end of the war. I was here when the armistice was signed. A little like *Pork Chop Hill*, not quite as dramatic."

"Rough."

"I always thought it was rougher for the Korean civilians. At least we could shoot back and rotate out." Priestly let a few seconds pass, then said, "I have a proposition." A few more seconds went by. "We need another squad leader."

Lorne didn't say anything. The stardom of running a squad versus the hassle.

"It's not a pay grade promotion," said Priestly. "You'd be getting acting jack stripes."

Lorne said, "Why me, Sergeant Priestly?"

"Because you have your head screwed on."

Lorne deepened his smile. "I don't know as I have the proper attitude for a sergeant."

"How so?"

"I don't take readily to authority. Especially when it's AFU." The last three letters of SNAFU, situation normal—all fucked up.

Priestly didn't laugh. "That's actually a concern. But it's more important to be put together. What do you say?"

"Will that peckerhead Hendrick be in my squad?"

"He will."

"Now, Sergeant Priestly, how can you ask me to be squad leader and stick me with Hendrick?"

"Because nobody else wants him."

"That's funny. How long does Hendrick have to go?"

"He just re-upped for six."

"You're shitting me. They let him re-up."

"They not only let him, they dangled a couple thousand re-up dollars in front of his nose."

Lorne shook his head.

Priestly said, "Word has it he's the only first-term soldier to ever re-up out of Korea. They're ecstatic down at division. But anyhow—he'll be on special duty as a driver half the time, out of your hair."

"What about that other idiot, Rothman? Do I get him too?"

"You do," said Priestly. "What's the matter with Rothman?"

"He's a pain in the ass."

"He does his job."

"He's a stickler for the obvious. It drives you nuts after a while."

Priestly laughed. "A stickler for the obvious—I like that. So, Lorne, are you in?"

• • • •

A HALF HOUR LATER, Lorne pulled his squad together at the far end of the platoon hut. They sat around on a bottom bunk and foot lockers. Lorne could see his were the dregs. The three E-5s had filled out their squads to nine and ten men with their personal picks. Lorne had himself, Hendrick, and Rothman. He had a New York City Italian everyone called Joe DiMaggio who sang "Maria" and other songs from *West Side Story*. He had a Russian everyone called Ivan, an actual Russian who would become a US citizen after giving the army three years. He had three Anglo-Saxons from the Midwest or thereabouts that he could never tell apart.

DiMaggio said, "Do we still call you Lorne?"

"That's not appropriate," said Rothman. "He's now our sergeant."

"Here's the deal," said Lorne. "I'm not lording it over you. We still sleep together, piss together, play cards together, all of that." Lorne tried to remember the rest of his prepared remarks. "But if I tell you to do something, it has to be done. Okay?"

The men nodded, except for Hendrick, who leaned back on the bunk and scratched his balls.

"There's no problem unless there's a problem," said Lorne. "You know what I mean?"

The men nodded, except for Hendrick.

Rothman said, "Sergeant Boyle, can you tell us what the drill is down here?"

"Training," said Lorne. "A drag but a lot of free time. A lot of liberty for the ville."

The squad dispersed, except for Hendrick, who had fallen asleep. Lorne shook him until his eyes opened. "What do you want?" he said.

"I want you to grab your parka and step out back with me."

Hendrick smirked at Rothman, pulled his parka off his bunk, and followed Lorne out the rear door. As the door closed, Lorne turned, grabbed Hendrick with both hands by the front of his parka, and threw him against the side of the hut. Hendrick staggered and regained his footing.

Lorne said, "What the fuck's the matter with you? Stinking drunk in the middle of the day."

Hendrick raised a finger. "I'll thank you to keep your fucking hands—"

Lorne slapped him across the face.

Hendrick's finger was still in the air. "Try that again," he said.

Lorne slapped him again.

"Goddamnit," said Hendrick. "I'm reporting you."

Lorne swept an arm down the hill toward the command post. "Let's go."

Hendrick lowered his finger. Lorne stepped closer and said, "I don't care what you do with your re-up money or how drunk you get at night. I'll even help you get undressed and tuck your dead ass in. But on duty you're sober, you got that?"

Lorne re-entered the hut and closed the door behind him. He dropped his parka on his bunk and went to the top shelf of his wall locker but didn't know what he was looking for. *Jesus, that was stupid!* It would have been one thing to slap him around to straighten him out, but Lorne had slapped him around because he was pissed. He was still pissed, more at himself now than at Hendrick. Lorne felt a presence, Rothman standing next to him.

In a soft voice, Rothman said, "That was a near thing, wasn't it, Sergeant Boyle?"

What's he talking about? Was he watching out back?

Rothman said, "Finding those men ... Jenkins and the others. I thought they were dead."

Lorne dropped his arms from the wall locker. He knew his wide face failed him at times like this, always seemed to be smiling. He tried to put what he felt into his voice. "It scared me too. But it turned out okay."

"I've been thinking about it, Sergeant Boyle, about what we could do next time we're up there. You know how Joe carries those PPS-43 submachine guns."

"I didn't know that's what they were called."

"I've been researching it. They're real good close in, but at a distance we got it all over them with our M14s. So if a firefight broke out, say, between Seiler and their outpost, we could knock most of them down without getting touched ourselves."

Jesus, thought Lorne. "Specialist Rothman, we can't shoot across the MDL."

"We could say they shot first."

"We cannot take it upon ourselves to create an international incident." *Where was Rothman's head? At times, too many brains; at times, none at all.*

"Well, what did they create when they killed our guys?" asked Rothman.

"They didn't kill our guys. They were sleeping."

"They killed that other patrol."

"Look," said Lorne, "when we first met on Seiler, you told me they were fair game when they come across."

Rothman nodded.

"Then that's our game. The best thing we can do is stay alert. Not do something stupid like getting caught in our sleeping bags."

"We've hit them before," said Rothman.

"I heard that story too," said Lorne. Scuttlebutt had it that an American squad crossed the MDL, middle of the night, and shot up a North Korean outpost. "It was a rogue operation if it happened at all."

Rothman shifted his weight from one boot to the other. "It was just a thought." Rothman was a few weeks ahead of Lorne in Korea, a few weeks ahead in pay grade, no doubt. Lorne wondered if there was resentment, Rothman thinking he should have gotten the stripes. He didn't behave that way, probably realized, smart as he was, that he didn't have the necessary command presence; probably realized that something was a little awry upstairs.

Rothman said, "Thanks for the talk, Sergeant."

• • • •

LIFE BELOW THE RIVER settled into dull drill. Command of the company fell to a succession of lieutenants. The training schedule was treated as a loose guideline, if followed at all. Ambush patrols on the south side of the Imjin River provided a taste of excitement, but for the most part, weapons were stowed.

Life in the ville proved more interesting. Lorne could truck to Changpa-ri or walk the kilometer to Nullo-ri. Nullo-ri didn't have the cowboy feel, the wide-openness of Changpa-ri, but there was no lack of OB lager and spread-legged girls. The first night Lorne walked to Nullo-ri, he stopped at the guard shack at the main gate. The guards weren't military police, but ordinary infantry drawn from headquarters company. Lorne said to the specialist on duty, "Do you write up everybody coming in past curfew?"

"Depends," said the specialist. He returned Lorne's smile. "I've never known a lieutenant or non-com to get written up."

So Nullo-ri had that advantage. Didn't have to worry about making the truck back to base. Didn't have to worry about making curfew. Could stay out all night—get up before dawn and be back on the compound for reveille. On those occasions, Lorne eschewed the road in favor of the rice paddies—less chance of being caught in the open by a vehicle. He would enter the platoon hut by the rear door, his squad asleep except for Rothman. Rothman might be reading or cleaning a piece of gear. He'd look up and say, "Morning, Sergeant Boyle."

Chapter Three: March 1967, Unit 124 Training Camp

During the early weeks of January 1967, Jun-seok's regimen of abuse and endurance was interspersed with weapons training, martial arts, land navigation, and the usual political education. He noticed the other teams were like his, a captain and two lieutenants. Sometimes the teams trained together. Other times, the lieutenants were pulled off for separate training, the newer lieutenants receiving special treatment.

As the winter passed, cadre and candidates dispensed with long underwear and quilted outerwear in favor of polished green pants, shirts, and jackets. Jun-seok no longer felt he might die, frozen under two ragged blankets on his wooden sleeping platform in an unheated barracks.

One day in early spring, he sat cross-legged on level ground with eleven other candidates. Each of the twelve lieutenants held a hand grenade in his right hand, forward of his chest, fingers tight around the spoon.

Their captain instructor said, "Pull pin."

Jun-seok hooked his left forefinger through the ring of the grenade pin and yanked.

"Release spoon," said the captain.

Jun-seok loosened the fingers of his right hand until the spoon flipped free and the striker clicked over, igniting the four-and-a-half second fuse.

"Position the grenade," said the captain.

Jun-seok placed his grenade to the side of his face above the right cheekbone, his movements mechanical, knowing this was no time to falter.

"Make the fierce face," said the captain.

Jun-seok parted his lips and widened his mouth, keeping his teeth together.

The dummy grenade popped, its small charge driving out a wax plug, which careened off the top of Jun-seok's shoulder. Jun-seok maintained his cross-legged, fierce-faced position.

"You will never," said the captain, "be taken alive."

"We will never be taken alive," said the lieutenants in unison.

The candidates removed the grenades from the sides of their faces and recovered pins, spoons, and plugs. They stood to attention.

"Dismissed," said the captain.

Chong stood nearby. "Excellent suicide," he said.

Jun-seok stole glances left and right. He had taken a liking to Chong but wished his behavior less cavalier. Maybe the difference in attitude was due to their formative years, Jun-seok's rural, his parents working on a collective farm; Chong's closer to the county seat, his father a supervisor in a factory. Sure, Jun-seok's parents pilfered extra rice from the collective farm and kept an illegal garden for cabbage and cucumbers. They raised dogs and rabbits, and when government honchos came around, gifts of meat and kimchi fell into their hands. But regarding political matters, the family attended all meetings and workshops. They took care to treat commissioners and party cadre with deference.

"Don't get me wrong, little brother," said Chong. "I don't plan on being captured by the Americans or their puppets, but do we have to obsess over it?"

"Without the repetition of training, we would falter when the time comes."

"Well spoken," said Chong.

Here we go again, thought Jun-seok. Why the sarcasm? If our superiors want us to practice suicide by grenade, do the practice. If our superiors want us to make the fierce face, make it. And they're correct: better a quick death by grenade than torture and humiliation by the Americans.

"I'm not spouting doctrine," said Jun-seok. "It's a military necessity."

"I don't know," said Chong. "I think we should practice to live, not die." Chong walked toward the mess hall. "The dying will take care of itself."

"What are we doing?" said Jun-seok. It was mid-afternoon, no time to be near the mess.

"The captain's pleased with your progress," said Chong.

Jun-seok felt his stomach tighten. Compliments scared him, made him feel like he was being set up for a fall.

"He won't say it, of course, but he's pleased with our team's progress. I've talked him into a short furlough."

Jun-seok stopped. Chong turned and said, "Doesn't that appeal to you?"

"I just don't want to risk a lapse in my training."

Chong laughed. "Comrade Pak, don't you think you've reached a point in your training where you're allowed a little pleasure?"

"If you say so, Comrade Lieutenant."

Chong laughed again. "This weekend, we're leaving together on a three-day pass. But first—" Chong nodded toward the mess. "Something more immediate."

Chong and Jun-seok entered the mess, a cinder block building with a concrete floor, by its rear door. Along the floor lay sacks of rice, barley, dried meat, kimchi, and other foods. Halfway down was a wall with a door to the kitchen and eating area. To the left of the door, a raised platform held three rooms with sliding doors and a veranda for removing footwear—quarters for the kitchen staff. Chong pushed open the door to the kitchen and whistled. Twenty seconds later, one of the cooks, a woman in her fifties, came to the door.

"Didn't I see you yesterday?" she said.

Chong stood aside and nodded toward Jun-seok. "I've got a cherry boy for you."

"Just what I need. Can't you see we're busy?"

Chong placed a hand on her shoulder. "You can spare a few minutes."

She pushed Chong's hand away. She glanced at Jun-seok, who felt his face warming.

"Wait." She turned back to the kitchen.

Chong slid the door to the first raised room open. "Take your boots off. Don't just look at me. Take your boots off, Comrade. That's an order."

As Jun-seok unlaced and pulled off his boots, Chong said, "Leave her a few coins but don't be overgenerous." He motioned Jun-seok into the room.

Jun-seok looked around at a sleeping mat and blankets, a chest, and a small pile of clothing. He looked back out. Chong said, "A few coins—that's enough. Believe me, she does okay for herself."

The cook reappeared carrying a basin of water, steam rising into the cool air. She stepped onto the veranda, kicked off her rubber shoes, and stepped into the room. Chong disappeared behind the steam. The cook set down the basin and slid the door closed.

"Wash your genitals," she said.

Jun-seok stood mute.

"Look," she said. "We haven't got all day. Strip down and wash up."

Jun-seok let his jacket fall away and pulled at his shirt.

The cook wore an apron over a green uniform. She tossed the apron aside and pulled off her shirt. As Jun-seok dropped pants and underclothes, he examined his prospective partner. Old enough to be his mother, with a coarse face, coarser hands, and missing teeth. But the vision of her sagging breasts and mottled vagina poured blood into Jun-seok's cock, for this was the real thing, the unspoken pleasure.

The cook sat cross-legged on the mat, then lay back and opened her legs. Jun-seok felt a touch of blindness, everything out of focus, as he stumbled forward. He lowered his knees between hers, his cock throbbing like the piston of a motorbike. He lunged forward, lying atop the cook.

"Slow down, Comrade," said the cook. "You're not in yet."

But Jun-seok's libido had surged past control. He gasped as his insides emptied.

"Oh," said the cook, "now we have a nice mess."

Jun-seok lay panting on top of her, the urgency dissolved, mortified by his loss of control, shamed by a failure of mission.

"Get off me," said the cook. "In the name of the Great Leader, grab a towel."

As Jun-seok scrambled from the mat, the cook issued a low laugh followed by soft words. "Don't be upset, Comrade Lieutenant. It'll go better next time."

• • • •

TWO MORNINGS LATER, Jun-seok and Chong climbed over the tailgate of a ZIL-130 on a supply run to Koksan-up. They wore dress uniforms and carried furlough papers allowing them transport to their home villages. In Koksan-up, they showed their papers to the driver of a truck going north. Jun-seok clambered into the back and sat on a carton. Chong joined him a minute later and said, "Want to stop off and meet my parents? You'll like my father. He's just like me."

Jun-seok shook his head. "My papers don't permit it."

"No problem," said Chong. "I gave the driver a pack of cigarettes. He'll look the other way."

Jun-seok felt queasy from toes to anus. "Is that a good idea?"

"Hey, let's have a smoke ourselves," said Chong. He removed a pack of cigarettes from his jacket. They lit up.

Jun-seok thought about the invitation and that he was being rude. "I'd like to meet your father," he said, "but who am I going to bribe to get a ride up to my village?"

"It's only twenty kilometers. That's nothing for you, especially without a pack full of rocks." They tilted sideways as the left wheels of the truck entered a deep rut and emerged. "Actually, I think you could move faster on foot on these roads."

Jun-seok pondered the invitation. He didn't want to jeopardize his position as an officer and a Unit 124 candidate, but he didn't like being rude.

Chong said, "You can leave in the wee hours and double-time up the road. Believe me, you won't see anything, but if you do, just jump off the road until it passes."

Jun-seok said, "Some extra training, eh?"

"As your big brother," said Chong, "I order it."

A while later, Chong stood and called out, "Hey, driver, slow down. Okay, stop. Thanks for the lift."

Jun-seok and Chong went over the tailgate, ran into woods, and found a path. They entered an area of wooden huts with verandas and raised floors. Jun-seok noticed that even here, where the people worked in factories, small gardens surrounded their houses, and small rice paddies lay between them. Jun-seok and Chong encountered neighbors, it being daylight and impossible not to be seen. Chong waved and greeted everyone, exchanging bows with his seniors, and military salutes with some young boys. Nobody challenged Jun-seok.

Chong's house and family reminded Jun-seok of his own. Two rooms on a raised floor with a kitchen off to the side. A picture of Kim Il-sung in the first room. Chong's mother acted just like Jun-seok's would, looking him over, darting her eyes about, fitting him into the environment. She leaned into Chong's ear, and Chong said, "His papers are in order. Don't be such a worrywart." Chong flashed his teeth, and his mother's frown melted to a smile.

Chong had a sister in her early twenties, standing with her eyes to the floor. Unmarried, thought Jun-seok. Attractive, but then all young girls looked attractive to Jun-seok. Chong's mother said to her, "Run to the factory. See if your father can leave early."

Jun-seok and Chong sat on the floor of the first room. Chong said, "I saw how you looked at my sister."

Jun-seok tried to think of words of protest, but knew anything he said would fall flat. Chong laughed. "She's nice-looking, don't you think?" Chong leaned forward. "Hey, I could see you as a brother-in-law some day."

Chong's mother hustled between the first room and the kitchen, laying out cups, chopsticks, tea, slices of octopus, kimchi, and rice cakes. Jun-seok's mouth watered at the thought of octopus and rice cakes with real tea.

"When you reach home," said Chong, "you'll see your family is getting extra rations too." Chong turned his head to the wall and said, "Thank you, Great Leader."

His mother shook a finger and said, "Don't do that, Myung-seung."

Jun-seok too had wearied of Chong's carefree attitude. Dismissal and imprisonment were not jokes. The mother said in a whisper, "A uniform does not change your *songbun*."

"But our commissions and special training do," said Chong. "Look at the treatment you get now. Look at the extra rations."

"It could evaporate in a second."

Chong shook his head as his mother turned to the kitchen. "The cup is always half empty for my mother." He peered at Jun-seok. "Not you too?"

Jun-seok picked at a rice cake with his chopsticks. "There are many uncertainties," he said.

The front door slid open, and a man who could only be Chong's father entered. Same short stature, same round walk, same exuberance. He placed a liter bottle of makkoli in the middle of the floor as Chong rose and gave a quick bow. Jun-seok followed suit.

Chong's father said, "Son. And your esteemed comrade." He turned to the wall. "And Great Leader."

The men sat as Chong's mother and sister brought rice and strips of seasoned pork. Chong's father shook the bottle, unstopped it, and poured drinks. "And so, Myung-seung, what is our people's army up to?"

"I'm sorry, Father, but that's a state secret."

Chong's father laughed. "As it should be. I will wake up one morning to hear the glorious news, that we've polished off the running dogs, and I'll know where you are."

"They'll fall of their own accord," said Chong. "Maybe with a little nudge. What do you think, Lieutenant Pak?"

Chong's mother, who was bent over delivering more food, said, "Do we really need another war?"

"Take care," said Chong's father gesturing toward the wall, "of what you say in front of the Great Leader."

Chong's mother swept her arm. "You take care. Ears are everywhere."

Chong's father addressed Jun-seok. "I hope you're not upset by a little horseplay."

By midnight, the makkoli had run its course. Jun-seok bowed and thanked Chong's father for his hospitality. The father said, "Look after my son."

"It's the other way around," said Jun-seok.

Chong walked with Jun-seok to the main road as his eyes grew accustomed to the starlight and quarter moon. "I'll have no trouble," he said. "Four or five hours."

"Good training," said Chong.

Jun-seok took off at an easy lope. It felt pleasant to have but a few kilograms in his backpack. It felt agreeable not to be under observation. He felt an edge from the makkoli but was not drunk.

Chong's mother had mentioned the war, and Jun-seok understood her trepidation. He had been entering his teens, hoping the war would last until he could join and become a hero. One day, sirens sounded, and everyone fled their huts and fields for the shelters dug into the side of nearby hills. Jun-seok felt safe surrounded by the earth, the bombs but distant thuds. It was exciting. But when the all-clear sounded, even the cries of those ahead of Jun-seok did not prepare him for the destruction. Every hut in the village had been reduced to rubble. Half the rice crop had turned into craters. Along with the other youth, Jun-seok went to work with shovel and basket, transforming their bomb shelters into permanent living quarters. And that's how they lived out the war, like moles.

It was still dark when Jun-seok slipped into his childhood home, rebuilt after the war. His mother woke and shook his father. His father opened his eyes and said, "Son. Long time no see. Is everything okay?" He sat up. "You must be a big shot these days. Suddenly we're getting special treatment."

"Which we don't need," said Jun-seok's mother.

Jun-seok's father looked at his wife then Jun-seok. "We're glad you're doing well but don't like the extra attention."

"What they can give, they can take away," said Jun-seok's mother.

"We kick a third of our extras back to the commissioners," said Jun-seok's father. "A third we give to our neighbors."

"Against a rainy day," said Jun-seok's mother.

"I think that's wise," said Jun-seok. "I came up with a friend. His family is very offhand about the special treatment, and careless in their private talk."

"That's a dangerous game," said Jun-seok's father.

Chapter Four: March 1967, East of Dongducheon

On her seventeenth birthday, Lee Min-hee's mother presented her with a comb of plain wood, beige, lacquered, with a few Chinese characters imprinted in gold. The family sat in a square on the floor for the evening meal, the two younger brothers across from Min-hee and her mother, the first son to their left, the father to the right. Her older sister had married and moved to her husband's compound.

Min-hee's father, smelling of sake and kimchi, leaned forward. "Let me see that."

Min-hee's mother, about to place the comb in the bun of Min-hee's hair, instead passed it to the forefingers and thumbs of her father. He snapped it in two and filled the small room with his voice. "You know what you are?"

Min-hee and her mother sat with heads bowed. The brothers looked straight ahead. Across from Min-hee, her youngest brother's throat bobbed.

"You're an extra mouth."

His words roamed the room, now directed at Min-hee, now at her mother, now at the sons. Min-hee understood his anger, having heard him vent since she could remember. Half a century of Japanese rule, a bloody civil war that resolved nothing, Chosons and Chinese, Hanguks and Americans, a country not their own. But his concern always came back to livelihood—work, food, rent, education for the sons. His scrutiny returned to Min-hee.

"I can tell you this. Don't look for a dowry. I'm sorry now I provided one for your sister. What good has it done?" Not always his sentiment: four years before, Min-hee's father had oozed enthusiasm over his older daughter's engagement. The bridegroom's father was a manager at a factory in Chuncheon, and Min-hee's father began thinking he already had a foreman's job there. But an offer of employment never came. Maybe the bridegroom's father thought the dowry, all that Min-hee's family could afford, miserly. Maybe he didn't like Min-hee's father. Maybe no employment existed, everyone just hanging on these days.

A month after her father broke the comb, Min-hee visited her sister at the compound of her husband's family. By this time, her sister had two children, a toddler and an infant, and could use some help. That evening, Min-hee's sister put a proposal to her husband, to let Min-hee stay with them.

"She can help with chores and look after the children."

They were sitting in a circle on the floor of the first of two rooms.

"That way I can spend more time looking after your mother."

The husband ran his eyes over Min-hee, knees to forehead.

"Why not?" he said.

Min-hee slept in the second room with the children. At night she heard grunts from her brother-in-law, the clamor of lovemaking no doubt, although she didn't hear the same sounds from her sister.

One day, two months later, Min-hee sat alone in the first of the two rooms, mending a pair of socks for her sister's father-in-law. Her sister had taken both children and her mother-in-law to the market. The door slid open, and her brother-in-law stepped in. He sat cross-legged next to Min-hee so their knees almost touched.

"No work today, brother-in-law?"

"We should get to know each other better," he said.

Her brother-in-law pressed a hand against the folds of Min-hee's skirt and tightened his fingers on the inside of her thigh.

Min-hee dropped the socks into her lap and wriggled away. "Please don't do that, brother-in-law."

Her brother-in-law wriggled next to her. "You don't have to be coy," he said.

Min-hee scooted to the far corner of the room, drew her knees to her chin, and wrapped her arms around her drawn-in legs.

"Where do you think you're going?" said the brother-in-law. "Who do you think you are, anyhow?"

Min-hee lowered her head into her knees and closed her eyes. The brother-in-law had risen to his feet and stood over her.

"You eat my rice," he said. "You sleep on my floor."

He squatted so his face came close to Min-hee's. "You're nothing without me," he said. "Think about it."

Next morning Min-hee tied what she owned in her spare wrap-around skirt. She understood that she couldn't stay where she was and couldn't go back where she'd been. She understood that no marriage would ever be arranged for her—and from what she'd seen of her mother and sister's marriages, wasn't sure that she wanted one. With her last few *won*, she boarded a bus for Dongducheon. This town, which sprawled along the northern outskirts of Seoul, housed the large American military base called Camp Casey. Min-hee had a childhood friend named Kim Soo-jin, who had moved there the year before and found work as a barber. *I can learn to cut hair and slap on cologne. I can be an independent woman.*

In Dongducheon, Min-hee located a shop next to the bus station that mailed and received letters. A middle-aged woman looked at Soo-jin's address, took Min-hee outside, and pointed down the wide main street of packed dirt. On the street were many American soldiers. It was spring, and they sauntered in boots, green cotton pants and shirts, and polished field jackets. Their skin spanned a spectrum from faint pink to dark brown. Many were big, a hundred eighty centimeters in height, with deep chests and wide shoulders. Min-hee walked with head down but eyelids up.

Soo-jin lived in one of a long line of rooms fronted by a narrow veranda. Girls sat on the veranda, some in long Korean dresses, but most in tight western dresses, or mini-skirts with blouses. Several girls had dyed their hair, one to blond and one to red. Several had clipped their eye folds for the western, round-eye effect.

Soo-jin's room had a large bed and a wardrobe. Min-hee wondered at the extravagance. And who would want to sleep on a piece of furniture instead of a heated floor? Soo-jin wore a mini-skirt.

"Why do you have such furnishings?" said Min-hee.

"The Americans," said Soo-jin, "they don't like to fornicate on the floor like Korean men."

Min-hee looked at Soo-jin who was awaiting her reaction. Soo-jin shrieked. "You should see your face!"

Soo-jin, sitting cross-legged on the bed, patted the bed cover for Min-hee to join her. "Yes, I'm a comfort woman. What the GIs call a working girl."

"What does *ji-ai* mean?"

"It's GI. It's the English word for American soldier."

"What about your job as a barber?"

"What was I supposed to tell you? 'Hello, everyone back home, I've got a nice job as a Yankee whore?'"

Min-hee bowed her head. "So there's no real work with the Americans."

"There's some," said Soo-jin, "but there's many more girls than jobs." She lifted Min-hee's chin. "Are you planning to stay in Dongducheon?"

"How can I go back?"

Soo-jin sighed. "You can stay with me. Except when I'm entertaining." Soo-jin took Min-hee's hand in hers. "But here's the thing. After a while you'll have to take care of yourself."

The two girls sat in silence. Min-hee felt her nose and eyes moisten. She said, "The Americans scare me."

"They're less scary than Korean men," said Soo-jin. "And they have more money. Do you know about SOFA?"

Min-hee shook her head.

"It's an English word that means Status of Forces Agreement. Do you know about that?"

Min-hee had no idea even in translation.

"It means that if an American soldier hits a Korean or makes other trouble, he can go to a Korean jail."

A surprise. Min-hee thought the Americans did what they wanted.

"All GIs are afraid of SOFA. They'll never beat you like a father or brother, or husband."

That evening, Soo-jin took Min-hee to a room at the end of the veranda occupied by an old woman—not yet sixty but ancient in a town filled with GIs and working girls. She had a craggy smile and gray hair tied in a bun. Soo-jin called her *mamasan*, a word formed from English and Japanese.

Mamasan's room had sparse furnishings like a traditional Korean household. Min-hee sat on the floor facing her, and Soo-jin left. Mamasan said, "You must stay here until eleven."

"Why eleven?"

"Curfew for GIs. Unless Soo-jin gets an overnighter. But that doesn't happen much these days." Mamasan shook her head. "Business is not like it used to be."

"Why is that?" said Min-hee.

"Too many girls."

· · · ·

A FEW MORNINGS LATER, Mamasan slid Soo-jin's door open and let herself in. Min-hee and Soo-jin were sitting on the bed. Mamasan sat on the floor and unfolded a small bundle of clothes: a mini-skirt, blouse, underpants, bra, and high-heel shoes. Four girls from adjacent rooms scooted through the door into sitting and kneeling positions on the floor, one the redhead, another the blond.

Soo-jin said, "Mamasan makes some of her living selling clothes. She's giving you these with payment after your first work."

Min-hee looked at Mamasan and the four girls on the floor. She turned her head and looked at Soo-jin.

Soo-jin said, "If you stay here, you have to work. It can't be avoided."

Mamasan said, "I know how it is. I used to be a comfort woman, but I'm too old for that today. A blow job now and then."

The girls on the floor laughed and pinched their noses.

Soo-jin said, "I hope I never have to do that."

Mamasan said, "You young girls know nothing. A blow job is good. You can't get pregnant. You can't get VD if you wash your mouth right away."

"What's VD?" said Min-hee. Another English word.

Soo-jin said, "It means a disease that gets passed around through sex."

Mamasan said, "You must be very careful not to get pregnant. You must avoid disease." She shook a forefinger. "Always have your own rubbers on hand. Always wash your pussy before and after. Wash the soldier's cock too."

The blond girl said, "You've gained so much wisdom over the years, Mamasan." She turned to Min-hee. "Mamasan started out servicing Japanese soldiers."

"That's true," said Mamasan. "I've serviced Japanese, Korean—both Hanguk and Choson—Chinese, American, Australian, and English."

"And the Americans are the best," said the girl.

"They're all the same," said Mamasan.

"Not true," said the girl. "GIs fall in love. You can become a wife and go to America."

Mamasan's face reddened and her voice rose. "That's bad thinking. It will lead to misery."

"Many working girls go to America."

"One in a thousand," said Mamasan. "You listen to too much mush on the radio. Don't get hooked up with a GI thinking he'll take you to America." Mamasan straightened her posture and looked up at Min-hee. "Are you a virgin?"

Min-hee felt her face flush. "Of course, what do you think?"

The girls laughed. Mamasan laughed too, then said, "The first time can be difficult, but not as bad as you think."

Soo-jin said, "I know. We must give Min-hee a lesson." She flopped on her back, opened her legs, and moaned English words. "Oh so good. So good."

The girls on the floor laughed and two of them rolled to their backs moaning in English. "Oh so good. So good. You number one. You have best cock ever."

Mamasan clapped her hands. "Knock it off. This is serious business."

Soo-jin said, "Min-hee, now you give it a try."

"What? I can't do that. Not in front of everyone."

Mamasan said, "Soo-jin is right. You must practice."

Soo-jin said, "If you can't do it here, how are you going to do it with a GI? Come on. On your back. Spread your legs."

Min-hee lay on her back, moaned once, and said, "I can't do this. I don't know English."

Soo-jin enunciated the English words. "Oh. So. Good."

"Oh so," said Min-hee.

"Oh so good," said Soo-jin and threw herself on top of Min-hee, rubbing her lips against Min-hee's, and gyrating between her legs.

Min-hee cried out. "Stop it."

"Not until you say oh so good like you mean it."

Min-hee emitted a small moan. In English, she said, "Oh so, oh so."

The girls on the floor fell against each other laughing. Even Mamasan leaned sideways with her half-toothed mouth open.

"That's a good start," Mamasan said. "Now we need a cucumber so you can practice unrolling a rubber."

"What exactly is a blow job?" said Min-hee. She and Soo-jin had resumed their cross-legged positions on the bed.

Soo-jin said, "Do you know how a man's cock works?"

Min-hee pulled back her shoulders and puckered her mouth. "Maybe I don't know every detail."

"It's okay," said Soo-jin. "I'll explain. Okay, normally the man's cock hangs down and is not so big. But when he gets hot, the cock goes straight out. It gets big, real big, and hard like a cucumber. Then when the cock gets rubbed, especially when it gets rubbed inside your pussy, the man gets hotter and hotter. He breathes faster and faster."

On the floor, two of the girls were simulating males in heat.

"And then suddenly white fluid gushes out."

The girls on the floor laughed as Min-hee gasped.

"That's the semen," said Soo-jin. "But if he has on a rubber, the semen stays in the rubber, and can't get you pregnant. Or give you VD."

Min-hee said, "So that's the blow job?"

The girls on the floor laughed anew.

"No, no," said Soo-jin, "that's fornication. What the Americans call fucky-fucky. A blow job is when you put the man's cock in your mouth and suck on it until the semen comes out."

"Ew," said Min-hee.

"Ew," said the girls on the floor.

Mamasan shook her head.

Min-hee wanted to run from Dongducheon but had nowhere to go. What would she do as an independent woman, mend and wash clothes? Become a concubine for a married Korean man?

Mamasan leaned forward and patted her knee. "You won't find it so bad," she said.

"Okay," said Soo-jin. "Now you need an American name. GIs like American names. My name is Suzie Q."

Min-hee tried to pronounce the name. "Soo-chi-koo," she said.

The blond girl said, "No, Suzie Q. Don't you ever listen to the radio?" She tapped her palms on the floor. The other girls joined in with a four-four beat.

"Oh Suzie Q," wailed the blond girl.

The other girls wailed along, "Oh Suzie Q. Oh Suzie Q."

Soo-jin clapped her hands. "I have a good name. And it uses your family name. Sally Lee. What do you think?"

Min-hee said, "Sa-ri Ri?"

"No, no, Sally Lee."

"Same thing."

"No, no, for Americans they sound different. It must be Sally with the ell sound. It must be Lee with the ell sound."

"Okay," said Mamasan, "let's get down to business. I think, for this first time, we should leave Min-hee in the room and someone should bring a GI to her."

"I agree," said Soo-jin, "and I'm thinking we can make good money if we wait for payday and get a GI who wants a virgin."

"Not a bad idea," said Mamasan.

"And I think I have just the soldier. A sergeant E-6 who likes to hang out and have a few drinks and not grab a girl right away. Always has money, even at the end of the month."

The blond girl said, "Yeah, I know who you mean, but he's a big guy. His cock's too much for a virgin."

"Don't you know anything?" said Mamasan. "Cock size has nothing to do with body size."

"Yeah," said the redhead, "I think it's just the opposite. The little dark ones have big cocks. The big blond ones have small cocks. The ones with red hair, smaller."

"No, you can't tell till you get their pants down," said Mamasan.

"Stop, everyone," said Soo-jin, "I've done it with him. He has a medium cock. And he's nice. He treats you like you're his yobo."

"Ah, a yobo," said one of the girls. "A good deal if you can get it."

"Not a good deal," said another girl. "You can make more money as a josan."

"Maybe so, but if you're a yobo, you don't have to hustle all month. You can relax and your yobo will bring things from the PX."

"What's the *pi-eck*?" asked Min-hee.

"That's the GI store," said Soo-jin.

"And you can always do a little work on the side," said the blond girl.

"Bad idea," said the girl who had started the yobo discussion. "What if you get caught? What if you get VD and give it to your yobo?"

Soo-jin clapped her hands. "Okay, listen. I'll talk to this sergeant next time I see him. I'll tell him how he can spend the night with a cherry girl from the country. I'll get twenty dollars."

The girls laughed. "You'll be lucky to get ten," said the redhead.

"No," said Mamasan. "Hold out for twenty."

• • • •

THREE NIGHTS LATER, Min-hee sat cross-legged on Soo-jin's bed in blouse and mini-skirt. The door slid open and Soo-jin looked in. She motioned for Min-hee to sit with her feet on the floor and scooted into the room. Behind her, a soldier sat on the veranda removing his boots. Seconds later, he filled the doorway, stooping and sidling sideways to enter the room. Soo-jin took his hat and field jacket, and placed them in the far corner. Min-hee took note of his insignia, three stripes on top of a rocker. Staff sergeant E-6. Big bucks.

Soo-jin spoke to the sergeant in English. Min-hee heard her new name, Sally Lee. Soo-jin said to Min-hee, "I told him you're a little nervous. He said he understands."

The sergeant pulled a black leather wallet from his back pocket and extracted a twenty-dollar note in American military scrip. Soo-jin took it in two hands with a short bow and backed out of the room. "See you in the morning," she said.

Min-hee wondered why she had bothered with a skirt and blouse when they appeared only to be a hindrance, soon discarded along with the soldier's shirt, undershirt, pants, underpants, and socks. She lay on her back with the sergeant half on her, half on his side, pressing his lips against her. Min-hee didn't know how to kiss and wished now she'd let Soo-jin give her a lesson. She felt her lips forced apart and realized the sergeant was pushing his tongue into her mouth. She felt the folds of her labia forced apart, and realized the sergeant was pushing a finger into her pussy. Now comes the cock, thought Min-hee.

Not yet. The sergeant released his lips from Min-hee's and placed them on her neck. Next he placed them between her collarbones. At least I can breathe, thought Min-hee. This is going to be a long night.

• • • •

MIN-HEE OPENED HER eyes to scant light filtering through the room's single window. On the side of the room away from the bed, the staff sergeant buttoned his shirt and pulled up his pants. Min-hee lay still and silent as the door slid open and the sergeant slid out.

Minutes later Soo-jin and Mamasan entered the room, trailed by the four girls from the adjacent hooches. Min-hee sat up, and Soo-jin joined her on the bed. Mamasan and the other girls squatted and sat on the floor.

"So," said Soo-jin. "How'd it go, your first fucky-fucky?"

Min-hee crossed her arms. "You didn't tell me about the other stuff."

Mamasan and the girls leaned forward.

"What other stuff?" said Soo-jin. "He's not a weird guy."

Min-hee turned down the corners of her mouth. "First he kisses me on the lips and all over my face and neck. He keeps kissing and kissing."

Mamasan put up a finger. "Americans like to kiss," she said. "It's true, that's a difference from the others."

"So that goes on for a while. Then he moves his head down and he starts"—Min-hee faced away then came back—"he starts sucking on my nipples. First one, then the other. It doesn't hurt but it feels funny."

The girls clapped. "Get used to it," said one of the girls. "GIs like to suck tit."

"But that means he likes you," said the blond girl.

Min-hee closed her fists and set her mouth in a pout. "Then he starts kissing lower. He goes past my belly and first thing I know—his tongue is down there."

The girls clapped louder. "Oh that means he really likes you," said the redhead.

Mamasan said, "I don't understand why they do that, but they do."

"Then he comes back up and puts that same tongue back in my mouth. Finally I put on the rubber like you showed me with the cucumber and he gets between my legs. He keeps asking, okay, okay, and other things, but I don't understand. I say oh so good like you taught me."

"Did it hurt?" said Soo-jin.

"It felt funny, like I was making a poop out the wrong hole. Then suddenly he goes all tense like a strangled chicken, and he falls on me with a big moan."

The girls clapped.

"How many times did you do it?" said Soo-jin.

"Three."

"Did he use a new rubber each time?"

"Yes," said Min-hee.

"Did you washy-washy each time?"

"You're off to a better start than most of us," said the blond girl.

"Don't let it go to your head," said Mamasan. "This is the only time you'll get twenty dollars."

When they were alone, Min-hee asked Soo-jin about the money. "You have to pay Mamasan rent," said Soo-jin. "And you owe her for the clothes. But I'll get a few dollars back for you."

• • • •

ONE MORNING IN EARLY spring, Mamasan slid Soo-jin's door open and beckoned. Min-hee stepped onto the veranda followed by Soo-jin. A man who looked like Mamasan's twin stood next to her, his feet together, his hands behind his back. His eyes scanned Min-hee top to bottom, not with lust, but like he was checking out a head of lettuce. He smiled.

Min-hee and Soo-jin slipped into shoes and stepped into the alleyway.

Mamasan said, "Papasan here is from Changpa-ri, up on the Imjin River. Have you heard of it?"

Min-hee nodded. Changpa-ri had come up in conversation. Some of the girls thought of it as a place of adventure, others as a place of last resort.

"It's very far north," Min-hee said.

Mamasan said, "It's as far north as you can go without crossing into the combat zone. But every night hundreds of horny American soldiers come across the river for liberty."

Papasan said, "It's a rough place, but business is good. I can give you a room with a bed and wardrobe."

Soo-jin put an arm over Min-hee's shoulder with her forehead against her neck. "It's best for now, Min-hee. There are too many girls in Dongducheon."

Min-hee could see it was a done deal. She had been getting enough business to pay half the rent with a few dollars left over. But two girls, even the best of friends, in one room proved awkward, especially if one of them got an all-nighter.

"We'll still be the best of friends," said Soo-jin. "We'll write all the time."

That afternoon, Min-hee bounced north over pot-holed dirt roads in a minibus with a beat-up body, collapsed suspension, and steering that put the vehicle at an angle to its direction of travel. The bus overflowed with men and women of all ages, toddlers, infants, rice, fish, vegetables, chickens, dogs, and the odors of kimchi and tobacco smoke. Min-hee wore a wrap-around dress and rubber shoes and carried her belongings—her trade clothes and cosmetics—in a bundle formed from her other wrap-around dress. She'd approached the bus with bundle on head in the traditional manner but doubted that she fooled anyone as to her occupation.

The bus disgorged its passengers in a square in front of a bar with a sign in English letters. Min-hee knew from Papasan's directions that this was the Lucky Club. She put her back to the midday sun and walked north on the chalky main street to where a second wide dirt road ran off to the left, down a slope toward, she knew, the Imjin River. To her right, on top of the T formed by this intersection, crouched another GI establishment, the Half Moon Club. Min-hee's new home was a room behind the Half Moon, but first she wanted to view the famous river and the combat zone on the far side.

The road to the river had a modest slope. Like the main street, its edges sprouted clubs and working girls. At the river, the ground dropped away in a precipice. A thin span of steel and concrete with an American name, Libby Bridge, ran straight to the high embankment on the other side of the waterway. On the near side squatted a guard shack manned by American military police. On the far side, Min-hee could make out sandbagged bunkers with protruding machine guns.

Min-hee walked to the left side of the military police shack and looked down upon the broad waters of the Imjin River. From a map she'd seen, she knew it flowed southwest, taking many twists and turns and a half loop before entering the Han Estuary and the Yellow Sea forty kilometers away. She thought back ten years to lessons of geography and history, before she understood the meaning of being a second daughter where none were wanted.

Min-hee turned away from the embankment, placed her bundle on her head, and

retraced her steps up the road. She crossed the main street to the Half Moon Club and found her papasan out back in an alleyway with verandas and rooms similar to Dongducheon. He slid open the door to the fourth room—linoleum floor, papered walls and ceiling, bed, nightstand, and wardrobe.

"You'll find me fair," he said. "The rent is fixed, once a month, five days after the GI payday, ten dollars. But if you're having a hard time, tell me. We'll work something out."

"Okay," said Min-hee. Less rent than Dongducheon. She could get by on twenty, she thought, maybe make enough to put something away.

"The club is always busy at night. A good place to work."

"Okay," said Min-hee.

"Or you can pick up GIs on the street. But don't go to the other clubs. The girls there will get angry."

That evening, Min-hee walked to the front of the Half Moon Club and watched as truck after truck, spewing diesel exhaust skyward from vertical pipes, crossed east on Libby Bridge and unloaded hordes of off-duty GIs. The soldiers leaped over tailgates and charged up the road with shouts and laughs. Some dropped off at clubs on the way up. The bulk of the formation fanned out on the main street, turning left and right toward the Last Chance Bar, the Lucky Club, and other places. Some came straight on for the Half Moon.

These GIs wore a patch on the left shoulder with the profile of an American Indian. This, Min-hee would learn, was the insignia of the 2nd Infantry Division. They called themselves the Indianhead Division and called the area north of the river Indian Country. Some soldiers had patches on their right shirt pockets depicting an outline of Korea with a line crossing its middle. This was called the Imjin Scouts patch, awarded after twenty missions in the DMZ.

The GIs referred to the town as Chang or the ville. Min-hee learned to be forward, to walk up to soldiers for a dance at the Half Moon Club under low lighting and wailing rock 'n' roll, grind against their cocks, get them in the hooch, get them out. She learned the American pay grades: private E-2, little money except on payday; private first class E-3; specialist E-4; sergeant E-5; staff sergeant E-6, big bucks; sergeant first class E-7, bigger bucks. Sometimes an officer: second lieutenant O-1 or first lieutenant O-2 if she was lucky. Lieutenants weren't allowed in the ville but came anyhow.

Min-hee learned that the army paid once a month on the last day. The first week of every month, she could get five dollars from an E-2 for a one-timer. The last week of the month she would be lucky to get two dollars from a sergeant E-5 for an all-nighter. She didn't like taking more than one one-timer a night, but felt compelled near the beginning of the month to grab what she could. It was a catch-as-catch-can business, and the second half of the month might see no income at all. She couldn't work when her period came on.

Min-hee took care to use a rubber. She took care to washy-washy.

Chapter Five: May 1967, Camp Walley

L orne Boyle had rotated back north with its three-day stints of barrier, outpost, and patrol, and one-night stands in Changpa-ri. On patrols, Lorne led one of the five-man teams, no longer carrying sleeping bags but setting up proper ambushes, two men awake at all times. The weather had turned pleasant, with warm days and cool nights. The DMZ saw new leaves, fresh grass, flowers, bounding deer, wild pigs, and pheasant. The soldiers wore cotton fatigues with sleeves rolled up, flak vests, steel helmets on barrier and outpost, soft caps on patrol.

One morning in late June, Lorne came into Camp Walley after three days on Outpost Seiler. He looked around the platoon hut, empty except for the few returning soldiers, platoon and squad integrity lost with men drawn as needed for DMZ duty. Lorne cleared and dropped his rifle, dropped his helmet, dropped his flak vest, and flopped on his bunk. His next remembrance was being shaken awake, Priestly's face in his.

Priestly said, "We're wanted at the command post."

Outside, Priestly said, "It's fucking Hendrick. He didn't—" Priestly's eyes moved toward the main gate. Lorne turned to see a jeep approaching with an officer, a major, riding shotgun. Lorne and Priestly brought their heels together and threw up salutes at the braking jeep. The major returned their salutes then reached out and grabbed Lorne's dog tags. Lorne saw a cross on the officer's left lapel and realized he must be the brigade chaplain.

"Why are these taped, soldier? I can't read them."

Lorne, still at attention, said, "So they don't jangle on patrol. Sir."

"Are you Catholic?"

"Protestant. Sir."

The major turned his face to Priestly.

"Protestant. Sir."

"I want some Catholics," said the major, "and I want them now."

"Sir," said Priestly. "I'll see what I can do."

The jeep pulled away.

"He didn't come in last night," said Priestly. "Nor this morning."

"Hendrick?"

"He went into Chang last night and didn't come back."

"But he's not our problem. He's detached for driving."

"Apparently he's not detached when he fucks up."

Lorne and Priestly entered the command post, and Lorne got his first up-close of the new first sergeant, a real sergeant E-8, a big guy from the Midwest named Steiner whose voice ranged from loud to shrieking. He jabbed a finger at Lorne and said, "When's the last time you checked on him?"

"I don't know, First Sergeant, I've been on Seiler three days."

"That's your answer? You've been on Seiler three days?" Steiner turned to Priestly. "Who's that officer in our camp?"

"Catholic chaplain," said Priestly.

"Oh Jesus," said Steiner. He turned to the company clerk. "Levine, get some men down to the mess hall so the chaplain can run his service."

Levine looked over his typewriter. "Catholics, First Sergeant?"

"I don't give a fuck what they are. Just get them down there."

Levine jumped up, grabbed his baseball cap, and exited the command post.

Steiner jabbed again at Lorne. "I want you to draw a jeep, and a driver, go across the river, and bring that piece of shit back."

"First Sergeant, we'll never find him."

The veins on the side of Steiner's bald head bulged. "That's your answer, Acting Sergeant? We'll never find him?"

Priestly said, "Top, it's impossible to find anyone in the ville. He'll come in when his money runs out."

"Find him!"

Outside the command post, Lorne said, "It's a fool's errand."

"I know, I know," said Priestly.

"Where's he gonna go in Korea? He has to come back in some time."

"Sergeant Boyle, would you do me this favor? It's a nice day for a ride."

Lorne was not happy. He'd wanted to get a little sleep. He'd wanted to get his gear in order and check on his squad as best he could and go into Changpa-ri for the evening. He drew a jeep and driver from the motor pool. The driver said, "What the fuck we going to Chang for in the middle of the day?"

The driver parked in the square in front of the Lucky Club. Lorne said, "I'm gonna take an hour to look around."

"I'll be here."

• • • •

MIN-HEE SAT ON THE narrow veranda in front of her room, palms down, swinging her legs, keeping her knees bent so as not to scrape the ground. The air was getting sticky, early summer with monsoon season on the way. She wore a wrap-around dress, not yet made up for the night.

From the front of the Half Moon Club, a GI approached. This time of year the GIs wore olive drab uniforms with the shirt sleeves rolled up. This GI was white with a wide face and sticking-out ears. His sleeves had three stripes, a sergeant E-5 or acting sergeant E-4. Middle of the month—Min-hee calculated three dollars for a one-timer but would take two.

However, he didn't behave like a customer. He spoke some English words and lifted a hand to indicate height and pinched the skin of his arm. She heard the word AWOL and understood. AWOL meant running away from the army. This sergeant was looking for an AWOL soldier who was tall and had white skin.

Min-hee shook her head. "*Ubseo*," she said. The Korean phrase *ubseo*, or *ubsumnida*, meant not here or does not exist. All the GIs knew it and mangled it to *oop-so*. They did that with everything. *Mianhamnida* meant I'm sorry—the GIs said *mian-hum-chum*. *Irriwa* meant come here—the GIs said *iddy-wa-wa*.

The sergeant had a smile that seemed a permanent part of his face. "What your name?" he asked.

"Sally Lee."

The sergeant pointed to himself. "Lorne. Can you say?"

"Rawn," said Min-hee, still swinging her legs, still leaning back on the palms of her hands. "So Rawn, wanna go hooch?"

The sergeant looked back toward the main street. He made driving motions with his hands. "No can do."

He gave Min-hee more English words, which she didn't understand, then pointed to a watch on his left wrist. Min-hee peered closer and saw seven o'clock. She pointed to where she sat. "*Yeogi?*"

"*Yeogi*," said the sergeant.

Min-hee memorized the English letters on the sergeant's name tag: BOYLE. When he left, she called out to the girl in the next room, "Hey, Jeong-ja."

The door to the third room slid open, and Jeong-ja stepped onto the veranda. "Yeah, I heard. I think he's in love with you."

"Let's see if he shows up first," said Min-hee.

• • • •

PRIESTLY SAID, "I DON'T imagine you had any luck?" He and Lorne were standing in the motor pool.

"Got a date for tonight," said Lorne.

Priestly guffawed. "That's really hard to do in Chang."

"This feels different."

"It always feels different." Priestly was still grinning.

"I guess we report to our new first sergeant," said Lorne.

"I'll take care of it," said Priestly. "You know, this top's okay."

"If you say so, Sergeant Priestly."

"He knows how to run a company. That's the big thing. If he's nice, that's just frosting."

"I don't mind frosting."

Priestly shook his head. "We're getting a new CO, too, an actual captain."

"A real lifer?"

"I said captain, not lifer."

"Same thing."

"Not these days," said Priestly. "They're asking two-year lieutenants to ship over a year. Automatic promotion to captain."

"And they don't turn into lifers?"

"They might want to, but Vietnam won't last. The army needs them one year, maybe two, then they're gone."

"Why are we all of a sudden getting all this attention in Korea?"

"Because of all the shit along the DMZ. Have fun in Chang tonight."

Camp Walley kept a PX in a corner of the Quonset hut that housed the supply room. It also served as the EM club, the NCO club, and if a lieutenant wandered in, the officers' club. Lorne purchased two cold cans of Coca-Cola and walked to a ton-and-a-quarter idling by the camp gate. He climbed in the back and, with a quarter of the company, bounced south and east, across Libby Bridge, feeling like a kid on his first date.

· · · ·

MIN-HEE TAPPED ON THE wall to Jeong-ja's room. She was still listening to her favorite soap, Lost Love, on her transistor radio, which meant it was between six and seven. "Almost time," said Jeong-ja through the wall.

Min-hee exited her room made up in a red mini-skirt and matching lipstick, heels in hand, slipped them on, and stepped off the veranda. As she heard the sign-off tune from Lost Love, a soldier approached in the western sun. Min-hee shaded her eyes, unable to get a clear picture. No matter, she thought, a soldier is a soldier. But it was him, Rawn Boyle, the sergeant who said he'd come back at seven.

Boyle sat on the veranda and removed two red-and-silver cans of Coca-Cola from a paper bag. "You like?"

"Yeah, rike," said Min-hee.

She sipped her coke. Boyle talked to her. He smiled all the time. She didn't understand what he said. Earlier in the month, this would have annoyed Min-hee—time was money—but mid-month business was slow: might as well relax, have a good time. She ran numbers in her head and decided three dollars would be her rock bottom price. Five if he stayed over.

Min-hee leaned back and slid her door open. "Wanna go?" she said.

"Sure," said Boyle. He leaned over and unlaced his boots.

Min-hee and Boyle sat on the bed. Boyle crossed his legs under him, Korean style. "Okay," said Min-hee, "four dollar can do."

Boyle said words that sounded like *koolyer-jets*, but Min-hee had no idea what they meant. Boyle continued to smile and look around. He said more words. Min-hee said, "No wanna fucky-fucky?"

Boyle motioned a calm-down with his right hand. "Yeah, yeah, we fucky-fucky. Koolyer-jets."

He pulled a wallet from his back pocket and placed military scrip on the night table, a five and a single. "Have to go eleven," he said. He pointed at his watch. Okay by me, thought Min-hee. Six dollars for an all-nighter and he's not even staying all night. She unzipped her mini-skirt. Boyle put a hand on her hand. "Koolyer-jets," he said.

An hour passed before they were undressed and in coitus. A half hour later, Boyle came back for seconds. Slow start, strong finish. A quarter before eleven, Boyle pulled on his fatigue shirt and pants.

"Okay?" said Min-hee. "You rike?"

"Yeah," said Boyle, "I like. Come again? Okay?"

This was the first time a soldier had asked to see Min-hee again. Good for business, she thought, bad if he became a pest. But this soldier had three stripes and had paid her six dollars, middle of the month. "Yeah, okay," she said.

Boyle held up the fingers of his right hand minus the thumb. "Four nights, come again." He pointed to seven o'clock on his watch. "Okay?"

Min-hee now knew he was a fighting soldier. The headquarters and supply and other soldiers who didn't fight, which was most of them, came to town whenever they wanted. The fighting soldiers worked three nights in the DMZ then had one night off. "Can do," she said.

• • • •

FOUR DAYS LATER, MIN-hee stepped outside to the sign-off tune of Lost Love. A minute later, Boyle sauntered into the alleyway, a wide smile as always. He pointed toward the main street and asked her a question, but she didn't understand. When he asked again, Jeong-ja slid open her door and scooted onto the veranda. "Min-hee, he wants to take you to a movie. I tell you, he's madly in love."

"Yeah," said Min-hee, "maybe he just likes movies."

"You wait. Tonight he'll ask you to be his yobo."

Min-hee checked Boyle's smile—he looked oblivious to their discussion. "What should I do," she said to Jeong-ja, "if he asks me?"

"Depends on what he offers. I think—yeah, if he offers twenty-five, take it. Too bad he's not an E-6." Jeong-ja turned her head to Boyle and said in English, "Sally say yeah, movie number one."

Min-hee and Boyle walked to the main street, turned right, and a minute later arrived at a cement block building filled with folding chairs overflowing with working girls and other Koreans. Min-hee glanced about. Boyle was the only American. He looked at her with closed lips pulled wide. She returned his strange smile then turned to the front as the projector's stream of light hit the screen. The audience as one went silent and leaned forward to appraise the opening credits. *Divorce American Style*, Dick Van Dyke, Debbie Reynolds, Jason Robards, Jean Simmons, Van Johnson, English with Korean subtitles.

Min-hee clapped, laughed, and sighed with the rest of the audience. She loved the plot with its on-and-off relationships and intrigue. The setting appeared to her as a fantasy land. She couldn't imagine living in houses with many rooms, indoor toilets, and electricity. How much of it was made up?

That night, in Min-hee's room, Boyle extracted his brown leather wallet. They had not discussed price. It was later in the month, but Min-hee hoped for the same six dollars. She also had Jeong-ja's words bouncing in her head, half hoping he'd ask her, half hoping he wouldn't.

Boyle rubbed the wallet between the palms of his hands, looking down, then up. Then he asked the question. "You wanna be yobo?"

Min-hee didn't know how to ask how much in English, much less in a polite manner. She knew how to say, three dollar can do, five dollar can do, but this occasion demanded a more nuanced vocabulary. She put three English words together as a question, not sure if they fit the occasion. "What you say?"

Boyle pulled a ten-dollar note from his wallet and laid it on the nightstand. He reached again in his wallet. Another ten, a five, and five one-dollar notes followed.

Min-hee looked over the military scrip. Thirty dollars a month, the same as five times a month at six dollars a visit, but that wouldn't last. She pointed at Boyle's stripes. "E-5?"

Boyle shook his head. "E-4."

This was disappointing, but what was Min-hee going to do, wait for an E-5 to come along? The offer was generous for an E-4. A guaranteed income with no hustling while it lasted.

"Okay," she said.

"Okay?"

"Okay. Be yobo."

They were sitting on the bed and Boyle edged next to Min-hee. He placed his arms around her shoulders and kissed her. When he took his lips away, he hugged her. Like Debbie Reynolds and Dick Van Dyke.

• • • •

NEXT MORNING, LORNE started a 3-day patrol, drawing Rothman, DiMaggio, Ivan, and a man from another squad for his team. They meandered to the MDL, followed it east for a hundred meters, and dropped back a kilometer to their night ambush site. They sat around eating C-rations and smoking.

Rothman said, "What's the word on Hendrick?"

"Still gone," said Lorne. "Wouldn't bother me if he stayed gone."

Ivan farted and said, "His next trip will be to the Eighth Army Stockade."

"I bet not," said Lorne. "Would you mind moving downwind?"

"Why not?"

"He's their poster boy," said Lorne. "He'll probably get busted back to E-2, no more."

"Four years," said DiMaggio, "and still a private. Hey, Rothman, you put in your papers for re-up?"

"Fuck you," said Rothman.

DiMaggio laughed. "So what are you gonna do without the army holding your cock?"

"I'm using the GI Bill to become an aeronautical engineer."

"Goddamn," said Ivan, "you're not as dumb as you look."

"Fuck you," said Rothman.

"What are you doing, Sergeant Boyle?" said DiMaggio.

"Going back to the farm," said Lorne.

"Back to the farm?"

"Yup. There's a lot of money in chickens if you're smart about it."

"Sergeant Boyle," said DiMaggio, "you been in the best mood I ever seen you. Because Hendrick is gone?"

"That helps," said Lorne, "but mainly I've found the love of my life in Chang."

The men fell back laughing, even Rothman. DiMaggio said, "I find a new love of my life every time I go to the ville."

More laughter.

The long shadows turned to no shadows, and the team set up for the night, two men to Lorne's left and two to his right. Lorne went to each set of two soldiers and said, "One of you awake at all times."

Lorne picked up the handset of the prick twenty-five and checked in with charlie zero. At the other end, he recognized Levine's voice. Levine said, "Everything okay, over?"

Lorne pressed the push-to-talk button. "Okey dokey, over?"

"You guys have a good night, out."

At first light, the radio crackled again. It was charlie zero, but Priestly's voice. He said, "Meet me at the iron drop gate. In an hour, over."

"What's that for?" said Rothman.

"Guess whatever he has, he doesn't want it on the air," said Lorne. "Okay, guys, let's finish chow and saddle up."

At the drop gate, another team appeared, led by Hank. When asked what was up, he answered, "Your guess is as good as mine."

Ten minutes later, Priestly came into sight. The two teams gathered around. Priestly said, "We got hit. Early this morning."

"Hit?" said Hank.

"Joe came in last night and set a couple of satchel charges. They went off a few hours ago."

"Camp Walley?" said Lorne. "The camp got hit?"

"Two dead, and we sent out seven wounded."

Jesus, thought Lorne, they just walked into Camp Walley and blew up a hut. Here we are, guardians of the DMZ, and they just walked into our camp?

"Sergeant Priestly," said Rothman. "Anybody from our platoon?"

Priestly shook his head. "Admin and supply. Levine and a new kid."

"Levine's dead?" said Lorne.

Priestly nodded. "Did you hear anything out here last night?"

Lorne shook his head. "Just some animals rustling around. It wasn't Joe."

"Same here," said Hank.

"Let the other two teams know," said Priestly. "See you in a couple of days."

As Priestly faded south, Hank pulled Lorne aside. "Those fuckers. What are they trying to prove?"

Lorne said, "I hear it has something to do with us being all out in Vietnam, and them opening another front here."

"I think they just like being assholes," said Hank.

"I hear we hit them once."

"Oh," said Hank. "I was on that."

"You're shitting me."

Hank shook his head. "It was before I became an acting jack. We were up on Seiler without a lieutenant, and we got sick of looking across at the gooks and their hatchet throwing and decided to whack them."

"When was this?"

"Oh, almost a year ago. So we crossed over about zero two hundred, six of us, and shot up their outpost. It wasn't thought out. We just emptied a couple clips each and tossed a few grenades. Then ran back. Let me tell you, I never ran so fast in my life."

"I'd be scared shitless," said Lorne, "being on the wrong side of the MDL."

"You think I wasn't?" said Hank.

"What happened after?"

"Well, we buttoned down Seiler the next day, but there was no retaliation. I don't think the gooks knew exactly what happened or who did it. We got yelled at."

"Yelled at?"

"Yeah. I got called in by a lieutenant colonel. He kept saying, are you nuts? But there was no court martial over it."

"You think our brass was secretly happy we whacked them?"

"I don't think so," said Hank. "I think they just wanted to bury it. The gooks complained at Panmunjom, and we gave them their own shit, I hear. We said, sorry, Joe, we don't know what you're talking about."

"You must be near the end of your tour," said Lorne.

"Twelve and a wake-up," said Hank. He sighed.

"Don't tell me you're gonna miss it?" said Lorne.

"I'm gonna miss Chang. I'm gonna miss my pussy."

"But not this," said Lorne, sweeping his arms about.

"Actually, I kind of like it out here. No inspections, no marching, nobody bothers you, the occasional lieutenant. And it's exciting."

Life in the zone did have a certain charm, thought Lorne. Three days of running around with loaded rifles, one day off for fucking. But there was the downside of taking a hit, the anger, the helplessness.

"I guess you're too short to pull another raid across the MDL," said Lorne.

"I would never do that again, short or not," said Hank. "Like the man said, we were fucking nuts."

• • • •

TWO DAYS LATER, LORNE watched an engineering crew bulldoze the remains of the admin hut off its cement slab, the plan being to slap down a new hut. Next morning found Lorne on the barrier with seven men and four hundred meters of trench. Toward evening, the lieutenant running Lorne's sector called a meeting outside his command bunker. The soldiers sat on sandbagged entrenchments with their legs hanging. The lieutenant stood next to the door to the bunker and said, "Would you guys mind keeping your fucking eyes open?"

The soldiers flicked ashes from their cigarettes, and looked into the trenches.

"If you see someone climbing over the fence with a submachine gun and a satchel charge, you have permission to shoot him. Okay?"

"Yessir," said the soldiers, and drifted away to their trenches and bunkers. Lorne wanted to ask the lieutenant where he'd been when the hooch was blown up. Why didn't *he* stop Joe from coming through the barrier? Why didn't *he* catch Joe coming onto their compound? Was the sarcasm necessary?

Lorne spread himself and his seven soldiers in two-man teams across their four hundred meters. This is nuts, he thought, but to his soldiers, he said, "One man awake all the time. I'll be checking."

As Rothman and a new man went into position, Rothman said, "It's a near thing, Sergeant Boyle."

"What are you talking about?"

"I mean if Joe comes climbing over the fence, it's a near thing whether we engage him or not. It could go either way."

"If Joe comes climbing over the fence," said Lorne, giving a side glance to the new man, "you nudge your buddy and start shooting. There's nothing near about it."

"The thing is, you may be scared so shitless, you can't react."

"You may be scared shitless," said Lorne, "but you better be pulling that trigger."

"I heard scuttlebutt that someone down the line saw Joe and just let him go. Didn't want to mix it up."

"That's not happening on my watch. Our watch. You got that?"

Rothman bobbed his head. "I hear you, Sergeant Boyle."

Lorne had no doubt as to his personal reaction if he saw Joe. And it made sense to shoot while he had the advantage. But—Lorne remembered a night in the DMZ when an animal, a large animal, deer or wild pig, approached his team's ambush position. The strength drained from his arms and legs, as if his bones had dissolved. Even though, in the back of his mind, he knew it had to be an animal, not Joe. The guys laughed over it the next morning. Lorne understood what Rothman meant about freezing, about fear taking over the body. This wasn't the movies.

· · · ·

IN JULY, THE MONSOON rains started. On patrol, Lorne called a halt for noon chow. He squatted and pulled his arms in and his head down so his poncho formed a tent. He applied his P-38 opener to a can of franks and beans. *Where's my fucking spoon?* Every time he moved, his socks squished. He heard Rothman's voice. *Doesn't he ever shut up?* Lorne poked his head back up through the neck hole of his poncho.

Rothman, squatting alongside, said, "This really sucks, Sergeant Boyle."

"That's correct, Specialist Rothman."

"I was thinking, this is a good time for Joe to come down, take advantage of the situation."

"I don't think so. I think Joe has more brains than us, knows enough to get in out of the rain."

"I'm not so sure about that," said Rothman. "We wouldn't see him coming, wouldn't hear him."

"Look, I'm gonna duck back under here and finish my lunch. Okay?"

"Okay, Sergeant Boyle. Good talking to you."

Chapter Six: June 1967, North of the MDL

Jun-seok and Chong followed Captain Ho, who followed an officer from the 17th Foot Reconnaissance Brigade. They wore polished green and carried PPS-43 submachine guns. An enlisted man from the 17th Foot headed the short column, and two more enlisted men brought up the rear.

A high, chain-link fence topped by barbed wire crossed in front of them as far as Jun-seok could see in either direction. The land about the fence lay barren, except for jutting watch towers. A kilometer ahead, on the other side of the fence, appeared a forest. The lead enlisted man unlocked and swung open a gate in the fence, and the team passed through.

"You are now in the famous DMZ," said the reconnaissance officer, a senior lieutenant. "Let's pick up the pace." The lieutenant looked tough and worn, in the mold of Captain Ho, although thin in the shoulders, with a hawk nose.

The team double-timed across the kilometer of open ground into hardwoods and tall pines. They slowed and followed a path for twenty minutes until the lead enlisted man raised his hand. Jun-seok could see by light through the trees that they were coming to another open area.

The point man led the group forward until only single trees and brush separated them from the open ground. The reconnaissance lieutenant said, "Pick a place where you can squat and get a good view."

Jun-seok chose a viewing spot on the well-trampled forest floor. He squatted and gazed across two hundred meters of open, grassy terrain; on the other side, more woods started.

The reconnaissance lieutenant said, "Look to the right, about forty-five degrees. What do you see?"

"An outpost," said Ho.

Indeed, to their right front rose a small hill topped by sandbagged trenches and enclosures.

"Look again," said the reconnaissance lieutenant.

"Aha," said Ho. "Two outposts."

"The nearest one is ours," said the reconnaissance lieutenant. He passed binoculars to Ho. "The one to the south belongs to the running dogs."

When the binoculars came to Jun-seok, he put them into focus and examined the Americans on the farther outpost. They wore helmets and flak vests.

"Their rifles are M14s," said Jun-seok.

"Correct," said the reconnaissance lieutenant.

"There's another type, with a scope. Resting on top of some sandbags."

The reconnaissance lieutenant took the binoculars. He said, "An M1 sniper rifle. Another reason not to expose yourself during the daytime."

"Will they shoot at us?"

"They're not supposed to shoot across, but best to play it safe."

Jun-seok passed the binoculars to Chong.

The reconnaissance lieutenant said, "You see that path on the other side of the field? Parallel to us? It runs between the two outposts? See the signposts every hundred meters?"

Chong nodded and passed the binoculars to Ho. The captain nodded and passed the binoculars to Jun-seok.

Jun-seok examined the path. It lay on the other side of the clear area just before the trees picked up again. It did not look like a constructed path but earth worn down by many footsteps over the years. He could make out the signposts.

"That's the Military Demarcation Line," said the reconnaissance lieutenant. "The dividing line between the imperialists and us."

Minutes passed. Captain Ho said, "Are we waiting for something?"

"The American patrol," said the reconnaissance lieutenant. "Their headquarters company sends out a special patrol every morning. They call it the MDL patrol."

"How do you know that?"

"We listen to their radio transmissions."

A half hour later, the reconnaissance lieutenant said, "Here they come. Look—the other side of the outposts."

The Americans walked single file on the path between the two opposing forces. They wore flak vests and soft field caps, and carried M14 rifles. Their left shoulders bore a patch with the head of an American Indian in profile. The Yankees looked ahead and to the north, into the trees where Jun-seok's patrol squatted.

"Don't worry," whispered the reconnaissance lieutenant. "They don't see us. But what do you notice?"

"They're sloppy," said Ho.

"They have Negroid as well as Caucasian soldiers," said Chong. "Wait. There's a Korean—no, two Koreans—with them."

"Yes," said the reconnaissance lieutenant, "they force Koreans into their army. But what do you really notice?"

Nobody spoke up.

"How old do you think they are?" said the reconnaissance lieutenant.

Of course, that's it, thought Jun-seok. He considered himself to be immature at thirty-one, but these American soldiers were only boys. When the binoculars came to him, Jun-seok examined their faces. He guessed three or four of them were in their twenties, the rest in their teens.

Jun-seok's patrol dropped back ten meters.

"So that's who we're up against," said Ho.

"I wanted you to see their faces before we go over," said the reconnaissance lieutenant. "But it's important not to get complacent. That's when we lose our edge."

"Now what?" said Ho.

"We'll be taking a long break. Until after dark."

The team sat and munched rice balls. Chong put his head close to Jun-seok and said, "What do you think, little brother, are you nervous?"

"Yeah, I'm nervous," said Jun-seok. "Aren't you?"

"More excited than nervous. Too bad we can't smoke."

"Discipline is essential," said the reconnaissance lieutenant. Jun-seok turned to see he was squatting a meter from them. "Remember, our mission is to observe and become familiar. Not to make contact. Follow the lead of my men."

• • • •

TWO HOURS PAST DUSK, in faint starlight, the patrol stepped from the trees into the open field. They felt their way along a north-south ditch that gave them cover from the American outpost. But at night the main requisite was silence. The three enlisted men went first, followed by Ho, Chong, Jun-seok, and the reconnaissance lieutenant. They reached the path, the border between the two forces, without incident, and squatted there in anticipation of the waning moon. They needed more light to keep from thrashing about in the woods on the American side.

Jun-seok entered a half sleep. Take any opportunity for rest, he had learned. He could sleep sitting, squatting, standing up, walking. Hours went by. Jun-seok felt a shoulder tap and came out of his doze. The patrol moved, sometimes with rapid steps, sometimes at a crawl. The enlisted men knew the terrain, speeding up on paths and open areas, passing through brush with great care. During the break that afternoon, one of them had told Jun-seok they could smell the American ambush patrols from the cigarettes they smoked before going into position at dusk.

Jun-seok had only to keep sight of Chong's back and watch the placement of his own feet, cringing at every cracked twig. The patrol zagged south, walked up an incline, and settled in squats on a ridge of brush and trees. As dawn approached, the reconnaissance lieutenant motioned for Ho, Jun-seok, and Chong to take positions that allowed them to see through the brush. He put his palm down with a grimace, an exhortation to take small steps and push brush aside with deliberate motions.

Jun-seok's bowels tightened. In front of him, not more than a hundred meters, at a lower elevation, ran a chain-link fence with barbed wire. On their side of the fence, for a width of forty meters, to the base of their low ridge, the land lay cleared of vegetation. Twenty meters from the fence ran a line of barbed wire with red triangles, indicating a minefield. On the other side of the chain-link fence, Jun-seok saw sandbagged entrenchments and bunkers. He saw Americans in helmets and flak vests smoking cigarettes and on occasion looking around.

Toward noon, the reconnaissance lieutenant signaled the patrol to withdraw from the ridge. The men backed off with care, emptied their bladders, and settled in for a snack.

The reconnaissance lieutenant huddled with Ho, Chong, and Jun-seok. "All you need to get through," he said, "is a knife and bolt cutters." A knife to probe for mines and bolt cutters for the fence. "They used to have a wooden fence. Have you seen American cowboy movies?"

Nobody responded—American movies were not permitted in North Korea. The reconnaissance lieutenant smiled. "I thought you might have seen one as part of your training."

Jun-seok had seen four, including one with cowboys and American Indians, all from military projectors, billed—as the reconnaissance lieutenant had suggested—as training films. But he was not about to admit it. Even Chong didn't venture a smart remark. Jun-seok doubted if a skilled reconnaissance officer was political, but one never knew.

"Their old fence looked like the wall of a fort in those cowboy movies." The reconnaissance officer pointed northeast. "They still have some sections like that."

"Do we go back as soon as it's dark?" said Ho.

"No," said the reconnaissance lieutenant. "We wait for the moon. So we'll observe some more, then get some sleep."

Jun-seok positioned himself on his back and rested his head on a rock. *This commando work is not all bad.* Chong lay next to him and whispered. "Isn't this the balls?" His face glistened like a recruit's before the reality of military life set in. He put his lips closer to Jun-seok's ear. "We're in the belly of the beast."

The belly of the beast or not, it was clear to Jun-seok they were where they shouldn't be. Their emergency instructions—what to do if discovered—were to empty a clip and run north. The purpose of the exercise, they were told, was to remove the jitters of working in enemy territory. Jun-seok fell asleep thinking Chong was dispensing with the jitters better than he.

When Jun-seok opened his eyes, it was as if he still had them closed. He couldn't see a meter. He sensed his comrades waking up. Waiting. Halfway between midnight and dawn, a sliver of moon appeared through the trees. Now he could see three or four meters. Ho tapped his shoulder, and he took his position behind Chong.

The men moved north in a zigzag fashion, the same way they'd come in, as far as Jun-seok could tell. An hour out, Chong slowed and stopped. Looking past him in the dim light, Jun-seok discerned the profile of the point man with his face up, like a hunting dog, sniffing the air. Then he turned left with short, deliberate movements, slower than any on the way down. Jun-seok realized this was a time for more silence than ever and willed every fiber of his body not to emit the slightest sound. He brought his boots down a centimeter at a time, lifting and trying another spot if he felt a twig about to break.

The point man repeated his previous motions, stopping, sniffing, moving left, at still a slower pace. He dropped to his hands and knees. The rest of the patrol dropped likewise, one by one. They proceeded with a technique learned in night training. With one hand, clear away twigs and leaves, then place the knee there. Clear another spot and place the other knee. Not a decibel of sound. Jun-seok never imagined he'd be using this training technique for real.

Hours passed. At times, Jun-seok thought he could smell stale smoke from American cigarettes, but maybe not; maybe it was his imagination. One thing he knew, they were near an American ambush patrol, or they wouldn't be going through this exacting maneuver. They had moved but a hundred meters in the past hour.

Ahead, the point man rose. The rest of the patrol followed his lead, walking with half steps. To their right rear, shards of dawn pierced the branches. The point man put up his hand, and the reconnaissance lieutenant walked forward. He whispered with the enlisted men, looked about, came back, and called a huddle.

"Our bad luck," he said. "The Americans set up an ambush on our exit route."

"They know we're here?" said Ho.

The reconnaissance lieutenant shook his head. "They don't know anything. They set up night ambushes on their side of the MDL at random. Like I said, it's just bad luck." He looked to the southeast. "And now we have daylight."

The reconnaissance lieutenant motioned the patrol forward another two meters. From this vantage point, Jun-seok saw the trodden path of the MDL crossing in front of them twenty meters farther. The ground between them and the border contained high weeds and a few thin hardwood trees. The reconnaissance lieutenant pointed his finger to the right. "The ditch we came in on is over there."

Jun-seok, Ho, and Chong looked over the ground, the open terrain, the worn path, the ditch. They'd be okay once they got in the ditch, but twenty meters of American DMZ lay between it and them.

"Where's the Yankee outpost?" said Ho.

The reconnaissance lieutenant tossed his head to the left. "You can see it if you step out. And they can see you if they look. But it's a good distance, about three hundred meters."

Jun-seok envisioned the outpost, the American boy-soldiers in their flak vests and helmets. But in possession of lethal weapons.

"We'll make a run for it," said the reconnaissance lieutenant. "Otherwise, we'd have to sit here another day. Too dangerous."

"What about that sniper rifle?" said Jun-seok.

"It's a concern, Comrade Lieutenant," said the reconnaissance lieutenant. "Even with their M14s, they could get a lucky hit. Look, one of my men will go first." The reconnaissance lieutenant turned to Ho. "Then you, Comrade Captain, then Lieutenant Chong, then Lieutenant Pak. Okay?"

The reconnaissance lieutenant opened his arms to his remaining two enlisted men. "We'll go last. That's the most dangerous."

The three officers from Unit 124 nodded.

"Two-second intervals," said the reconnaissance lieutenant. "Run fast in a crouch. Make yourself small. Don't look around—just run."

The men formed a queue. The reconnaissance lieutenant tapped the butt of the first enlisted man, and he sprang forward. Jun-seok counted to himself, one thousand and one, one thousand and two, and the reconnaissance lieutenant said to Ho, "Go, go."

The captain bounded after the first enlisted man; two seconds later Chong leaped forward. Jun-seok heard, "Go, go," and pumped his legs into a dead run. On the second stride, he heard shouts, foreign voices, at a distance to his left, and knew they'd been spotted. He tucked his head and pumped his legs.

Ahead Chong twisted his body toward the American outpost, which slowed his run and froze him for a second in mid-stride. And he smiled—to reassure his little brother? For the sake of the adventure? And he wasn't in a crouch. With his body still twisted and his right knee in the air, Chong said, "Aw." The report of a rifle reached Jun-seok's ears as Chong lurched right, then left, and a cheer sounded from the American outpost.

Jun-seok caught up with Chong and threw a shoulder under his left arm. The reconnaissance lieutenant caught up and went under the other arm. Chong's feet stopped working as Jun-seok and the reconnaissance lieutenant dragged him to the ditch.

"Put him on your back," said the reconnaissance lieutenant. "We have to get out of here." Jun-seok bent over, felt Chong being pushed on his back, and grabbed the limp arms that draped his shoulders.

"Go, go," said the reconnaissance lieutenant.

Jun-seok forced every step of the two hundred meters, putting forward one foot, then the other, ignoring fatigue and pain, with the reconnaissance lieutenant lifting and pushing from behind. He didn't hear any more shooting from the Americans. As the distance to the trees shrank, the enlisted man up front and Ho ran back to help. A minute later, Chong lay on his back on needles and dirt under a large pine.

Jun-seok dropped to his knees and opened Chong's bloodstained shirt. Near his left nipple, blood gurgled.

"We need a compress," said Jun-seok.

Ho pulled Jun-seok to his feet and back a meter. "He's better off to bleed out."

The reconnaissance lieutenant said, "What's his *songbun*?"

"Wavering," said the captain.

The reconnaissance lieutenant nodded. "Even if he survived, he'd be out of special operations. He'd be out of the officer corps."

"Why?" said Jun-seok. "Is it his fault he was shot?"

Ho pressed closer to Jun-seok and pointed at Chong. "Look how peaceful he is." It was true. Chong's eyes had closed. He shook every third or fourth breath—the breaths coming with less frequency—but exhibited no pain. "Not a bad way to go."

• • • •

THE NEXT DAY, HO SAID, "Comrade Pak, you've been a soldier long enough to know these things happen."

Ho and Jun-seok were in their barracks standing over Chong's sleeping platform.

"I understand, Comrade Captain."

"His sacrifice has made the rest of us stronger."

"Of course, Comrade Captain."

Ho pushed a forefinger through the loose items next to Chong's folded pants and shirts. He separated two photographs, one of Chong's parents and the second of Chong in dress uniform on his day of commission as a lieutenant. He also pushed aside some *won* notes and a watch.

"Take these," said Ho. Jun-seok lifted his eyebrows. "If you don't, someone else will."

"Won't they be returned to his family?"

"Not through official channels," said Ho. Jun-seok felt like a twelve-year-old being explained the facts of life. Ho looked at him and added, "If not mendacity, then bureaucratic incompetence."

"They'll return only his body?"

Ho didn't respond. Jun-seok bent and picked up the items. He placed them in a pocket, taking care not to bend the pictures.

Ho said, "I've arranged a furlough for you. Next week."

"Are we still a team, Comrade Captain?"

"We are. More than ever. But I think you need a furlough. When you return, you'll be breaking in a new man."

The captain clapped Jun-seok on the shoulder. "A few days off. When you come back, you'll be fit, ready to go. Correct?"

"Correct, Comrade Captain."

"That's the spirit. Let me see your fierce face."

Jun-seok thought, is this a joke? But the captain didn't look like he was joking. Jun-seok parted his lips, keeping his teeth together. He spread the corners of his mouth. He made the fierce face.

• • • •

IN KOKSAN-UP, JUN-SEOK bribed the driver of a northbound truck with a pack of cigarettes, and as the truck slowed before Chong's village, dropped over the tailgate. The least he could do for Chong's family was to pay his respects and deliver the personal items. Jun-seok waited for dark and moved on the back paths as though he were in the DMZ. He watched Chong's house for a while before approaching and tapping. The door slid open to the bland face of Chong's mother, and Jun-seok slipped inside with boots in hand.

Chong's father sat cross-legged on the other side of the room. His eyebrows rose, then dropped. Jun-seok bowed. Chong's father nodded for him to sit. Chong's mother looked at her husband, then retreated to the kitchen.

Chong's sister stood by the door to the kitchen.

"I wish to express my condolences," said Jun-seok. He removed the two photographs and placed them on the floor. He removed the *won* notes and watch, and placed them on the floor. "We didn't know if Myung-seung's belongings would be safely returned. I wanted to make sure you got these."

Chong's mother returned with cups and a pot of tea—boiled barley—not leaves, not even a rice tea. She put out kimchi, and cakes made from barley.

Chong's father said, "It's kind of you to stop by. We suspected something had happened."

Chong's mother lowered herself to her knees with hands clasped. "Are you certain?"

The father leaned forward and lowered his voice. "What can you tell us?"

Jun-seok had prepared a story, an embellishment of what had happened, without mentioning the units involved and the Americans. But the father's words, they—suspected? Jun-seok sipped his tea and saw his hand was unsteady. He put the tea down and looked across at Chong's father, the mother in his peripheral vision, the sister in the doorway behind her. *What am I doing here?*

"You don't know your son died a hero's death?"

Chong's mother's head dropped. His father said, "We've heard nothing. But our extra rations stopped last week. Yesterday the factory dismissed me."

Chong's father looked at his wife. He looked at the picture of the Great Leader. His eyes came back to Jun-seok. "My supervisor said it was political and there was nothing he could do."

Jun-seok thought back to Chong bleeding out in the forest and Captain Ho's remarks and those of the reconnaissance lieutenant. Were their leaders angry because Chong had wasted the expense of his training by getting killed? Or was it his *songbun*, wavering, cast aside when not useful?

Chong's father said, "We thought Myung-seung had opened his mouth one time too many." The father shook his head. "He gets it from me."

"No, no," said Jun-seok. "He died in an enemy action. I was there."

"He wasn't tortured or sent away?"

"I tell you he died from an enemy bullet."

"And you were there?"

"If you hear anything different, it's like you say, political."

The mother remained kneeling with hands clasped. Behind her, Chong's sister sobbed. For a moment, Jun-seok thought Chong's mother wasn't crying but then, in the dim light, saw tears on her cheeks. He was pleased that he'd delivered the photographs but wanted to be gone. They hadn't received official notification? They hadn't received his body? Maybe it was bureaucratic incompetence as Captain Ho had said. Maybe a letter would arrive in a month or so along with Chong's ashes. Jun-seok didn't know what to think.

Chong's father pointed to the barley cakes. His voice was a hoarse whisper. "I'm ashamed we can't offer you better fare."

Jun-seok slipped out of the village an hour later and double-timed up the road. He awoke at dawn on the floor of his childhood home to the soft nudges of his mother's hand. "How long do you have with us?" she said. "We're off to the fields."

Jun-seok sat up. His father sat two meters away, chopsticks and bowl in hand. "I'm going with you," said Jun-seok.

"That's nice," said his father. "We can chat while walking over. I'm afraid we'll be late coming home. The harvest is in."

"No," said Jun-seok. "I mean I'm working with you today."

"You must get your rest," said his mother. "You have other duties."

Jun-seok's father put his bowl and chopsticks aside. He smiled. "Do you forget how hard and boring the work is? Bending over with a sickle, slashing, straightening up, all day. And you an officer now."

"That's why, Father. I don't want everyone to think I'm such a big shot I can't work a day in the fields."

Jun-seok's father massaged the stubble on his chin. He pushed against the floor with his left hand and rose to his feet. The years of bending and straightening had curved his back and narrowed his shoulders.

"Did you stop by your friend's? Lieutenant Chong, right?"

"Briefly," said Jun-seok.

"Is there something wrong?" said Jun-seok's mother. Always the sixth sense with mothers.

"Well," said Jun-seok, "Lieutenant Chong is no longer with our unit. I can't say any more about it."

"That's the army," said Jun-seok's father, "always moving men around. Look, I have to piss. I'll wait for you outside."

Jun-seok's mother placed a bowl and chopsticks in his hands. "Eat something before we go."

As Jun-seok shoveled and swallowed, he felt fingertips along his scalp.

"What are you doing, mother?"

"What, I can't touch my son?"

• • • •

UPON JUN-SEOK'S RETURN to Unit 124, Ho said, "Let's go meet our new team member. His name is Yoon. He looks like a baby."

Jun-seok and Ho walked outside where the temperature had started its downward trajectory toward the long winter. A new lieutenant stood at attention next to a knapsack of rocks, trying not to shiver. Jun-seok peered at the soldier's smooth face as he circled him twice. Crow's feet spread from his eyes. Early twenties, Jun-seok guessed, but he could be taken for sixteen at first glance.

Ho said, "So you're an officer now? A brand new lieutenant, eh?"

"Comrade Captain," said Yoon.

"Shut up," said Ho. Yoon pulled in his chin and stared forward.

"For the next two months," said Ho, "you're scum. If you survive, then you can think about your exalted status."

"Comrade Captain."

"I told you to shut up." Ho lifted his bludgeon. "Can't you obey a simple order?" The bludgeon slammed the side of Yoon's face. His knees wobbled but he held his stance.

Ho smiled. "You look cold, Comrade Scum. Lieutenant Pak, maybe you can help warm him up."

Jun-seok lifted the knapsack and held it out. "Take it," he said.

Yoon grasped the knapsack with two hands and tilted forward from its unexpected weight. He recovered his balance and put one arm through a shoulder strap, then the other.

"On the double," said Jun-seok.

Chapter Seven: July 1967, Changpa-ri

Min-hee wrote to Soo-jin in Dongducheon. I have a yobo, a white sergeant E-5. He has a nice smile and treats me great. Thirty dollars a month. How about that?

A week later, Soo-jin wrote back. Don't get too attached. If he gives you any trouble or doesn't pay up, drop him.

Later that day, Min-hee sat on the veranda with Jeong-ja listening to a soap. In this episode, a GI stood in front of his commanding officer and said, Captain, I'm in love with a Korean girl. I respectfully ask permission to marry her. Min-hee knew the commander wouldn't consent right away, and that there would be other problems. But she also knew that many episodes later, the wedding would take place, and she would go with him to America.

"Do you think that really happens?" said Min-hee.

"Yeah, one in a thousand. But you want some advice?"

"Not really," said Min-hee. "I've already had plenty."

"Well, I'll tell you anyhow. Don't plan on anything from that sergeant. You using a rubber every time?"

"GIs don't like rubbers," said Min-hee.

"GIs don't get pregnant."

Min-hee swung her legs back and forth with her palms on the veranda. "He's different," she said.

"He's not different."

• • • •

MIN-HEE'S ENGLISH IMPROVED and she had conversations with her yobo, Boyle. She was surprised to learn that he came from a farm.

"Cows," he said. "Two cows for milk."

"Yeah?" She understood. Like an ox, but for milk and meat, not work.

"Chickens. Hundreds. Tacsan." Everyone in Changpa-ri, Korean and American, used the Japanese words for many and few, tacsan and skoshi.

"What you do with chickens?"

"Eat them, chop chop." Boyle simulated using chopsticks. "You like?"

"Dog better," said Min-hee and laughed. The girls liked to tease the GIs about their aversion to dog meat. Min-hee didn't understand why someone would eat a filthy bird but turn his nose up at dog meat. The GIs also had trouble with kimchi, the Korean staple made from fermented vegetables, usually Chinese cabbage, laced with red pepper.

An American farm, thought Min-hee. Really? She had imagined all Americans living in houses with sidewalks and lawns, or in skyscrapers. Now she thought, well, yes, they must have farms too. They have to get their food from somewhere. Boyle brought a black-and-white photograph of him, his siblings, his mother and father. They looked the same, with wide faces, except for the father, whose face was thin and stern. Min-hee thought of her own family and wondered if she'd ever see her mother again. She said, "Look rike mom."

Boyle peered into the photograph. "I guess I do."

Min-hee turned her attention to the setting, the kitchen. "Whah this?"

"The stove," said Boyle. A stove without a stovepipe—Min-hee knew about those from the movies. She recognized the refrigerator and understood its function. It amazed her that the kitchen was a normal room in the house.

She pointed. "Water come here?" Boyle nodded. She had recognized the sink with faucets to bring in the water. But there was one aspect of this large basin she didn't understand. "How throw away water?"

"Go out bottom," Boyle said. Min-hee watched his pantomimes until she understood the water went away from the house through a pipe.

"Same with pee pee," said Boyle.

"Whah?"

Later that week, Min-hee and Jeong-ja visited Papasan in his plain room. No beds or wardrobes. A bare floor except for blankets, now folded. They sat in a circle cross-legged.

"Yeah," said Papasan, "the GI latrines and kitchens are like that. I've seen them. And I've been in hotels with bathrooms."

"So what happens?" said Min-hee.

"The sinks have faucets." He twisted a hand to demonstrate. "Turn one and cold water comes out. Turn the other and you get hot water."

"Like the movies," said Min-hee.

"And the old water runs out through the bottom of the sink and goes into the ground."

"What about the toilets?" said Jeong-ja.

"Those are very clever. You piss or crap in a bowl."

"Crap too?" said Min-hee. Everyone pissed in a bowl—then they threw it outside. But crap in a bowl? For that, Min-hee went to the town crap house or a rice paddy.

Papasan smiled. "It's a different kind of bowl, more like a sink with water in the bottom and a big drain. After you piss and crap, you push a lever, and more water pushes everything out the drain."

"And it goes in the ground?"

"Hmm," said Papasan. "Too bad it doesn't go in the rice paddy. A waste of good crap."

Min-hee told Papasan about Boyle's assertion that he lived on a farm with cows and chickens, but his house had a bathroom inside.

"Probably true," said Papasan. "Americans have everything. Even the peasants."

The room fell silent. Min-hee pulled her shawl tighter over her shoulders.

Papasan said, "Min-hee, how's it going with that yobo?"

"It's going okay."

"When does he go back to America?"

"Not sure. Three or four months maybe."

"You should find out. But he treats you okay?"

"Yeah."

"Except one time," said Jeong-ja, "he put hands on her."

Papasan's eyes widened. Min-hee's face warmed. "He had a bad dream," she said. "You shouldn't be talking about it, Jeong-ja."

"What happened?" said Papasan.

Min-hee returned Papasan's gaze. His manner was mild, not like a husband or big brother or big uncle. He never raised his voice even when he had cause to be angry. Min-hee had heard he took favors from the girls but never forced himself.

"One time," said Min-hee, "he stayed over, and in the middle of the night, I woke up. He was shaking me and yelling."

"I could hear him," said Jeong-ja. "He was yelling, 'Stay awake, you want to die? What's the matter with you?' Things like that. Very loud."

"Then he stops," said Min-hee, "and says, sorry, sorry. He gets very quiet, puts his arms around me and says, sorry, bad dream."

"What do you think, Papasan?" said Jeong-ja.

"I think it was a bad dream like he said." Min-hee could see Papasan was pondering the matter further. She and Jeong-ja waited in silence. Papasan pointed toward the river. "I think something bad happened over there."

"Yeah," said Jeong-ja. "Sometimes bad things happen to the fighting soldiers."

"So what's your story, Jeong-ja?" said Papasan. "Do you have a yobo on the horizon?"

Jeong-ja snorted. "If he has a bar on his lapel."

"I'll keep my eyes open."

"Why do GIs want yobos anyhow?" said Jeong-ja. "They have all this money. They can pick whoever they want, especially if they save at the beginning of the month and spend at the end."

"First of all," said Papasan, "they're young. They don't know enough to save now and spend later." Papasan put his hand in his chin. "Here's what I think. Men like shelter. They run around and do wild things, but in the end what they really want is someone they can come home to."

Min-hee had never talked to a Korean man in such an informal manner. She said, "Papasan, how did you come into this business?"

"Min-hee, that's not polite," said Jeong-ja.

"No," said Papasan, "it's okay to ask. After the war, I had nothing. I don't even know what happened to my family. Dead? Taken up north? You girls are too young to remember."

"Were you in the military?" said Min-hee.

"Who wasn't? So after being discharged, I went from job to job, but only the Americans had money. You still see it today. A GI private has more than an officer in the Korean army."

"So you don't really like the Americans?" said Jeong-ja.

"Not true. If not for the Americans, our so-called brothers from the north would run over us again." Papasan looked at the floor. "And sometimes our so-called brothers from the south."

"I don't know about that," said Min-hee.

"You don't want to know." Papasan smiled. "Plus the GIs bring us money." Papasan pointed out the door. "I don't want to end up like old Ho next door."

Min-hee and Jeong-ja nodded. They understood. Next to the Half Moon was a compound with girls and a mamasan. They had a large room where everyone ate together, sitting on the floor in a rectangle. Min-hee and Jeong-ja sometimes gave the mamasan a few won and joined them. Old Ho was the mamasan's father or uncle. He wore the traditional flowing robes of an elder, had a white goatee, and sat at one end of the rectangle.

The first time Min-hee ate there, the old man yelled at the girl sitting to his left, angry because he wasn't being served first.

The girl said, "Shut up, you old goat."

The old man raised his raspy voice, "You need a thrashing, bitch."

"And who's going to do it?" She cupped a hand toward his chin. "I'll pull your billy goat hairs off."

The other girls laughed as Min-hee quivered at the disrespect. But then she thought, well, here's one advantage to being an independent woman, even a working girl. Don't have to take crap from an old goat.

* * * *

ONE DAY IN LATE SEPTEMBER, Lorne trucked across the river to Changpa-ri for his off-day. Out back of the Half Moon, Sally Lee stood on the portico in front of her hooch. Something about her wan smile slowed Lorne's approach.

Sally crooked a finger and said, "*Irriwa, yobo.*" Come here.

Lorne closed the distance between them, his shoulders level with her midriff, he on the ground, she on the platform. Sally took his right hand and placed it against her stomach. "*Na baby ga-jut-seo-yo.*"

Lorne caught the baby part. *Jesus, isn't she supposed to be avoiding situations like this? How stupid, not using a rubber every single time.* Sally still had Lorne's right hand pressed against her stomach. With her other hand, she pulled his face between her breasts. Lorne felt a flush of what, pride at impending fatherhood? Love for the impending mother? Back in the world, a pregnancy led to the altar.

But Lorne and Sally weren't back in the world. And Sally wasn't the girl next door.

On the return ride to Camp Walley that night, jammed in the back of a ton-and-a-quarter, Lorne pondered. Could he take this yobo arrangement any farther than the end of his enlistment and his tour in Korea? Could he approach his commander, the new captain, about his situation? Could he write back home about it? As Lorne stared into the middle of the truck, his thoughts shifted to a more immediate issue, for three soldiers away, staring back, sat Hendrick.

Hendrick put on a half-smile and said, "Reporting for duty, Sergeant Boyle."

Lorne put on his own smile and said, "Laugh while you can, Private Hendrick."

Next day, mid-morning, Lorne bent over boxes of C-rations with twenty other men bound for patrol duty. They pulled cans from cardboard boxes and stuffed them into socks, tied the socks together, and draped them over their necks. Nine rations, three days.

Eyes rose as the nearby door to the command post opened and Priestly stepped out followed by Hendrick. Priestly pointed, and Hendrick walked toward the platoon hut. "On the double," said Priestly. Hendrick increased the speed of his shuffle.

Priestly walked over and said to Lorne, "He's going out with you. Give him a minute to get his shit."

Lorne said, "I'd thought he'd be heading down to Eighth Army Stockade."

The other soldiers laughed.

Priestly motioned with his head, and Lorne followed him away from the others. Priestly said, "The captain gave him an Article-15."

"That's it?" said Lorne. "I thought the new commander was tough."

"It's not the captain," said Priestly. "He recommended a court martial, but battalion said no."

Lorne shook his head.

"It's the re-up officer at division," said Priestly. "An embarrassment if their golden boy goes to the stockade."

"Yeah," said Lorne, "their golden boy."

"This isn't new," said Priestly. "Some soldiers keep fucking up but keep sliding along."

"What'd the captain give him? Were you there?"

"Busted back to E-2. Loss of pay, loss of liberty, the usual." Priestly looked toward the knot of men stowing their C-rations, then back to Lorne. "We're rotating down to Blue Lancer the end of the week. This should be your last patrol."

"Suits me," said Lorne.

"And you're getting a new man. Hope you don't mind a KATUSA." A Korean soldier integrated into an American unit.

"A KATUSA's fine."

"We'll see. He's already had a dust-up with the first sergeant."

"Oh?"

"Had the top's head arteries popping. Anyhow, he's still gearing up. You'll see him when you come back in."

• • • •

THREE DAYS LATER, A deuce-and-a-half turned onto Skyline Drive, and replacements poured out from the second battalion, thirty-eighth infantry. Lorne and his compatriots along the barrier piled into the emptied truck for the ride back to Camp Walley.

Before entering the platoon hut, Lorne released the magazine from his rifle and pulled the bolt back, ejecting the live round in the chamber. As he picked up the round and pushed it into the magazine, Lorne watched the other men clear their weapons, paying particular attention to Hendrick.

In the hut, a KATUSA looked at Lorne's name tag and came to attention. "Sergeant, Private First Class Kim Yeong-su, reporting.

Sorry to miss time on DMZ. Had to get gear and settle administrative matter."

Lorne looked at Kim's name tag. Kim YS. "You speak good English, Private Kim."

"Much fluency, Sergeant. I have request."

"What's that?"

"Do you have influence with first sergeant?"

Lorne laughed. Several nearby men laughed.

From the end of the hut, Priestly shouted attention. Lorne dropped his rifle, helmet, and web gear on his bunk, and put his heels together.

"At ease, men," said a new voice. "As you were, men."

An officer, a second lieutenant, tall, skinny, glasses, red hair, had entered the hut with Priestly.

"Listen up," said Priestly.

The lieutenant nodded to both ends of the hut. "Men," he said. "I'm Lieutenant De Groot, your new platoon leader." He nodded to Priestly. "Of course, I defer to Sergeant Priestly on all matters of importance." He laughed, and the men took the cue.

De Groot stepped closer to the man to his front. "Where are you from, soldier?"

"Sacramento, California, Sir."

"Whoa," said De Groot. "The other side of the continent. I'm from New York, but not the city—up the Hudson." This prompted another round of laughter.

As the lieutenant continued his meet and greet, the men packed. Hours later, Lorne hauled his duffel, cold weather gear, and combat gear outside and looked at the lined-up trucks. Also a jeep with Hendrick at the wheel. Lorne found Priestly and said, "What's with the jeep?"

"The lieutenant's going ahead to set things up."

"Mind if I hitch a ride into Chang then catch the trucks when they come through?"

"Just don't miss the trucks," said Priestly.

Lorne tossed his gear in the nearest truck then jumped in the back seat of the jeep. Hendrick said, "What you got cooking in Chang?"

Lorne leaned forward. "You been drinking?"

Hendrick flushed.

Lorne said, "You're gonna fuck yourself and everyone else you keep it up."

De Groot took shotgun and Hendrick started the jeep. As they crossed Libby Bridge, De Groot said, "There she be. Changpa-ri." He twisted his body. "Sergeant Boyle, I hear Changpa-ri is wide open, like Dodge City in the Wild West."

"There's no showdowns in the streets, Sir. But the rest of it's true." De Groot laughed.

Lorne hopped out at the Half Moon, and a minute later Sally slid open her door. "Yobo," she said, putting her arms over his shoulders and around his neck.

"No can stay," said Lorne.

Sally pouted. "No can stay?"

Lorne put up two fingers. "Two nights come again. Moving to Blue Lancer. Nullo-ri."

"No more DMZ?"

"No more DMZ."

Sally smiled. "No Joe Chink at Blue Lancer."

"Yeah," said Lorne, "no Joe at Blue Lancer. See you, two night, okay?"

Lorne still fantasized about bringing Sally to rural Alabama, to Pop's chicken farm west of the Chattahoochee. It seemed exotic, different, a crossing of racial boundaries he could get away with. Something he could stick in the face of his old flame, Lorraine.

But then he imagined his mom saying, "So nice to meet you Sally, honey, and what did you do in Korea before you met Lorne?" That would always be a punch in the gut, whether his mother said it or not. He'd be marrying a woman who'd been down with who knows how many other men, for money. He'd be marrying a woman, when he thought about it, who might have set him up. And what would Pop do? Bounce their baby on his knee, saying, "Coo, coo. Aren't you a cute little cotton picker?" Everyone would see he'd been played for a fool. Still—the fantasy persisted.

• • • •

TWO DAYS AFTER THE move back to Blue Lancer Valley, the company officers and NCOs came together in the mess hall. All the lieutenants and sergeants, down to squad leader. Boyle took a table with the other three squad leaders from his platoon.

The captain and the first sergeant stood up front. Steiner nodded to Hirschfeld, who glanced toward the outside door before turning to his lieutenants and sergeants. "In a few minutes," he said, "Colonel Luppino, our battalion commander, is showing up. Lieutenant Colonel Vincent Luppino. First thing you should know, he puts his pants on one leg at a time like the rest of us."

Hirschfeld waited for the obligatory chuckles.

"The colonel wants to give us the big picture, explain our job here in Korea. A little motivation. Can someone here tell me who General Bonesteel is?"

Hirschfeld looked at the table of four lieutenants. De Groot's face flushed red as his hair.

"Nobody?" said Hirschfeld. "That's okay. I didn't know until a few days ago. He's our big boss, the commanding general of the US Eighth Army, the commander of all forces in Korea." Hirschfeld glanced toward the door. "Look sharp."

Steiner opened the mess hall door and Hirschfeld called attention as Luppino crossed the threshold. Chairs scraped and men rose, throwing back their shoulders and bringing heels together.

"At ease," said Luppino. "Relax, men. Take your seats."

Luppino waited, leaning forward against the back of a chair, then pushed himself away. "Men," he said, "I'm going around to each company, first, to introduce myself and get some eyeball time, especially with my non-commissioned officers. But more important, to let you know firsthand what we're doing here. What, precisely, our mission is, which often gets left unsaid."

The colonel coated his bombast with sincerity, as if he wanted to reach out one-on-one to each buck sergeant and acting jack in the room. Boyle found himself drawn in despite his aversion to speeches from the brass.

"A quick primer on the Korean War," said Luppino. "Nineteen-fifty. North Korea invades South Korea. We not only push them back but overrun North Korea. The Chinese enter the war and push us back. We push them back. Nineteen fifty-three—everything stagnates on the thirty-eighth parallel, the DMZ. I have a question. Is the war over?"

Priestly raised a hand. "Sir, not really. There's an armistice in effect, but no peace treaty."

"Excellent, Sergeant. An armistice, which had been holding up. But I don't have to tell most of you, things have changed, things have heated up." Luppino folded his arms. "Has anyone here heard of a General Bonesteel?"

Heads bobbed and Luppino raised his eyebrows. He pointed at Boyle, "You, with the smile."

The squad leaders around Boyle chuckled.

Boyle said, "Sir, General Bonesteel is the commander of all US forces in Korea."

"Excellent," said Luppino. He gave Hirschfeld a nod and a smile. "Now last week he had us battalion commanders down for a meeting. And he wants us to pass what he said down the chain."

Once removed from the horse's mouth, thought Boyle.

"The war is on again," said Luppino. He put hands on hips. "Not technically, because technically the armistice is still in place, but in reality, because they're shooting at us."

Luppino dropped his arms and his voice. "But this is a different kind of war. It's not like what's going on in Vietnam, where we can drop bombs and cross the line. In fact, that's exactly the war we want to avoid. Here in Korea, we want to hold what we have like it's our precious child. We don't want to overreact to provocation. We don't want to take the bait."

Same old, same old, thought Boyle, for all the talk.

"Now," said Luppino, "that's what the general said. Here's what I say. When we go back up there, this battalion will patrol aggressively. We can and will keep our guard up. And if they cross the line, we will pounce." Luppino raised a finger. "If one of them crosses over looking for trouble, I'll tell you what I want. I want that intruder's body."

Easy to say.

"When we go up there, I want nobody walking through our sector. I want nobody in our sector, period, except us. Is that understood?"

"Yessir," said the men.

• • • •

IN EARLY NOVEMBER, MIN-hee met Soo-jin at the bus stop in front of the Lucky Club. Soo-jin wanted to see her childhood friend and check out the situation in Changpa-ri. She wanted to see the famous Imjin River. Shivery winds were finding their way down from Manchuria, across North Korea, across the DMZ, across the Imjin River, reminding everyone of the great freeze soon to descend.

Double wrap-around dresses and padded jackets had appeared. The GIs wore parkas and trooper hats.

Soo-jin stared at Min-hee in wrap-around and rubber shoes before leaning in for a hug. Soo-jin wore a mini-skirt, red jacket, and red shoes. They walked to Min-hee's room, removed their shoes, and slid open the door. Inside Min-hee loosened her wrap and Soo-jin removed her jacket. As they sat cross-legged on the bed, Soo-jin's eyes widened, and she shook her head. "Oh, Min-hee, what have you done?"

"I told you. I have a yobo."

"Min-hee, you must throw away the baby. Go to the hospital in Munsan-ni. Or come with me to Dongducheon."

"It's too late for that," said Min-hee.

Soo-jin pressed a hand against Min-hee's stomach. "No it's not."

"I want the baby," said Min-hee. "I want to be a mother."

Soo-jin shook her head. "This is not a game. This is not a soap opera. When your yobo's time is up, he'll go home and leave you here with another mouth to feed."

"I don't think he would do that."

"What are you talking about, Min-hee? The army tells him what to do. When they say go, he goes. And how often do you see each other, a few times a week? Do you even know him?"

Soo-jin stayed the night, sleeping in the bed with Min-hee. In the morning, Min-hee said, "Soo-jin, I can't throw away the baby."

Before boarding the bus, Soo-jin said, "I'm saving money to open a business. I have a few hundred put away."

"Dollars?"

"Of course, dollars. So if you need help, come back to Dongducheon."

• • • •

ONE EVENING AT THE beginning of December, Rothman sat next to Lorne on his bunk. He showed Lorne a short-timers' calendar, an Asian girl on a stool, legs crossed, one elbow on a knee, no clothes. The last two days, two and one, were her tits.

"That's nice," said Lorne.

"It's for you, Sergeant Boyle."

Lorne looked from the Asian girl to Rothman's face. Rothman said, "You're right behind me, aren't you?"

Lorne calculated in his head. "Forty-eight, I think. Forty-eight and a wake-up. I guess I am getting short."

"Thirty-five and a wake-up," said Rothman. "Anyhow, when I saw them, I thought you'd like one too. It's a present."

Lorne took the calendar in his left hand and held out his right. "Mighty kind of you, Specialist Rothman."

"Good thing we're down here," said Rothman.

"How's that?"

"Less chance of getting killed before we go home. That would really suck, getting killed when you're short."

"There's little chance of that, even up there."

"It's been a rough year, if you ask me, Sergeant Boyle."

"I know, the division got hit pretty hard. But the odds of you yourself getting it are very small."

"Still, I'm glad we're south of the river."

Lorne motioned backwards with his head. "I worry more about loaded weapons behind me than the ones in front."

"Just the same." Rothman pointed to the calendar and left.

Lorne fished in his footlocker and found a dull pencil. He shaded in number ninety on the calendar. He worked his way down to forty-eight, which filled in her legs.

Chapter Eight: December 1967, Kimpo Air Base

At Kimpo Air Base, a medic shot gamma globulin into both buttocks of Private First Class Marshall Jones: draftee, age 19, race Negro, religion Protestant, home town Rochester, New York, Military Occupational Specialty 11B Infantryman. "For hepatitis," said the medic. "But don't drink the water anyhow. Unless it's boiled."

Marshall moved to the next station in the airplane hangar and turned in his greenbacks for military scrip and Korean won. At the last station, a staff sergeant called out Marshall's orders: "First battalion, twenty-third infantry. Sorry about that, Private Jones." The two hundred soldiers from Marshall's plane laughed.

Next day, an olive military bus lugged Marshall and two dozen other replacements north. They entered Seoul, the capital city. Marshall pressed his face against the window and saw squat buildings, oxcarts, bicycles, military vehicles, pedestrians, food, smoke, dung. Bent-over Korean civilians exhaled plumes, either cigarette smoke or moisture-laden winter air. Housing thinned as the bus motored north on a narrow strip of tar amid frozen rice paddies and clusters of thatch-roofed huts. The oxcarts and bicycles dwindled to a dribble. Marshall looked left and right at the sunken paddies, partitioned by brown berms, leading into low, barren hills. He imagined that if astronauts ever made it to the other side of the moon, the side not seen from earth, they'd find something like this.

The bus pulled through a gate with an overhead sign, Camp Howze, Headquarters, 2nd Infantry Division, Second to None. Marshall stepped into piercing cold worse than the air base that morning. The soldiers he saw outside wore parkas and Russian-style trooper hats. Most of the buildings were Quonset huts, cans slit down the middle and set flat end down on slabs of cement. Dormer windows on the sides, doors on either end.

Marshall traded the bus for the bed of a ton-and-a-quarter truck. Four other replacements joined him, all in dress greens. The driver's face appeared over the tailgate. "Well, don't you boys look pretty." He pointed to a pile of drab olive that merged with the floor of the truck in the dark. "There's some parkas. Leave 'em here when you get out."

Marshall pulled on a parka, pulled up the hood, and sat knees to chin, back against the headboard as the truck exited Camp Howze and bounced north on pot-holed roads. He retracted his hands into the parka sleeves and crossed his arms. Nothing could be seen out the back but a trail of dust fading into black sky. At intervals, the soldier next to him stood, looked out, said Jesus or fuck, and sat back down. Marshall stayed as still as possible, conserving every calorie of warmth, adjusting to and accepting the cold.

The ton-and-a-quarter stopped bouncing, then stopped altogether, and the motor shut down. Marshall followed the others over the tailgate onto a strip of tarmac.

"Be sure you leave the parkas," said the driver. He pointed toward the outline of a double Quonset. "Battalion headquarters. You can warm up in there."

Marshall entered a room of desks and chairs surrounding an upright 55-gallon drum with a stovepipe running from its top through the ceiling. He pushed in with the other replacements as close to this source of warmth as he could. Three sergeants sat behind desks, not as if they belonged there, but like they were lounging, waiting. The nearest to Marshall wore the six stripes and inset diamond of a first sergeant. He had a drill-sergeant frame, balding pate, small nose, and close-set eyes, a white guy. His name tag said Steiner.

Another sergeant, Hispanic, six stripes and the inset star of a battalion sergeant major, entered from the next room with a clipboard. The replacements straightened legs and backs, and pushed back shoulders. The sergeant major, short, stout, peppery, looked at his clipboard and bellowed, "Reechards. Speak up, Reechards."

The soldier next to Marshall, Private Richards by his name tag, said, "Here, Sergeant Major."

The sergeant major pointed to his rear. "You stay put." Battalion staff, thought Marshall, I wouldn't mind that.

The sergeant major dropped his eyes again to his clipboard. "Honays!"

Marshall rolled his eyes toward the ceiling. This was the third time in his short army career that a Mex or PR had mispronounced his name. He'd learned that J sounded like H in Spanish but hadn't figured out the *ays* part yet.

The sergeant major flushed and corrected himself. "Jones. Answer up, Jones."

"Yo. Here, Sergeant Major."

The sergeant major looked over his clipboard at Marshall, then tilted his head toward the first sergeant with the close-set eyes, Steiner. "Yours, Paul."

Steiner rose and hooked a finger, and Marshall followed him outside. The black air sucked away what little heat he'd gathered by the stove. He threw his duffel in the back of a waiting jeep. Steiner, who wore a field jacket and baseball cap, and seemed oblivious to the frigid air, called, "Ten-hut." Marshall locked heels and threw his shoulders back. Steiner came alongside his face.

"Yo? You say yo to the sergeant major, Private?"

"Sorry, First Sergeant. It's been a long day."

Steiner walked to the other side of Marshall's face.

"A long day. And you roll your eyes at the sergeant major?"

"With all due respect, the sergeant major—" Marshall was about to complain about being called Honays, but thought better of it and clamped his mouth. His shoulders shook from the cold. Pain ran from his knuckles to the tips of his curled fingers.

"You know what, Private Jones. I think we'll march to the company area." Steiner motioned with his head and the jeep pulled away. Steiner raised his voice to a parade-ground bark and called, "Forward ... march." Marshall's left foot stepped off.

Steiner called cadence. "One hut, two hut, three hut." At least they were moving, thought Marshall. "Pick up the step, Jones." I am in step, thought Marshall. I can march in step.

Marshall and Steiner crossed the tar road in front of battalion headquarters. They marched down a slope under stars and a quarter moon.

"Look around," said Steiner.

Ahead, Marshall made out a large ditch. About the time he thought Steiner was marching them into it, a foot bridge emerged. On the other side of the ditch crouched Quonset huts, with stovepipes and windows sticking out. A cinder block latrine. Another cinder block building, probably the mess. As they drew closer, Marshall saw a slope rising on the far side of the huts and buildings, and up the slope four more huts.

"Does this look like you're back on the block?" Steiner said.

"No, First Sergeant."

Steiner raised his voice. "I can't hear you, Private! Does this look like you're back on the block?"

"No, First Sergeant! Not that I remember it."

"Don't get smart with me, Private."

Steiner marched Marshall past the cinder block mess to the far side of the second Quonset hut and called, "Detail ... halt."

Steiner opened a door and Marshall followed him inside as an overhead fluorescent sputtered to life. Marshall saw two desks, chairs, a typewriter, filing cabinets, and a door to another room. The company command post. Marshall examined the stove in the center of the room as his fingers tingled and thawed. Same as battalion headquarters, an upright 55-gallon drum with a stovepipe out the top. Marshall now saw that a five-gallon jerry can hung on the side and dripped diesel fuel through a regulator into the drum.

Marshall realized he stood alone in the room. Steiner must have let him in and closed the door behind. His duffel lay on the floor nearby. A minute later, the outside door opened to the entrance of a black soldier—but not a brother, from another generation. He wore a parka with the hood up, his hands in his pockets. Marshall straightened his body to the position of attention.

The older soldier circled Marshall and the stove once. He stopped, facing Marshall, and said in a low voice, "I'm Platoon Sergeant Abel Priestly."

"Sergeant," said Marshall. "Private First Class Marshall Jones."

"The first sergeant tells me you're a smart ass."

Great, thought Marshall. "Sergeant, I can explain. There was a misunderstanding."

Priestly put up a hand. "Relax, Private Jones. You'll fit right in with third squad. Grab your shit."

Marshall followed Priestly up the hill to the second of the four Quonset huts there. The interior of this hut had no partitions, just two long rows of double bunks, gray metal wall lockers, olive wood footlockers, and stoves at each end. Marshall followed Priestly down the center aisle as lounging soldiers gave them the once-over. At the midway point, Priestly pointed to the right and said, "Third squad."

At the end of third squad's space, near the end of the hut, four soldiers had pulled footlockers next to a bunk to form table and chairs for a game of cards—double-deck pinochle. One of the card players, three stripes on his shoulder, looked up, then stood. He had green eyes, cropped blond hair, wide cheeks, and big ears. He looked at Marshall, then Priestly.

"Guessing you got me my new man, Sergeant."

Marshall's cracker antennae rose. The three-striper's voice wasn't the snotty, drawn-out drawl that Marshall detested, but originated—no doubt in Marshall's mind—south of the Mason-Dixon. From his four months at Fort Benning, Marshall guessed Georgia or Alabama.

"New as a baby's backside," said Priestly. He turned and his parka faded down the aisle of the hut towards the far door.

Marshall stood face-to-face with his squad leader, who seemed to smile. Seconds passed. Marshall looked into his face, not sure whether to come to attention, whether to report, or what the protocol was at this level. Then Marshall's lower peripheral caught a motion and he realized his squad leader's right hand stuck out. Marshall extended his right hand and they shook.

"I'm Lorne Boyle," his squad leader said. "Marshall Jones, right?"

Marshall nodded.

Boyle said, "Nice to meet you." He flipped his chin toward the card game. "I'm engaged at the moment. Tomorrow morning we'll get set up."

Marshall's gaze followed Boyle's to the card players. The player sitting head-on to Marshall looked like a high school nerd, tall, black hair, black-rimmed glasses, an angular Caucasian face. His name tag read Rothman. He nodded at Marshall. The other two card players were also white—a small guy who looked Italian or Greek, and a husky guy, Polish or Russian. They flicked their eyes at Marshall. A fifth soldier, an onlooker, stood behind Rothman, rocking heel to toe like Howdy Doody with a loose string, but blond hair instead of red and no freckles. He looked at Marshall like he wasn't there.

Boyle turned and pointed back to the middle of the hut, the beginning of their squad area. "You'll be bunking with Kim."

Marshall now noticed a short soldier with tawny skin, but not Mex or PR, his skin more ocher than brown, eyes more almonds than walnuts.

"Hey, Kim," said Boyle, "show the new guy around."

Marshall carried his duffel to the double-bunk at the beginning of the squad area. The soldier's name tag read Kim YS. He said, "Hope you like top bunk. Bottom already in use."

"You Korean?" said Marshall.

"Very observant. Have promising future in infantry."

Marshall unsnapped the top of his duffel and dug for fatigues. He unbuttoned the jacket of his Class A uniform and undid the necktie. Kim chattered. "Okay. Up front first squad and second. Across way weapons squad. Then us, Acting Sergeant Lorne Boyle, commanding."

"Is this the whole squad?"

"No, two more, probably at EM club. You make nine."

Marshall claimed his wall locker, happy to stow his Class A uniform and don fatigues.

"Okay," said Kim. "Out back, piss tube. Down hill, latrine for shit and shower. Mess hall and command post down there. Also senior sergeants' quarters. Also supply room."

Marshall looked up and down the aisle. Thirty, thirty-five men. Three more huts on the hill. A hundred forty, Marshall guessed, plus a half dozen senior sergeants down the hill. "Any officers?"

"Plenty officers." Kim raised an arm and pointed. "They live officer hill."

Kim spoke with what Marshall would call an Asian accent. His uniform looked close but not quite American.

"You wonder about me," said Kim. "I'm KATUSA. That mean Korean augmentation to US army. Some think it mean attached but proper word is augmentation."

"Your English is real good."

"Tell me about it. You think I should be in infantry squad? I should be company clerk. Or work on battalion staff."

Marshall thought of a wisecrack. "You should talk to the first sergeant about it."

Kim said, "I talk to him already."

"Really? What'd he say?"

"He say keep rifle clean, mouth closed, get out."

"I'll tell you this," said Marshall. "You got balls. He looks like one mean mother."

"No," said Kim. "He really big pussy."

Cards slapped and Boyle shouted. "Kim, goddamnit, it's pussycat."

"Same thing."

"It's not the same thing."

The card players laughed. Laughter rippled from the other squads.

Marshall lowered his voice. "What's the deal with Sergeant Boyle?" Marshall knew an acting sergeant was an E-4 with temporary stripes. Appointed due to the lack of a real E-5.

"He short timer. Six weeks left, go home. See lot of shit in DMZ. Trouble in ville."

"Is he okay?"

"Yeah."

Glad to hear that, thought Marshall.

"But no get on wrong side."

Shit, I could have done without that addendum.

"How come he smiles all the time?"

"This smile mean that. That smile mean this. You learn after a while. No get on wrong side."

Marshall pointed at Kim's name tag.

"What's the YS for?"

"Yeong-su, My name Kim Yeong-su. GI no can say. Call me YS."

Marshall practiced the name in his head. "Yeong-su," he asked, "who's the goofy guy standing over the card game?"

"What goofy mean?"

"Dumb. Out of it."

"Oh, that Hendrick."

"What's his problem?"

"He re-up and go AWOL."

"AWOL?"

"Yeah. Only GI to ever re-up in Korea. Get re-up money and go AWOL one month."

"And?"

"And get Article-15, then come back to squad." Kim touched the side of his head. "Nothing on top floor. Three years in army, still private, but have military license."

"Yeah?"

"So sometime drive jeep or truck. Very scary."

"I have a military license," said Marshall.

"Good," said Kim. "When we need driver, you take Hendrick's place."

Wonderful, thought Marshall. He'd just violated the first rule of soldiering, never volunteer.

"Where did you say we piss?"

Kim pointed past the card players. "Piss tube out back. Can't miss."

Marshall took a step toward the rear of the hut, but Kim blocked him with a hand. "Put on parka first."

Chapter Nine: December 1967, Blue Lancer Valley

"**D**ump it," said Boyle.

Marshall heaved an armload of gear onto his top bunk, made—hospital corners, blanket drum tight—with no effort on his part. That morning, he'd learned that GIs in Korea didn't make bunks, shine boots, or pull KP. Each soldier chipped in a few dollars a month for a Korean houseboy. In the mess, the army employed Koreans for kitchen police.

Boyle pulled a wool fatigue shirt and wool pants from Marshall's pile. "Best to put these on over your cotton fatigues."

"To keep from itching?"

"For another layer of warmth," said Boyle.

Boyle picked up two black, oversize, rubber galoshes. "These are Mickey Mouse boots—won't use them today." Boyle placed them at the bottom of Marshall's wall locker. "They're only for standing around."

Marshall held up a two-piece mitten. The canvas shell had a horizontal slit along the palm. The inner wool part had a sheath for the forefinger as well as the thumb.

"Trigger-finger mitten," said Boyle. "Just stick your forefinger through the slit if you have to shoot."

Marshall turned the mitten over in his hands. *Some of this stuff is neat. Trigger-finger mittens.*

"Now put on your field jacket," said Boyle.

"Whoa, Sergeant, I thought we'd be wearing parkas."

"We'll get to that. Okay, good. Now put on your flak vest and web gear," said Boyle touching each item, "over your field jacket. Let's see, this time of year, you want your trooper hat." From the pile, Boyle grabbed a heavy Russian-style hat with ear flaps.

"Unless you're the first sergeant," said Marshall. "Man, he just stands there in a baseball hat and field jacket."

"The first sergeant," said Boyle, "doesn't spend much time in the field. Ten minutes and he's back to his stove. Okay, now the parka—put it over everything else. Watch how the other guys do it."

"What about—"

"Or, some of the guys like to put their web gear over the parka. Whatever feels best."

"What about my helmet?"

"Depends on how cold you are. You can wear it on your head, or over your trooper hat, or over your hood."

"Over the hood?"

"Just kind of balance it on top of everything. You get used to it. Watch the other guys."

Marshall stowed his extra gear in his wall locker and watched the others dress. A few minutes later, the platoon trooped down to the supply hut, across from the command post, which Marshall had visited earlier to draw the cold weather and combat gear. The supply sergeant unlocked the weapons rack and handed out M14 rifles. Marshall checked his serial number and joined his platoon outside. Priestly wandered into their midst. "Listen up, men. We'll form two ranks, do a right face, and march to the gate. Then split to either side of the road."

"Ammo?" said Rothman.

"No ammo. Sergeants, pull your squads together. Sling arms."

Marshall leaned into Kim. "What's with the ammo?"

"Training exercise. Not good to load rifle."

Marshall happened to be looking at Hendrick, who'd stopped rocking on his feet, but now pulled the bolt of his rifle, wrapped his finger around the trigger, and dry fired the weapon. What the fuck, thought Marshall, although Hendrick's behavior seemed more absentminded than provocative. Rothman glanced sideways at

Hendrick. As Hendrick pulled the bolt a second time, Boyle walked to his front with a rippled smile, the edges of his mouth turned down. "Private Hendrick, are you looking to get your ass kicked? Close the bolt and put that thing on your shoulder."

The two soldiers stared at each other as Hendrick released the bolt of his rifle, loosened its sling, and shouldered the weapon.

A sleeve tug from Kim diverted Marshall's attention from the mini-drama between Boyle and Hendrick. Kim pointed to a ton-and-a-quarter pulling a short one-axle trailer. "Ammo wagon follow us."

"What for if we're not using it?"

"In case Joe Chink show up."

"Does that happen?"

"Never happen down here. But who know? Good to have bullets."

"What do you mean, down here?"

"Down here. We not on DMZ. We in reserve."

Marshall's adrenaline dissipated. This wasn't the show, just bullshit training.

At the gate, Marshall's squad split to the left side of the road, walking single file. The columns rambled between rice paddies, then scattered hooches, then T-boned against the main street of a village.

"Nullo-ri," said Kim.

The columns turned left, away from the village center. Two kilometers out, the soldiers stopped along a hillside of dead, flaxen-colored grass and clumps of barren bushes, and unslung their rifles. Marshall's squad made a left face and picked its way up the scrub-brush slope. Boyle approached, the corners of his mouth turned up.

"Make like you're looking for something, Private Jones."

"What exactly are we doing, Sergeant Boyle?"

"We're rooting out Joe. Look lively. Poke your weapon around in the bushes."

"No disrespect, Sergeant, but wouldn't Joe just shoot us if we did this shit?"

"He probably would, Private, but the important thing right now is to get with the program."

Marshall thrust the muzzle of his M14 in and out of a winter-dead shrub, and walked around it. Boyle circled on the other side.

"Sergeant Boyle, what's with the training? I thought we were supposed to be guarding the DMZ."

"Oh you'll get your crack at that. The battalions rotate up and down every four months."

"You been up there then?"

"Twice."

"How is it?"

Boyle dropped his smile and stared north. "Quiet most of the time." He turned his gaze toward Marshall. "But every so often... Look sharp. Here comes the lieutenant."

"Problem?"

"I'm guessing a meet and greet."

Boyle stopped poking in the brush, straightened, and pushed his shoulders back. Marshall followed his lead.

"Sir," said Boyle. "New man. Private First Class Marshall Jones. Lieutenant De Groot."

The lieutenant reminded Marshall of a South American llama, which he'd seen once at the Seneca Park Zoo, or a scarecrow made up with military surplus. Tall, not filled out, parka drooping from narrow shoulders, helmet perched on top of his hood, a black, vertical line on the front of the helmet designating his rank. He wore round, herringbone eyeglasses, non-military, chestnut in color.

"Welcome aboard, Private Jones. Where you from?"

"Rochester, New York, Sir."

"Ha. So you're used to this weather. I'm from Scarsdale."

"New York, Sir?"

"Westchester County. Just north of the city."

Ah, the city. New York City. Three hundred and fifty miles from Rochester. "Small world, Sir."

De Groot clapped his mittens, his breath mingling with Marshall's and Boyle's. His rifle was still slung. He looked from private to sergeant and back again, and said, "Carry on, men."

Marshall and Boyle resumed their search for North Korean intruders.

"So we got a platoon leader plus a platoon sergeant?" said Marshall.

"Here's the scoop," said Boyle. "If the lieutenant tells you to do something, say yessir and do it. Unless it's something stupid. If it's something stupid, say yessir and come see me or Sergeant Priestly."

Lieutenant De Groot had it wrong on one point. Rochester hadn't prepared Marshall for Korea. Rochester had buildings with central heating, and cars that warmed up after the motor ran for a few minutes. Marshall said, "We doing this all day, Sergeant Boyle?"

"Naw, another half hour or so. Then we'll go back and crap out. And tomorrow's indoor training—VD lecture, I think."

• • • •

NEXT MORNING, HALF the company assembled in the mess hall after morning chow. No rifles or helmets, no web gear, no quadruple layers, just parkas thrown over wool fatigues. Most of the men had dropped their parkas over the backs of their chairs. No senior sergeants. No officers except De Groot, who stood in front of a table near the serving area shifting from one leg to the other. He lifted a clipboard, looked down, looked up, pushed at the bridge of his glasses. He had red hair cut to a flattop.

One of the squad leaders said, "Listen up." Conversations drifted away, and eyes fell on the lieutenant.

"Okay, men." De Groot laughed. "You have more experience in this than me since officers aren't allowed in the ville."

A round of laughter ensued. De Groot's eyes went back to the clipboard. "Okay, first on the list is rubbers. It says here, use them." More laughter.

Marshall found it hard to believe. These guys took sex as an everyday event, a normal part of military life in Korea. He wondered whether it wasn't another cruel joke the army played, sticking it in front of your nose, letting you sniff, then yanking it away. Boyle sat kitty-corner at Marshall's table, his eyes open but somewhere else.

The training session lasted less than an hour. Guys grabbed their parkas. Chairs scraped back. De Groot put down his clipboard, put on his parka, picked up his clipboard, and left.

Marshall said, "What do we do now, Sergeant Boyle, crap out?"

Boyle, halfway out of his seat, said, "Yeah, for the rest of the morning."

"So, Sergeant Boyle, how come they were joshing the lieutenant?"

Boyle sat back down. "Now, that's a good story."

Marshall leaned forward, the mess hall clearing out, he and Boyle the only ones at their table. Boyle said, "A couple weeks ago Sergeant Priestly and the mess sergeant took Lieutenant De Groot into Changpa-ri. They call it breaking the new lieutenant's cherry."

Marshall thought about his own cherry.

"They set him up with a girl out back of the Lucky Club. But when she saw him, she hollered she wasn't wasting no night with a private. So Sergeant Priestly reaches across and tugs at the lieutenant's parka so she can see the gold bar on his shirt collar, and her eyes light up with dollar signs."

Marshall felt his forehead go quizzical. Boyle said, "A lieutenant's good for ten dollars for an all-nighter. Which reminds me—"

"So the lieutenant got laid?"

"If he didn't, he should hand in his commission."

"So he's kind of like one of the guys?"

"He's not like one of the guys," said Boyle. "Maybe he puts his pants on a leg at a time, but he sleeps on officers' hill, he eats in the officers' mess, when you see him you salute him, he's not one of the guys. Same with me."

"What do you mean?"

"I mean I'm a sergeant and sometimes I have to act like one."

"Right, Sergeant."

Boyle adjusted his lips to a straight-across smile. "But it shouldn't be a problem as long as we all keep our shit together."

Boyle started to rise again, said, "Oh," and sat back down. "What I was going to say. There's a truck going into Chang tonight. I'll make sure you have a pass."

Blood fell away from Marshall's head, and his sphincter tightened. He wanted little more than getting laid, but the prospect of actual engagement unnerved him. He needed a few more days in Korea. He needed ... he didn't know what. "You think I'm ready?"

"Since you were thirteen, I'm guessing." Boyle put a hand on Marshall's arm. "Here's the deal. Middle of the month, don't pay no more than three dollars for a one-timer."

"Right, Sergeant."

"Three dollars. Repeat it."

"Three dollars, Sergeant."

"If it was near payday, you'd have to do five. But mid-month, three dollars for an E-3 is plenty. Got it?" Marshall nodded.

"Okay," said Boyle. "Truck leaves at eighteen hundred. Sign out at the CP first. Coming back, the pickup in Chang is twenty-two hundred. Don't miss it."

"I got a question, Sergeant. Instead of taking a truck to Changpa-ri, why don't we just walk to Nullo-ri?"

"It doesn't feel right because when we're up north, we go to Chang. It's the closest ville this side of the bridge. So it's like our home ville, but you could walk into Nullo-ri if you want."

Marshall shook his head. "I'll take the truck to Chang."

* * * *

THAT NIGHT, A QUARTER before eighteen hundred, Marshall said to Kim, "You going into Chang?"

"KATUSA no go to ville."

"Why not?"

"Working girl no want Korean. Want GI with money."

Marshall had already noticed the KATUSAs sat apart. Most of them didn't have Kim's English. He noticed nobody else in his squad hung out with Kim.

Kim said, "Hey, you have good time in Chang. Use rubber. No catch VD."

Down the hill, Marshall found a ton-and-a-quarter idling by the command post. He hoisted himself into the back among twenty other bodies. The truck dropped into gear, chugged out the main gate, and bounced along the potholed road.

One of the men sang out a marching cadence, "I got a girl in Changpa-ri."

Another man hollered, "Stuff it for chrissake."

A third man yelled, "Stuff it yourself."

The first man sang out again and half a dozen others joined in the refrain. "I got a girl in Changpa-ri."

Marshall didn't know whether the marching song bothered him, or he liked it. He had other issues, foremost what lay ahead in Changpa-ri, but also the conversation with Kim.

The first man sang, "I love her and she loves me."

Again a refrain. "I love her and she loves me."

"Am I right or wrong?" sang the first man.

"You're right."

"Well, tell me if I'm wrong."

"You're right."

Marshall felt a tap on his shoulder and turned to see Boyle's light smile in the scant light. "We'll unload by the Lucky Club," he said. "Just follow the other guys who go in there."

"And?"

"And it'll take care of itself."

Take care of itself?

"Stop worrying," said Boyle. "It's like taking orders but more fun."

"You going in the Lucky Club?"

"I don't do clubs anymore."

Marshall pressed closer to Boyle. He didn't know how far he should go with his squad leader, but in the instant he wanted to bond with this southern white who didn't act like a cracker. In Boyle's ear, Marshall said, "Have you noticed the Koreans get treated like shit in their own country?"

"What of it?" said Boyle.

Not the expected response. "That doesn't bother you?"

"A lot of things bother me."

Marshall and Boyle bounced along on the floor of the truck jammed in with the rest of the men. Nobody else had tuned into their conversation. In a whisper, Boyle said, "Look, I don't like the way people are done sometimes. I don't like the way you personally are done in your own country if that's what you're driving at."

"I wasn't meaning to—"

"But there's not much I can do about it. Right now I got myself to take care of, plus a squad. Don't know which is worse."

The truck stopped, the tailgate dropped, and boots fell to the ground. Boyle jumped out and Marshall scrambled to keep up. Boyle said, "Just follow them in." He put a mitten on Marshall's shoulder. "I don't have to hold your hand, do I?"

"No, Sergeant."

Boyle dropped the mitten and slipped into the dark of a path on the north side of the club. Marshall watched his outline recede, then turned his boots toward the Lucky Club. He opened its door and crossed its threshold.

Through a fog of cigarette smoke, soldiers tipped brown bottles of OB Lager. Along two walls leaned girls in tight dresses and skirts, black and red, and high-heel shoes. Real girls. Sexy-looking girls. Marshall loosened his parka, pulled off his mittens and trooper hat, and stowed them in the parka pockets. He looked around to see what the rest of the soldiers were doing.

One of the girls, clad breastbone to crotch in snug red, pushed away from the wall. Coming my way, thought Marshall. She had hooded eyes and glossy black hair. Marshall hadn't seen a girl this close since before basic training, much less an Oriental sex machine.

As she approached, Marshall's ears filled with the bass chords and high-pitched wailing of The Animals regarding a house in New Orleans known as the Rising Sun.

The girl said, "Wanna dance?"

"Yeah," said Marshall. "Cool. Cool."

Marshall went into slow dance position, like prom night back in Rochester, taking the girl's right hand with his left. But as the palm of his other hand reached the small of her back, she tossed her left arm around Marshall's neck and stepped into him like clay to a mold. On their second step, in synchronicity with a bass note from The Animals, the girl pressed her groin against his. Marshall's cock, which had been hanging at ease in his army-issue boxers, surged like the prow of a warship.

The girl said, "Wanna go hooch?"

That or go blind.

She guided Marshall out the rear door of the Lucky Club and down a covered walk lined with sliding doors fronted by a narrow veranda. Marshall sat on the veranda and pulled off his boots. He scooted through a door into a square chamber with a warm linoleum floor, wallpapered walls and ceiling, a lacquered wardrobe, a nightstand, and a bed that took a third of the room.

"Whah your name?" said the girl.

"Marshall."

"Number one name. My name Donna. You rike?"

"Yeah," said Marshall. "Number one."

She motioned for Marshall to sit alongside her on the bed. "Figh dollah can do."

Boyle's advice regarding customary payment dawdled in the back of Marshall's mind as he looked into Donna's eyes.

"Can do?" she said.

Marshall nodded. "Can do."

The corners of Donna's mouth rose and she patted the top of the nightstand. "Okay, Marshall, put heah and we off to lace."

Marshall pulled a brown wallet from his back pocket. He knew its contents, a ten, a five, and six singles in military scrip, and some won notes. He extracted the five-dollar note and smoothed it face up on the nightstand.

Donna crossed her forearms below her stomach, grasped the hem of her dress, and shed it in a single motion. She unhooked her bra and dropped her panties. Marshall gaped at protruding nipples on small breasts and, between her legs, a tuft of pubis. He kept thinking, this has to be a trick, that at any moment military police would break down the flimsy, sliding door yelling, "Back to barracks, soldier, no poontang for you." Or Donna would stand and bark, "Now I have money, you get out, big fool, no poontang for you."

Donna said, "Whah you think, GI? Time to take off clothes."

Marshall ripped his arms from the parka and tossed it to the floor. As he fumbled away the buttons of his fatigue shirt, Donna pulled it up and over, tossed it on the floor, and pushed Marshall onto his back. She unbuckled his belt, unbuttoned and unzipped his fly, yanked down pants and shorts, and gave his erect cock a gentle slap.

"Look rike you ready for lock 'n loll."

From the nightstand drawer, Donna extracted a Trojan and unrolled it onto Marshall's cock. She scooted under the bed covers and held them open for Marshall. "Okay," she said, "you rike on top? We have good time."

Marshall rolled onto Donna and pressed his face against hers. She reciprocated with a smack of her lips. Marshall lowered his mouth to Donna's right nipple then the left. Donna pulled Marshall's face back level with hers and opened her legs. Marshall pushed and floundered, growing frantic, until Donna, with deft fluctuations of fingers and pudendum, encased his cock. "Oh, oh, you so good," she said.

Through his teen years, Marshall had half convinced himself that sex was sex, that vaginal penetration would produce no greater pleasure than, say, masturbation. But that was false, he now realized, false, false, not believing the rapture that clenched his body, that if he died in the next second, it would be okay.

Under him, Donna moaned, "Oh, oh. So good. You so good. You number one lover. You best ever. Oh, you—you come?"

Indeed the wave had crested, ebbed, and vanished. Marshall pressed his lips against Donna's a last time and rolled to his back. Donna sat up, lifted Marshall's shirt from the floor, and said, "You want cigarette now?"

As Marshall lay on his back blowing filtered smoke toward the papered ceiling, Donna removed the condom from his cock and applied a cloth of warm water. "Washy washy number one," she said.

That was quick, thought Marshall, but dwelled on his frenzy going in, and the release afterwards. And ... he'd done it, He wouldn't die a virgin.

From the Lucky Club, The Animals wailed. Marshall said, "Why do they keep playing that same song over and over?"

"Whah you say?"

"The House of the Rising Sun. Over and over."

"Ah, house of rising sun. Number one song."

"Why?"

"You know."

"I don't know."

"You know." She paused as if revealing a trade secret. "GI get hot, wanna go hooch."

Marshall blew more smoke to the ceiling. This is so different from Rochester, he thought. Donna dried his genitals and wriggled on his boxers.

"You rike? You have good time?"

Chapter Ten: December 1967, Blue Lancer Valley

L orne brought his squad to the front end of the hut, where the entire platoon gathered around Priestly and De Groot. Priestly explained they'd be pulling SCOSI duty for two weeks. Full combat gear, rifles, machine guns, ammunition, two-hour shifts from dusk to dawn, a warm-up tent between shifts.

A man raised his hand. "What does SCOSI mean, Sergeant?"

Priestly said, "It's something south of the river. I don't remember it all."

Lorne shook his head along with the other squad leaders. He knew what SCOSI was but had no idea what the acronym stood for. The army was full of acronyms.

De Groot, who stood to one side of Priestly, said, "Security and Counterespionage Operations South of the Imjin." Everyone looked at him as if to say, wow, so that's why we have lieutenants. De Groot pointed his finger at an imaginary map on the door. "If we take a left in Nullo-ri, go out to the river, take a right, then go up to Changpa-ri ..." Lorne followed De Groot's finger on the familiar roads. "Does everyone know where the Half Moon Club is?" The platoon laughed. "So if we take a left at the Half Moon, we drop down to Libby Bridge and cross the river." Everyone nodded.

De Groot backed his finger up to the Half Moon. "But if we keep going"—he ran his finger north—"we're in the bell area where the river does a U-turn. The SCOSI positions are here, on the west side of the bell. Second line of defense"—De Groot pointed toward the DMZ on his imaginary map—"against infiltration from the north."

Priestly pointed to De Groot's imaginary map. "Now that you show us, Sir, it's obvious. If we cross the river at our SCOSI positions, we're just a few clicks from the DMZ." A click being GI talk for a kilometer.

• • • •

THAT NIGHT THE SQUAD bounced along in the back of a ton-and-a-quarter, crammed among other squads, down a man because Hendrick had pulled driving duty—in fact, drove the truck they bounced in. Blackout lights, hooded bulbs, threw small arcs in front of the truck, making it hard for the enemy to see, but the driver couldn't see much either. The truck stopped, and the squad piled out, parkas, helmets, flak vests, rifles, Mickey Mouse boots. A nice night except for the cold, with the moon and stars casting soldier shadows.

Lorne formed his squad in a single rank, the road at their back, the Imjin River a hundred meters at Lorne's back. "Listen up," he said in a loud whisper. "We're about to lock and load. What are the rules?"

Rothman said, "Safeties on, Sergeant."

"That's right, always, unless you intend to shoot. So do it, check your safeties."

The men pushed trigger fingers through the slits in their mitten shells and felt the outsides of their trigger guards. Safeties on.

"What's the other rule?"

"Keep 'em pointed downrange," said Rothman.

"Always. Port arms or point your weapons over the river. Okay, lock and load."

The men jammed magazines and released rifle bolts. Those metal clacks never failed to send testosterone coursing through the arteries, Lorne knew. And a few of his soldiers had never before chambered a round outside of training.

"Now double-check your fucking safeties."

Lorne waited for the men to run their fingers over their trigger guards.

"Now what's the first rule of engagement?"

No answer.

"Don't shoot at shadows," said Lorne.

A few men snickered.

"Funny, is it? Specialist Rothman, why is it we don't start shooting every time we think we see something?"

"Don't want to give your position away."

"That's a good answer, but there's something more important." Lorne walked up and down in front of the squad. "Listen," he said. "If you open fire, everybody gets excited. They think there's something out there. There's more shooting. Battalion wants to know what's going on, and we're sitting here with our thumbs up our asses saying, 'Oh, jeez, Colonel, we thought we saw something.'"

The squad emitted low laughs.

"Ha ha," said Lorne, "but believe me, pissing the colonel off is a whole lot more serious than giving your position away."

Jones said, "What if there really is something out there?"

"There's never nothing out there," said DiMaggio.

"No, no," said Lorne. "Fair question. If you think there's something out there, grab me or check with your buddy."

Jones didn't look convinced.

"But if you're totally one hundred percent sure there's a man on the ice, and you don't have time to check, you can open up. But you better be producing a body."

"So, Sergeant," said Jones, "if we're positive there's a man there, we can shoot him? Without warning?"

"We don't challenge. If you have to shoot, shoot."

Kim said, "Sergeant, sometime civilian cross river to look for scrap metal."

"The river's a free-fire zone. Everyone knows that. They know it. We know it."

"But, Sergeant," said Kim.

"Look, Kim," said Lorne. "I'd feel bad about shooting a civilian, but they shouldn't be there." *But not to worry, this isn't the show, not like being across the river. More like practice.* "Okay, ladies, let's go."

The squad stumbled single file across frozen rice paddies toward what looked like the edge of a cliff. Parkas passed going the other way, the squad they were relieving. "Have fun," one of them said.

"Keep going," said Lorne. "Watch your footing."

The squad dropped over the embankment into a trench, clods of brown earth, frozen and frosted. Leaning over the front parapet of the trench, Lorne made out the near shore of the frozen Imjin many meters below. His eyes lifted and crossed the ice to the shadows of the far shore.

To Lorne's right, Jones had let his body sink so elbows and rifle rested on the parapet. Despite cotton fatigues, wool fatigues, field jacket, parka, trooper hat, parka hood, steel helmet, Mickey Mouse boots, and the double-layer trigger-finger mittens, Jones threw off a shiver, then another. Lorne knew the feeling, that Jones couldn't believe the cold had already cut through four layers. That after ten minutes, he would say to himself, I don't think I can take the cold. After another minute, he would say, I think I'm dying.

Jones's head nodded.

Lorne edged next to him, leaned into his left ear, and whispered, "Stay awake. It's just two hours."

Jones's head bobbed up. He extended a mitten over the parapet and said, "It looks like something moving by the far shore ..."

"Shadows. If it flickers in place, it's nothing. Okay?"

"Okay, Sergeant."

Lorne placed a mitten on Jones's shoulder. "It's easy duty. Just boring and cold."

"Has anyone froze to death out here?"

"You won't freeze to death," said Lorne. "It's the army way." Enough clothing to stay alive but not enough to be comfortable.

Two hours later, the squad filed out of their entrenchment, passed their buddy squad filing in, and piled into the back of the truck idling on the other side of the rice paddies. They bounced along in the dark, parallel to the river, turned inland, and climbed a small hill. They piled out of the truck into a tent, and spread their olive drab bodies across the floor. No lights, nothing to do but sleep or smoke or chat in low voices.

• • • •

THIRD NIGHT OUT CAME a thin coat of snow, two centimeters in Army-speak, almost an inch. The men brushed it from their rifles as it fell, and their two hours passed. Lorne stepped from the trench over the embankment and found his left boot sliding and his right knee buckling. "Watch your footing. Slippery."

The squad stood at the top of the cliff waiting for the behind-schedule relief truck. Across the paddies, Lorne heard the whine of a motor. Soon blackout lights dotted the ground. *That fucking asshole. Must be Hendrick—he's all over the road.*

The relief soldiers piled out the back of the truck, and the two squads passed each other midway on the paddies. A man from the other squad said, "Good luck. You might wanna walk."

As Lorne approached the truck, he saw De Groot's long figure in the cab. Jones said, "It looks like the lieutenant riding shotgun."

"Yeah, he likes to come out with the men," said Lorne.

The squad clambered over the tailgate, mingling with another squad. The truck lurched forward and Lorne felt his eyes close, then nothing, then coming awake, the bed of the truck at a slant. From the cab came De Groot's voice at a high pitch. "You're going off the road, goddamnit."

Hendrick's voice: "Sir, I must ask you not to touch the steering wheel."

"Then keep the truck on the road, goddamnit."

Seconds later, the bed of the truck dropped forty-five degrees to the left. Lorne fell on soldiers to his port side and received bodies from the starboard. A boot pushed against his face, and a rifle butt struck his shoulder. He fought for air through arms and legs amid the clanging of ammo cans and helmets. Shouts of fuck and goddamn abounded. DiMaggio screamed, "Hendrick, you're dead. You're fucking dead."

Lorne felt a bare hand on the side of his face. "My glasses," said Rothman. Lorne drew closer to Rothman. His glasses had pushed up to his forehead.

Up front, Hendrick yelled, "Sir, you're stepping on me. I must ask you to not step on me."

Lorne saw starlight as the guys behind and above him crawled over the cockeyed tailgate. He followed, grabbing his helmet and dragging his rifle. Outside, De Groot lowered himself from the passenger door of the angled truck followed by Hendrick. As soon as Hendrick's boots touched the road, Lorne grabbed his left arm. Rothman, glasses intact and in place, stepped forward and grabbed his right arm. The two men frog marched Hendrick around the front of the truck, trailed by DiMaggio and Ivan.

De Groot said, "Where are you going with that man?"

"We can handle this, Sir," said Lorne.

Hendrick screamed, "Save me, Sir. Save me."

"Bring that man back. Release him."

"Sir," said Lorne as Hendrick shook himself free. *Just as well. That asshole's not worth a trip to the stockade.*

The two squads assembled on the road next to the truck. De Groot walked up and down surveying the damage. "Okay," he said. "Private Hendrick, get back in the cab. The rest of us, let's see if we can push this vehicle out of the ditch."

"Sir," said Lorne, "you can't let Hendrick back behind the wheel."

"Sir," said Hendrick, "it's my truck. I'm the assigned driver."

Lorne recalled some information Kim had passed to him. "Sir, Private Jones has a license."

De Groot said, "Really?"

Hendrick's dead eyes turned on Jones. "You can't take my truck. I'm the assigned driver."

Lorne stared at Hendrick. *Where does this guy get off? Doesn't he know how fucked up he is?* "Sir," said Lorne, "the circumstances are extraordinary. He'll kill us all if he keeps driving."

"Good point, Sergeant Boyle," said De Groot. "Okay, here's what we're doing. Private Jones, take the wheel."

Hendrick grabbed Jones's arm. "You can't do that. It's my truck."

Jones, who hadn't seemed to want the wheel, glowered at Hendrick's touch. "Let go of my arm, sucker." He turned to De Groot. "Is that a direct order, Sir?"

De Groot raised his eyes to the stars. "Yes, it's a goddamn direct order. I take full responsibility."

Jones hoisted himself through the passenger door and slid down the seat behind the wheel. He started the motor. With two squads pushing, the truck eased from the ditch and stood upright on the road. Ten minutes later, the men piled out of the truck and into the warm-up tent.

Across the way stood the command tent where De Groot and the senior sergeants hung out. They had called Lorne and Jones into their presence. They had a little stove and stools and lots of room. Lorne looked around the dull red glow. Cozy almost. De Groot said, "Private Jones, you'll be driving the rest of the week. Sergeant Boyle, Hendrick will rejoin your squad."

"Sir," said Jones, "I'm not assigned to that vehicle."

"We've cleared it with the motor pool. You and Hendrick will swap."

Jones stood in silence.

"That's all, Private Jones."

Halfway to the warm-up tent, Lorne turned to see Priestly following him and Jones. Priestly called out, "What's the matter, Private Jones? You don't like a nice warm truck cab?"

"I don't like being singled out, Sergeant Priestly."

"You got picked because you have a license."

The two men had stopped walking and faced each other midway between the two tents. Lorne stood near the entrance to the warm-up tent.

Jones said, "Here I am the new guy. And, if you haven't noticed, the only Black guy in the squad."

Bullshit, thought Lorne.

"Nothing to do with it," said Priestly.

Thank you, Sergeant Priestly.

"What about Hendrick?"

"What about him?"

"You should've seen the way he looked at me."

"He's a jerk. Forget about him."

"That's easy for you to say, Sergeant."

"Okay," said Priestly. "I'll talk to the lieutenant. When the weather clears, tomorrow, the next night, we'll ease Hendrick back into the driver's seat. Okay?"

Lorne and Jones found a space in the warm-up tent next to Kim. Kim whispered to Jones, "Good thing you have license. Save lives."

"Very funny," said Jones.

"Not making joke."

Lorne leaned back and closed his eyes. He wondered where Hendrick was in the tent and how much he could hear.

• • • •

A WEEK LATER, LORNE sat in the company mess for evening meal with the other three squad leaders from his platoon.

Half-engaged because he was eavesdropping on the conversation at the next table between Rothman, DiMaggio, and Jones.

"I don't get it," said Jones.

"Don't get what?" said Rothman.

"Why they keep letting Hendrick drive. Why he's even here."

"It's because of the re-up," said DiMaggio.

"They don't want to admit they were wrong," said Rothman.

Lorne watched Jones stare at his tray—watery spaghetti topped with ground beef and tomato sauce.

"Nobody ever re-ups out of Korea," said DiMaggio. "So the recruiters at division, when Hendrick raised his right hand, they got hard-ons."

"And now," said Rothman, "they don't want to hear any problems about him."

Jones said, "I never see Hendrick at evening chow."

DiMaggio laughed. "He likes to get a jump on his drinking."

Jones inserted his fork through the sauce and twine-like pasta on his tray. "Di, is this what they call al dente?" Lorne chuckled to himself. *Good one.*

DiMaggio twirled a mass of the mush on his fork. "This is what they call shit."

Jones addressed a question to Rothman. "When you and Sergeant Boyle grabbed Hendrick, would you have done anything serious?"

Lorne wondered about that himself. He didn't like losing his temper to the point of losing control.

Rothman said, "It's a good thing for him the lieutenant was there."

"No, really," said Marshall.

"Really," said DiMaggio. "Our good sergeant was as pissed as I've ever seen him." Rothman swallowed what he had in his mouth. "I can tell you this, Private Hendrick wouldn't have looked the same after."

Lorne looked around at his fellow squad leaders and nodded his head at the enlisted men's table. "They think I'm a good sergeant." A round of laughter ensued.

The fourth chair at the enlisted men's table scraped back, and Ivan sat down with a tray. "What's the talk?"

DiMaggio said, "Marshall here doesn't think our sergeant would've worked Hendrick over if the lieutenant hadn't been there."

"I still think we should take him out back," said Ivan. "A blanket party maybe."

Lorne had heard the talk but never knew one to happen. Catch a guy at night, throw a blanket over him, and everyone takes shots with their fists and boots.

Ivan, with fork in left hand, knife in right, sliced across the heap of red over white on his tray. He twisted the implements and sliced again.

"What the fuck are you doing?" said DiMaggio.

Ivan stared across the table at DiMaggio. Jones sat between them, opposite Rothman, such that Lorne caught the back of Rothman's head, Jones's face, and Ivan and DiMaggio in profile. DiMaggio's face had flushed. *Now what?* Lorne scraped back his chair, ready to intervene.

"What does it look like?" said Ivan. "I'm cutting my food."

"You don't fucking cut spaghetti, you dope, you twirl it. On your tray, or you can use a spoon."

"A spoon?"

"Yeah, like this. Jesus, don't you know anything?"

"Look," said Ivan, "it's my fucking food and if—"

As Lorne considered calling over, Rothman put up his hands. "Stop. Calm down, Di. Ivan, he's right. If you did that back in the world, you'd get thrown out of the restaurant."

Jones snorted. Ivan looked at him. "They're right," said Jones. "That's the way you do it."

"It's like if you were eating in the ville," said Rothman. "Would you bring a fork with you? No, you'd use chopsticks."

"Exactly," said DiMaggio, "when you eat rice, you do what the gooks do. When you eat spaghetti, you twirl it."

"You shouldn't use that word," said Rothman.

Jesus, Rothman, you were doing so well. Why start something else?
"What word?"

"Gook. It's a pejorative. How would you like it if I called you a wop?"

"That's different." DiMaggio extended his right arm forward toward a table of KATUSAs and lowered his voice. "Look at them. They're not like us." But as the words fell from his mouth, his eyes shifted to Jones, and DiMaggio's face flushed for the second time that evening.

Lorne had the urge to slap DiMaggio. *What a fucking jerk.* Jones gave DiMaggio a sidelong glance but otherwise let the incident slide.

"Oopso," said Ivan.

"What's that supposed to mean?" said DiMaggio.

"That's what they say," said Ivan. "The Koreans"—emphasizing Korean—"when something goes wrong."

"That's not what they say," said Rothman. "They say *ubseo* or more properly *ubsumnida.*"

"And it's not when something goes wrong. It means something does not exist." Rothman had on his flat school-teacher voice. "If you asked me where somebody was and he wasn't around, I'd say *ubsumnida.*"

"What if he was around?" said Jones.

"Then I'd say *issumnida.*"

DiMaggio pushed back his chair. "Well, boys, I'm *ubsumnida* from here."

As Rothman said, "very funny," and Ivan pushed his fork into his plate of sliced spaghetti, DiMaggio leaned toward Marshall. Lorne thought he heard, "Sorry about that." *That's good. Now I don't have to slap the shit out of Di.*

Chapter Eleven: December 1967, Blue Lancer Valley

"Who's that guy?" whispered Jones.

The company stood in loose formation between the supply room and the command post, watching De Groot, at attention, listen to a hand-animated monologue from a more senior officer. A few minutes earlier, Priestly had told Lorne the company was doing a sixteen-kilometer cross-country march to the bell area above Changpa-ri, east of the SCOSI positions; an overnight bivouac; and a sixteen-kilometer counter-march. The marches would be over hills and across rice paddies. No roads.

"That the old man," said Kim.

Lorne realized this was Jones's first glimpse of the company commander, Captain Adam Hirschfeld, medium height, dark hair, dark eyes, Mediterranean complexion, wearing field jacket, baseball cap, and gloves. De Groot raised his right arm. Hirschfeld returned the salute and walked away. The lieutenants and senior sergeants gathered around De Groot. A few minutes later, Priestly came out of the huddle and sauntered to the front of the platoon. "Okay, let's draw weapons and form up."

"Ammo?" said Rothman.

"No ammo."

"But Sergeant Priestly, what if we get attacked?"

"We're not getting attacked. The ammo trailer will rendezvous with us at the bivouac. Sleeping bags too."

Marshall's squad lined up at the door to the supply hut. DiMaggio said, "I don't like it, going into the bell with unloaded rifles."

"Do you know about odds?" said Lorne. "Like your chances for an inside straight?"

"Yes, Sergeant, I know about odds."

"Okay, the odds of us seeing Joe out there are just about nil. But running around with loaded rifles, the odds of us shooting each other are way above nil. And there's civilians out there."

"They shouldn't be there."

"It's not a restricted area."

"Still don't like it, Sergeant Boyle."

"You've got to look at the big picture," said Lorne. "Think like the captain."

"The captain's ass ain't out there," said Ivan. The squad laughed.

Very funny, thought Lorne. In the arms room, he took Jones aside. The squad needed a grenadier for the exercise, and Lorne had decided to give Jones a break. "I want you to draw an M79. And a forty-five."

"Why me, Sergeant?"

Why me, Sergeant? "Because I just told you to." *What's the matter with him? Is he turning into a fuckup like the rest of the squad?*

"Jesus, I'm doing you a favor. It's easier to carry."

"But what if something happens?"

"If something happens, you can have my rifle. Now shake the shit out'a your ass and draw your fucking weapons!"

Fifteen minutes later, the company ambled out the main gate and down the road to Nullo-ri. At the intersection with the main street, the men turned left, then right, leaving the road, headed north. They tramped single file across rice paddy berms and climbed into a set of low hills. They crested a ridge and dropped into another cluster of frozen rice paddies. Twenty minutes later, the company climbed a second set of low hills.

"You're right," said Jones.

"What's that?" said Lorne.

"The M79, it's easier to carry. Even with the pistol."

The company descended into a third set of frozen rice paddies and stopped. Ahead, De Groot and the other lieutenants knelt over a map spread flat on a paddy berm. The senior sergeants stood around them.

Kim said, "Every time we go out, get lost."

Smart ass, thought Lorne, but he's right.

Priestly walked over and said, "Okay, we're crapping out for a while."

Lorne's squad slid down with their backs against a berm and pulled C rations from under their parkas. "Anyone wanna trade for ham and lima beans?" said Jones.

"You funny guy," said Kim. The men removed right mittens, fished along their dog tag chains for P-38 can openers, and snipped open their cans. They produced spoons, replaced their mittens, and commenced gobbling their glop.

Kim said, "My uncle tell me some day there be something small like transistor radio tell you exactly where you are. No need map."

"Right," said Jones. "Do you know about Dick Tracy? He has a two-way radio you can wear on your wrist."

"No, really." Kim poked the ground with the top end of his spoon. "Let's say you here and get signal from two transmitters, and you know position of transmitters." Kim poked twice more on the ground and dragged lines that crossed his first poke. "Then you can triangulate where you are."

"Cool," said Jones, "So, Yeong-su, tell me, what's a smart guy like you doing in the infantry?"

"Long story. Why you in infantry, Marshall?"

"That's easy. I got a job out of high school, then a notice from my draft board."

"What you do for job?"

"Parts. Worked in a parts store."

"What's that?"

"You know, automobile parts. We buy from manufacturers and sell to garages and people who want to fix their own cars."

"Movies show lots of cars in America."

"Everybody has a car," said Jones. "Some people have two."

"Same thing in Korea some day."

"Maybe," said Jones. "Looks like you got a ways to go."

"Not funny," said Kim. "Americans think they better. Some day Koreans are better too."

Marshall put up his hands. "I'm on your side, Yeong-su."

"Piss me off sometime."

"Hey, I'm with you, brother." Jones slumped down, having stowed his empty C-ration can and spoon. "But what's your story? You sound like you should be in college."

"Go to university, not do well, get bored, too much party."

"I hear you."

"Father pissed, so pissed he not talk to me. Uncle pissed but give me advice. Say get army out of way, get in KATUSA program." Kim shuffled closer to Marshall. "I have to explain Korean way. My uncle is my father's big brother. Very important in Korea—he head of family. Also he work for up-and-coming electronics company. That how I know English."

"What do you mean?"

"Uncle insist I learn English. Pay for lessons when young."

Lorne's eyelids drooped. He pulled his mittened hands under his arms, the midday sun almost warming him. A nap would be nice, but Kim's chronicle had caught his attention.

"So I enlist for KATUSA program, but at end of basic training, they call me to admin building to discuss assignment. Have discussion with colonel, but he look like school teacher. Wear glasses with thick, black frames. No hair. Fat cheeks. Who is this guy? I sit on a chair in front of his desk."

Good story, thought Lorne.

"Colonel say in very important voice. He say I can choose not to go to KATUSA program. Can withdraw application and go in regular Korean army. So I say, 'Why would I want to do that, Colonel?' Colonel say, 'US army decadent. Soldiers lazy and weak.'"

Marshall laughed. "He's got us there."

"Yeah," said Kim. "Sound good for me, too. But colonel very serious. He say, in Korean army, become strong and disciplined. So I tell him, take chances with weak and lazy, Colonel."

Fucking Kim, thought Lorne, smart as a whip but always stepping in it.

"Colonel remove glasses and wipe them with cloth. His face very red. He replace glasses and put form with many boxes in front of him on desk. He pick up pen. He ask me, 'Do you have preference where you go?' So right away, I say yes. Tell him my English very good, best put to use in Eighth Army Headquarters in Seoul. Colonel smile. First time I see him smile. He say, 'You dismissed.'"

"Yeong-su," said Jones, "you should've told him you wanted to come up here. Didn't you ever read Tom Sawyer?"

"Yeah, yeah, I know, Tom Sawyer get others to paint fence. Big mistake. Colonel write me in for DMZ."

"What did your uncle say? Did you tell him?"

"Yeah, I go to uncle, tell him about colonel, tell him, 'Uncle, they send me to DMZ as rifleman.' Uncle say, 'When you ever learn? All the time, talk when you should listen, smirk when you should put on polite face.' And he right, always put foot in mouth."

Yeah, thought Lorne, at least Kim knows his problem.

"Don't beat yourself up about it," said Jones.

"What you mean?"

"Don't get angry at yourself. Just roll with it."

"That what uncle say. He very calm. He say, 'Look, Yeong-su, serve time, stay out of trouble. War was much worse.' Always talking about war."

"Which war?"

"What?" said Kim. "You here in Korea and don't know about war?"

"Well, I know there was a war, but I never studied it. Some of my friends, their dads went over."

"In 1950s ..." Kim seemed to be counting on his mittened fingers. "Almost eighteen years ago, the North Koreans, they come down. Everybody who can, run south. All the way to Pusan. South Korean army crushed. Then Americans and South Koreans push back, push North Koreans out and chase them all the way to China."

Then the Chinese came into the war, thought Lorne.

"Then Chinese come into war and push everyone south. Same thing again. Then Americans and South Koreans push back, and here we are."

Lorne looked around. He saw Hendrick asleep. He didn't see anyone moving. No officers, no sergeants. Okay by him. The sun felt good.

"Very bad for people then," said Kim. "Not me. Little kid. But father, mother, uncles. Many people killed, many people just disappear, never see again. Chosons shoot people as traitors. Hanguks shoot people as traitors."

"What's that?" said Jones.

"What's what?"

"Chosons and something else."

"Name of country. In north, Korea called Choson. Here, called Hanguk. Sometime get tired of hearing about war, but very bad time. So uncle say, 'Very lucky today. Much better. Don't complain. Stay out of trouble, finish military, finish education.'"

Good advice, thought Lorne.

"Uncle tell me he can get me job at Samsung. Tell me in ten years be rich. Finish army, finish education, stay out of trouble."

"What's Samsung?"

"Where he work. Transistors. Electronics. Very interesting."

Kim pulled off a mitten and worked his hand inside his parka. He extracted a palm-size gray radio and pulled the antenna up. Static then a Korean voice.

"What's that?"

"News. You know what piss me off, Marshall? March all day, sit in bunker, stand in trench, sleep in bunk, do toilet in cinder block latrine with GIs who think they better because Americans have money and Koreans none. Working girls give pussy to Americans but not Koreans. Even dumb-ass Hendrick get better treatment. Really piss me off."

"Yeah," said Marshall, "like I said before—"

"But in ten years have beautiful wife with degree from Ewha University. Have pussy on side whenever I want. Travel to Los Angeles in the United States and have round-eye pussy. And stupid American soldiers have nothing, no money, no pussy. Only hand job."

Kim clenched his teeth and parted his lips. The skin of his face peeled back like a kamikaze pilot in an open cockpit.

Whoa. Here was a KATUSA dimension Lorne had yet to see.

"Shit, man," said Jones. "What are you doing?"

Kim's face relaxed. He looked about. "Sorry. Sometime get worked up."

"That's wild, man. Do it again."

Kim drew in his head and hunched his shoulders. "Sorry."

Farther along the berm, Priestly's voice intruded. "Everyone. Saddle up."

Lorne pushed himself to his feet and stretched. The rest of the squad shuffled to their feet, except for Hendrick. Lorne walked over and cupped a hand on Hendrick's shoulder. "Wake up. Let's go."

Hendrick opened his eyes and swiped his right arm. He looked up. "I'll thank you to keep your hands off me, Sergeant Boyle."

Lorne squatted so he and Hendrick were at eye level. "You want to see some hands on you?" Hendrick glared. "Just give me some shit and you'll see some hands."

As Hendrick stood up, he turned his glare on Kim and Jones. "You think that's funny?"

Jones stared back.

The company lumbered off single file. Another set of hills, another set of rice paddies. More hills. In a few hours, the infantrymen reached their bivouac near the upper end of the bell, east of the SCOSI positions. Lorne's squad settled on a knoll facing west. The soldiers changed to their Mickey Mouse boots and watched the sun dip.

Two deuce-and-a-halves chugged up the river road, picked their way between hills, and shut down their motors at the foot of the squad's knoll. The first pulled the ammo trailer and the second carried evening chow. The men grabbed mess kits and headed down. Priestly walked along the chow line and said, "The truck with the ammo trailer has our sleeping bags. Grab one after you eat."

Lorne ate standing up. Chipped beef, mashed potatoes, gravy, peas—hot. He washed his mess tin, cup, and spoon, and grabbed a sleeping bag from the back of the ammo truck. He sat with his squad on the edge of their knoll watching the sky change to a deep blue, sleeping bags draped over their shoulders.

From the river, a kilometer away, south of the SCOSI positions, a machine gun opened fire, shooting north, up the river, tracer bullets streaking the dark air. Lorne recalled the night infiltration courses from basic and advanced infantry training. There, the machine guns were set on blocks, firing over the trainees' heads as they crawled forward. Getting under barbed wire obstacles required flipping onto backs and pushing through with boot heels. Lorne enjoyed that, looking into the starry night punctuated by tracer streaks a meter overhead.

"Hey," yelled DiMaggio, "shouldn't we be breaking out the ammo?"

Next to Lorne, Jones pushed his sleeping bag off his shoulders and jumped up.

Shit, thought Lorne, just what we don't need.

Kim said, "Sound like our gun. M60."

"What are they shooting at?" said Jones.

Lorne floated his voice across the squad. "Take it easy, ladies. I'm sure it's being checked out."

Jones leaned over and touched his weapons—his grenade launcher and pistol—resting on his pack on the ground. "Sergeant Boyle," he said. "How about that rifle you promised me."

"Calm down, Private Jones. Everyone, take it down a notch."

Priestly walked over. "The lieutenant's got a call into battalion." He walked away.

Rothman said, "What do you think, Sergeant Boyle?"

Lorne said, "I think it's not a good idea to load up right now with civilians wandering around." He had noticed a few women selling food and drink. "And we got each other wandering around. And half of us are about to wet our pants."

Lorne looked to the west. The machine gun had shut down. A few minutes later, Priestly reappeared, and the platoon gathered around. "We got an answer from battalion. The boys on Libby Bridge got excited over nothing. Squad leaders, set up for the night."

Lorne called his squad together. "Let's make this as painless as we can. One man on guard duty at a time, hour and a half. The rest of us can sleep. The man who's on, don't fuck up."

* * * *

MARSHALL UNROLLED HIS sleeping bag and sat on it. He pulled off his boots and stuck them under the head of the sleeping bag along with the grenade launcher, pistol, and web gear. He crawled in with everything else on, shivering. He closed his eyes. He opened his eyes. He shivered.

He thought about sex. He thought about how stupid it was to be thinking about sex but couldn't help himself. Here he lay in a sack on the ground half frozen to death thinking of Deidre Johnson from East High School in Rochester. She had, as they say, a rack, which Marshall lusted after, junior and senior years. Lusting only—she, the girl of his wet dreams—they'd never gone out. Lying on the ground in Korea, feet numb, nose numb, shivering—not a good time for a wet dream.

Marshall awoke thinking it was his turn for guard duty, but his eyes fell on a wrap-around skirt and rubber shoes. They rose to the wrinkled face of a mamasan, who squatted and pointed. Marshall followed her finger to the outline of a younger woman, a josan, a one-timer. "You rike?" said the mamasan. "Two dollah can do."

Not a good idea, thought Marshall, but his cock hardened. He reached under his wool fatigues into the right pocket of his cotton fatigues. "All I got is one dollar," he said.

"One dollah can do."

The josan unzipped the top of Marshall's sleeping bag and wriggled in. The mamasan said, "You give dollah." As Marshall extracted the crumpled piece of military scrip and pushed it into the mamasan's hand, he felt his flies being unzipped and the josan squirming underneath him. "No make noise," said the mamasan.

Two minutes later, the josan wiggled out of the sleeping bag and Marshall zipped up. There was no post-coital release, only remorse. No rubber, no washy-washy, only a wet spot in his shorts. He did feel warmer. So stupid! But why does the realization come afterwards and not before?

• • • •

MARSHALL'S EYES OPENED to shimmering starlight against a blue-black backdrop, and he realized the top of his bag had been unzipped. A face took focus, Hendrick, squatting over him. Marshall leaned on his elbows in an attempt to rise. Hendrick pushed a mitten toward Marshall's face.

"What do you want?" said Marshall.

"What do you mean?" said Hendrick. "You're on."

Of course. Marshall had guard duty after Hendrick, whose mitten held Boyle's watch. Marshall took the watch and pushed out of his sleeping bag into icy Mickey Mouse boots, impelled by a need to urinate. He checked the luminous hands on the watch, zero two thirty—he was on until zero four hundred. Marshall stepped down the knoll a few meters, undid his flies, and emptied his bladder. He turned and saw the glow of a cigarette, the guard for first squad. "Hey," said the other guard.

"Hey," said Marshall. An hour and a half later, he passed the watch to Rothman and crawled back into his sleeping bag, waking to the sound of the chow truck. He pulled on his boots, grabbed his mess kit and cup, and lined up. Someone up front lit a cigarette, and the man behind him used it to light his own cigarette. Soon the whole line had lit up, stomping and puffing, pulling off mittens to get at their cigarettes, putting them back on to keep from freezing, puffing even after having scrambled eggs and bacon bits dumped in their mess tins and coffee poured in their cups. Still puffing as they maneuvered their hot fare to a spot on the knoll.

Marshall washed his mess tin and cup in a barrel of hot suds, dipped it in a barrel of hot rinse, and scooted back up the knoll. He rolled his sleeping bag and draped his web gear over his body. As he picked up the M79, his web gear felt wrong. He patted around his waist, his right hand stopping on the holster, and his sphincter closed like a corked bottle. Panic rose through his bowels to his chest cavity. Marshall unfurled the sleeping bag, shook it, turned it inside out, and shook it again. He removed his web gear and dumped the contents of his pack.

Kim said, "What problem?"

Marshall turned to Kim and found Boyle next to him, smiling, but not smiling, behind him the faces of DiMaggio, Ivan, and Hendrick.

"My forty-five's gone missing."

Boyle raised a mitten and Priestly walked over.

"What?" said Priestly.

"Sergeant, it was in the holster last night. This morning it's gone."

"Where was the holster?" said Priestly.

"Under my sleeping bag. Under my head."

Priestly walked away with his head bowed. During the interval, Boyle asked Marshall, "Did anything unusual happen last night?"

"No, Sergeant."

Boyle moved closer and lowered his voice. "Think hard. Nothing?"

Marshall shook his head.

Priestly returned. "Okay, I'll hold the platoon back and we'll scour the area"

"Should we tell the lieutenant?" said Boyle.

"Let's hold off," said Priestly. "When we get back, if we don't have it, we'll go through the sleeping bags, everything. If we still don't have it, I'll go to the first sergeant." Priestly turned to Marshall. "What's missing? Just the pistol?"

"The pistol and two empty clips, Sergeant."

"Two?"

"One in the pistol, Sergeant, and another was stuck alongside in the holster."

The men lifted their heads as De Groot walked toward them. Priestly said, "Sir, we're gonna police the area for trash and catch up with you."

De Groot nodded and turned away.

"What will the first sergeant do?" said Marshall.

"He'll tell the captain," said Priestly.

"Is this bad, Sergeant Priestly?"

"It's real bad."

But looking past Priestly, Boyle's face scared Marshall more than the platoon sergeant's words. His lips were screwed lopsided like one side of his face tried to smile as the other side fought the smile. And those green eyes, drooping but glaring. Maybe Marshall should have told him about the mamasan and the josan, but the truth was hard; Marshall just wanted it to go away.

Chapter Twelve: December 1967, Blue Lancer Valley

Marshall sat on his foot locker, elbows on knees, head down, a scant diffusion from the overhead bulb outside the rear door the only light. He played the previous night over, the mamasan, the josan, two minutes, in a sleeping bag, in the field, stupid. He'd lied to his squad leader, couldn't help himself. Kim, snug in his bottom bunk, whispered, "You hear anything yet?"

Marshall leaned toward Kim. "Sergeant Boyle's not around."

"Maybe go to NCO club. Maybe spend night in ville."

Marshall's head shook. "Not this night."

Marshall recalled the books he liked to read as a kid. Knights on horses, Vikings in longships, brave, resolute, noble in every action. Not venal, not bowing to temptation when it interfered with mission. His thoughts swirled. This wouldn't have happened if I wasn't Black in a white squad. What's that got to do with it? No, that's what they'll say, look, the one Black guy in the squad, lazy, depraved, can't keep it in his pants for two seconds, wouldn't you know?

The far door of the hut opened. Boyle's boots advanced and stopped in front of Marshall. Boyle squatted so their faces were even. "Glad you're up," he said. "We're having a little after-hours meeting in the CP, and you're invited." Boyle moved his half-moon lips closer. "Should be quite the wingding. You, me, Sergeant Priestly, the first sergeant, the lieutenant, the captain. The colonel might even come down."

Marshall felt sick to his stomach. He felt like crying. He stood and fumbled in his wall locker for his parka.

"But first," said Boyle, "we need to have a little talk. Let's go out back."

Boyle eased into the center aisle, skirted the rear stove, and opened the back door. Marshall followed. Outside Boyle walked to the piss tube as Marshall pulled his parka tight. Boyle took his time, zipped up, and closed his parka, before walking back to where Marshall stood.

"The thing is, Private Jones, we can't deal with this unless we know the truth of what happened."

"I told you what happened, Sergeant Boyle."

Boyle draped his left arm over Marshall's shoulder. "I really like you, Marshall, I really do, but you're turning into a disappointment, lying to me."

Boyle's left arm scissored into a headlock, forcing Marshall to bend forward. Marshall said, "You're hurting me, Sergeant Boyle."

"I know," said Boyle. "And I don't want to. It grieves me to hurt you. But we've gotta out with the truth."

Marshall tried to straighten but Boyle tightened the headlock. He was shorter than Marshall by two inches and lighter by twenty pounds but held him like a vice. He said, "Tell me about that josan on our post last night. Did you consort with her?"

"Did I what?"

"Do you think I'm blind? I saw that mamasan and josan."

"I'm not sure I know—"

Marshall heard a thwack, and pain enveloped the area below his left eye. He flailed both arms and stuttered a step but failed to break the headlock. He couldn't believe that his squad leader had just punched him. "Against regulations," Marshall said. "Against regulations."

"Did you consort with that josan, goddamnit?" The headlock tightened, cutting Marshall's wind. Marshall squeezed his eyes. "Can't, can't—"

The headlock relaxed a notch. "Did you consort with her?"

With his breath back, Marshall said, "Yes, I consorted with her. Yes, yes."

The headlock fell away, and Marshall straightened his body. His neck hurt. His left eye throbbed. Boyle exhaled; he breathed in and exhaled again. "Now we're getting somewhere. Was that so hard?"

Despite the punching and throttling, Marshall felt relief that the lie no longer separated them.

"Now, Private Jones, while you were consorting, inside your sleeping bag, I presume, where was the mamasan? Was she in there too?"

Marshall let his head drop.

"Or was she outside in proximity to your weapons? Answer me, goddamnit."

"She was outside."

"In proximity to your weapons?"

"In proximity to my weapons."

"How could you be so stupid?"

"I don't know, Sergeant, I—"

"And you know what's double sad about this?"

Marshall shook his head.

"Losing your weapon isn't your only problem."

"I don't understand, Sergeant."

"You may lose your dick, too," said Boyle. "Fucking a josan in the field is about the dumbest thing a soldier can do. Have you not heard of VD?"

"What's gonna happen to me, Sergeant Boyle?"

"It's what's gonna happen to us, Private Jones. The army goes bull over a missing weapon. They'd rather have a body on the ground." Boyle looked to the stars. "Do you know how short I am?"

"A month or so, Sergeant Boyle."

"Less than a month. I've got less than a month left in Korea, Private Jones, less than a month left in the army. I don't need this. I don't need to be standing in front of the captain explaining why one of my men lost his dick and a forty-five."

"I'm sorry I fucked up."

Boyle stood silent. Marshall shivered and pulled his parka tighter.

"I'm sorry, too," said Boyle. His voice had gone calm. "But we'll get through it."

Boyle pulled Marshall under the circle of light from the bulb over the back door and touched the welt under his eye. Marshall winced.

"If anyone asks," said Boyle, "just say you tripped over the piss tube."

• • • •

MARSHALL FOLLOWED HIS squad leader past their hut, down the hill, into the command post, where they found Priestly and Steiner. Steiner said, "Shut that fucking door."

The room was cold. Priestly or Steiner must have just pumped up the stove. They still wore their parkas. Marshall and Boyle joined them, hands out, drawing in the fresh heat. They pushed their hoods back.

Steiner looked into Marshall's face. Marshall followed his gaze as it dropped to the bruised knuckles of Boyle's right hand. Steiner said, "Getting short, aren't we, Acting Sergeant Boyle?"

"Twenty-four and a wake-up, First Sergeant."

"Well, let's hope you get there without a court martial."

"I appreciate your concern, First Sergeant." Boyle lifted his right hand, rubbed the knuckles, and blew on them. Priestly looked away.

"We waiting on the captain?" said Boyle.

"And the colonel," said Steiner.

Marshall's intestines churned. He wanted to be out of the army. He wanted to go home.

"First sergeant," said Boyle, "can I offer a suggestion? We think that forty-five is in Chang." Steiner kept the palms of his hands over the stove and his thoughts to himself. Boyle continued. "There were civilians out there after dark. A mamasan floating around."

Steiner said, "We can't defend ourselves against a mamasan?"

"Top," said Priestly, "you know how it goes in the field. It's impossible to button down everything."

"It's dark, it's freezing," said Boyle.

"So that's what we're telling the captain? It was dark? It was freezing?"

"Here's the thing, First Sergeant," said Boyle. "If we get into Chang ASAP, we got a fighting chance at finding that weapon."

"Do we?"

"Whoever the mamasan fenced it to, they'll be looking to sell it. They'll sell it back to us if we can get to them."

"And what, pray tell, is your operations plan, Acting Sergeant?"

"Simple." Boyle extended his arm toward Marshall. "Private Jones draws a jeep in the morning. We go into Chang and start checking shops."

Steiner lowered his hands from the stove and turned to Boyle. "Let me get this straight. The plan is for you two fuckups to go on a joyride to Chang?"

"We'll take Kim with us."

"Which Kim?"

"Kim YS."

Steiner's temporal arteries bulged. His voice rose in volume and pitch. "Three fuckups."

"He speaks English," said Boyle.

"He speaks too much English."

Boyle's eyes flitted to the far window, and Steiner turned his head. "Fuck," he said, "here comes the captain."

"Think about it, First Sergeant," said Boyle. "It's a shot."

The door lurched open. Marshall's second look at his company commander, Captain Adam Hirschfeld, Vietnam veteran, Combat Infantryman Badge. Hirschfeld slammed the door behind him as Steiner called, "Ten-hut."

Hirschfeld strode past the four rigid parkas and at high volume said, "I'm not happy about this fucking situation."

He strode back toward the door. "I'm the opposite of happy."

He regarded the men still at attention. "At ease, for chrissakes."

Shoulders slumped while the captain plotted his next utterance. "Where is Lieutenant De Groot? Isn't he supposed to be right smack in the middle of this shit?"

"Sent a jeep for him, Sir," Steiner said. "Couldn't raise him through the switchboard." Steiner's eyes fell to the window, where headlights bounced and stabbed in the dark. "Not the lieutenant, Sir."

Hirschfeld looked. "Fuck," he said, "here comes the colonel."

Seconds later, the tick of the jeep motor stopped. The command post door opened, held by the colonel's driver, and Luppino crossed the threshold. "Aten-shun," called Hirschfeld. Once again, the men stood like poles, shoulders back, eyes ahead. With two hands, the driver removed the colonel's parka, which had hung about his shoulders like a cape. Luppino pulled off his gloves, gave them to his driver, and extended a hand. "As you were."

Luppino looked the perfect career officer, dark hair, short but not cropped, thin nose, thin frame, his appearance marred only by the stubble of a day-old beard. He turned to Hirschfeld. "Captain." He nodded to Steiner. "Top."

Luppino's gaze turned to the stove, and he nodded to Priestly and Boyle. The colonel stretched his neck, and Marshall wilted under his scrutiny in expectation of a query about the damage to his face. But the colonel pulled back without raising the question.

"Sir," said Hirschfeld, "we're waiting on Lieutenant De Groot. Did you want to start without him?"

Luppino folded his arms and leaned against the jamb of the door to the inner office. "We can wait." He looked at the enlisted men around the stove. "Smoke 'em if you got 'em."

Cigarettes emerged from pockets; matches and lighters sparked. By the time De Groot opened the door, smoke had filled the room and parkas had opened. De Groot hunched through the door and removed his fogged-up glasses. He squinted around the room, repositioning the glasses, and bobbed his head at the gathering. At Marshall, his eyebrows rose. "Private Jones, whatever happened to your face?"

Fuck, thought Marshall, glancing at Boyle then back to the lieutenant. "Sir, I tripped over the piss tube."

More eyebrows rose with all lips buttoned, until Luppino laughed. "Those fucking piss tubes. Worse than a minefield." The captain and the sergeants joined the laughter. De Groot laughed, and Marshall forced a chuckle.

Luppino stepped toward the stove, flashing his brown eyes on Boyle and Priestly as if in confidence. "Can you men give me some firsthand information? Some real facts? Not the usual bull."

"Sir," said Boyle. "It was after dark. Some Korean nationals were on our position. We shooed 'em off. But they were all over the place."

The colonel nodded. Priestly said, "Sir, the civilians are a problem when we're in the field south of the river."

"I understand that," said Luppino. "This isn't the first incident. Although ... we've never lost a weapon before." He turned to Boyle. "So in your opinion, Sergeant, this weapon is definitely gone?"

"Hard to say, Sir."

Luppino blinked. "Meaning?"

"There's a few places that could be poked into, Sir."

Luppino returned Boyle's smile. He stepped back and said, "Okay, we've got a clusterfuck here, but it isn't the end of the world. We need to get to work on it."

"Sir," said Hirschfeld.

Luppino looked at Boyle. "If by some miracle the gun turns up tomorrow, all well and good. We can bury the whole mess." He shifted his eyes to Steiner. "If it doesn't, a report has to go up to brigade. We'll need paperwork—an incident report, depositions. Top, you've been through the drill."

"Sir," said Steiner.

Luppino glanced at his driver and lifted his elbows. The driver placed Luppino's parka over his shoulders and handed him his gloves. The room came to attention. "Captain," said Luppino. "Lieutenant. Men."

The driver opened the command post door, and Luppino passed into the night. The door closed, the jeep motor fired, and the jeep putted away. As the men relaxed their shoulders, Hirschfeld said, "Lieutenant De Groot, since you're the responsible officer, it's only fitting that you be the investigating officer—who will resolve this fucking matter by the end of tomorrow."

"With all due respect, Sir, how can I be the responsible officer when I only learned of this matter in the past thirty minutes?"

"Oh, Lieutenant," said Hirschfeld. His voice had gone high-pitched. "I would suggest not using that as your defense at a court martial. Come over here."

De Groot stepped next to Hirschfeld, who pressed a forefinger against an inventory form on Steiner's desk and read with deliberation, "Pistol, Caliber .45, Automatic, M1911A1, serial number 947701C. Now look at the signature at the bottom, Lieutenant. Whose signature is that? Whose?"

"Sir, as the supply officer, that's my signature. But I'm also the mess officer, the training officer, and the recreation officer. I sign a hundred forms a day."

"Be that as it may, the signature is yours." Hirschfeld raised an arm and pointed toward the stove. "Now look at these men. To whose platoon do these men belong?"

De Groot opened his mouth, but Hirschfeld interrupted. "So you are culpable on two counts, Lieutenant. You are the signatory for the lost weapon. And you are the commander of the culpable parties."

Hirschfeld walked to the door. De Groot and the men stood to attention.

"I want a preliminary report by noon," Hirschfeld said. He walked out pulling the door closed behind him, and, once again, shoulders relaxed.

"Well, Sir," said Steiner, "it looks like we're up the proverbial shit creek."

De Groot didn't laugh. Steiner pressed the joke. "No paddle."

He looked into the lieutenant's face. De Groot's eyes were red, his lower lip trembling. Steiner put a hand on his elbow. "Sir, this is not your fault. You know how the captain can get."

Priestly stepped forward. "Right, Sir. If anything, it's us, we let you down."

Boyle, in line of view with Steiner, lifted his eyebrows.

"Sir," said Steiner, "Acting Sergeant Boyle has an idea."

De Groot nodded.

"Well, Sir," said Boyle, "that pistol is most likely being fenced in the ville. If we can find it, we can buy it back."

Steiner said, "Acting Sergeant Boyle proposes an expeditionary force to Chang. Himself, Private Jones, and Kim YS."

De Groot turned to Priestly with questioning eyes.

"Worth a shot, Sir," said Priestly.

"Changpa-ri," said De Groot. He seemed to have perked up. "Maybe I should lead the patrol."

Boyle's smile evaporated. "Not a good idea, Sir."

"Why not?"

Jesus, thought Marshall, just what we need, an officer along.

"You might scare them off, Sir."

"Right, Sir," said Priestly. "Better to send just enlisted men."

Steiner said, "While they're in Chang, Sir, we'll start the paperwork. In case they don't find it."

Boyle shifted from leg to leg. "One other thing. If we find it, we're gonna need scrip to buy it back."

Steiner's eyes narrowed. "How much?"

"Fifty dollars, maybe less. But fifty to be sure." He turned to De Groot. "Do you think you could throw in ten, Sir?"

Steiner said, "The first sergeant's pool can throw in ten too."

Priestly said, "We can get fifteen from the NCO hooch."

Boyle said, "I can get fifteen out of the platoon."

Marshall didn't share the flurry of excitement. He doubted they'd find the gun in Chang and knew he was fucked. He looked toward the door; he could use the latrine and a few hours sleep.

Steiner tapped De Groot's arm and pointed to a requisition form on his desk. "Could you sign right here, Sir?"

De Groot leaned over the form. "It's blank, First Sergeant."

"Right, Sir. I'll have the clerk fill it in later." He proffered a pen. "We need it for the jeep, Sir. If you don't mind."

Chapter Thirteen: December 1967, Changpa-ri

Cold sun at their backs, their jeep bounced west to the river, turned right, and bounced north to Changpa-ri. The three occupants shivered in winter fatigues and parkas, the jeep being semi-combat ready—windshield up but no enclosing canvas—to better repel an attack. Military logic, thought Marshall: how were they to repel an attack with frozen limbs and no weapons? Also, Marshall had noticed that the bigwigs from division, and the military police, drove in enclosed, heated jeeps.

Marshall held one mitten-covered hand between his legs and steered with the other, switching hands every minute. Boyle rode shotgun while Kim hunkered in the middle of the rear seat. Marshall glanced in the rear-view mirror at Kim's sullen mien, obviously not happy about going to Changpa-ri, a GI playground where Korean men found nothing but disdain. Uh, oh. The skin on Kim's face had tightened, his eyes bulged, and his lips parted—his kamikaze face. Boyle looked at Marshall looking at Kim and pivoted.

"Goddamnit, Kim, what the fuck are you doing?"

Marshall released his first laugh since losing the forty-five.

"And you, what the fuck's so funny?"

"I can't help it, Sergeant Boyle. I love that face."

"Goddamnit, Kim," said Boyle, "don't do that in the ville."

Marshall settled the jeep in the square in front of the Lucky Club and shut off the motor. The morning air was crisp, and the square uncrowded. No Americans, just Korean civilians squatting on haunches in chattering knots of two and three, waiting for the bus to Pobwon-ni or Munsan-ni. Boyle hopped from the jeep and walked to a path on the north side of the club. Marshall and Kim followed, Marshall with a backward glance to make sure the spare tire and gas can were chained and locked. He didn't need any further woes with government equipment.

The soldiers walked fifty meters, turned left for another fifty, and entered an alleyway of attached hooches fronted by a narrow veranda. At the top of the alleyway, Marshall saw the back of the Half Moon Club. Boyle walked to the fourth door from the club and tapped.

The girl who stepped onto the veranda wore a wrap-around dress and no make-up. Marshall thought her shorter than average, then realized the perception had more to do with girth. She was pregnant. She looked young, no older than his nineteen.

"Yobo," she said. Her eyes shifted to Marshall and Kim, then back to Boyle.

Boyle took her hand. "Yobo," he said. "Problem. Maybe you help." He motioned to Kim. "Tell her about the gun. See if she knows how to find it."

Kim walked to the veranda and spoke with sweeping, condescending gestures. The girl talked back, matching Kim's gesticulations, shaking her head. Kim turned to Boyle. "She no think gun in ville."

"What do you mean?"

"She say too dangerous for mamasan to take gun. Not in ville."

"Jesus," said Boyle, "I'd think that mamasan would be all over a gun."

Kim said, "Not the same as stealing diesel or binoculars. Bad news get caught with gun."

Boyle looked up at the girl and put two fingers to his eyes. "We look. You help."

She nodded her head and spoke to Kim in Korean. Kim said, "She say she look. No good if GI go."

Boyle reached inside his parka and withdrew four tens and two fives in military scrip and a piece of paper. "Kim, tell her to make sure the serial number matches this. If she finds it."

The girl slipped into rubber shoes and stepped down from the veranda. With scrip and serial number in hand, she departed by way of the Half Moon. Boyle turned to Marshall and Kim. "Go back and watch the jeep before we lose that too."

At the square in front of the Lucky Club, Marshall circled the jeep. Tires still there, gas can there, everything in order. Kim said, "First time I see his yobo."

Marshall said, "What happens when he goes back to the world next month?"

"She find new GI."

"What about the baby?"

"Maybe she keep. Maybe go to orphanage."

"Some of the guys marry their yobos, don't they?"

"Sometime that happen," said Kim.

Marshall cocked an ear to the negative tone of Kim's voice. "You don't approve?"

"She working girl," said Kim. "Not good for wife."

Marshall slumped in the driver's seat of the jeep, the sun hitting him through the windshield. Kim climbed in back. As Marshall's eyes closed, he thought, I guess things are fucked up for everybody. He wasn't sure how long he dozed, an hour or more, before the jeep shifted and he looked to the right. Boyle sat alongside. He said, "She didn't come up with anything." He turned to the rear seat. "What do you think, Kim?"

"Maybe mamasan take, but very bad to get caught. Go to jail."

Marshall said, "What happens now, Sergeant Boyle?"

"We all make statements. Lieutenant De Groot writes a report. It goes to battalion. It goes to brigade. Our asses get whacked."

Marshall started the jeep. As he pulled into the road, Boyle said, "Let's suppose the mamasan didn't take it. What else could have happened?"

"Don't know, Sergeant Boyle. We scoured the area before we left."

"I don't mean if it was lost. I mean if it was stolen but not by the mamasan."

Marshall, maneuvering the jeep south from Changpa-ri through and around the multitude of potholes, remembered Hendrick staring down at him in the middle of the night saying it was his shift. "You think it could have been one of our guys, Sergeant Boyle?" Marshall glanced sideways and saw Boyle's eyes set to the front and no smile on his lips. Marshall said, "He'd have to be a real asshole."

"Exactly," said Boyle.

• • • •

AT BLUE LANCER, MARSHALL dropped off Boyle and Kim in the company area, returned the jeep to the motor pool, and walked back to the company command post. Steiner pointed to the door to the second room and said, "Report to Lieutenant De Groot." Marshall stepped through the doorway, his first visit to the inner sanctum. To his left, the captain's desk, unoccupied. In the middle of the room, a stove. To the right, a second desk for the lieutenants, occupied by Lieutenant De Groot.

Marshall marched to the front of the desk, stopped at attention, and raised his right hand to his forehead. "Sir, Private Jones reports."

De Groot returned the salute and said, "At ease." He picked up a pen and circled it on a pad of yellow paper. "So when you bunked down," he said, "the pistol was under your sleeping bag, under your head? Along with the M79?"

"Yessir."

"Could you feel it there when you were in your bag?"

Marshall hesitated. "I think so, Sir. I think there was a bulge there. No, maybe I couldn't tell it from everything else there."

"Was it there when you pulled guard duty?"

Marshall paused a second time. "I didn't check, Sir."

"Who was ahead of you on guard duty?"

"Hendrick, Sir."

"Who followed you?"

"Rothman, Sir."

"Did you see the Korean civilians?"

"Yessir, before I bunked down."

De Groot's bespectacled eyes looked like they were examining the welt on Marshall's face. "Is there anything else I should know, Private Jones?"

"No, Sir. Can't think of anything, Sir."

• • • •

MARSHALL WALKED TO the mess hall and sat alone for lunch. Rothman came over with his tray, sat down, and said, "We're with you, Private Jones. This shit could happen to anybody."

"Thanks." Marshall pushed at his boiled carrots. They ate in silence for a minute.

"You short?" said Marshall. Rothman was a specialist E-4, must have been in Korea for a while.

"Eighteen and a wake-up."

Marshall lifted his eyes. "You're shorter than Sergeant Boyle."

"That I am." Rothman half rose from his chair and peeped out a window. "Something's up."

Marshall half rose and looked. Outside, he saw Priestly in a huddle with the first sergeant, the captain, and De Groot. Steiner split away and walked toward the mess hall. A second later, he pushed through the door barking, "Listen up, ladies. Finish your chow and form up outside. Let's go."

By thirteen hundred, the company had assembled between the supply hut and the command post. Steiner took roll call, the platoon sergeants singing out, "All present or accounted for."

Steiner looked up from his clipboard. "I want everyone in barracks right now. I want you standing by your bunk. I don't want you going to the latrine. I don't want you going out back. I want every swinging dick at his bunk right now. Dismissed."

The platoons broke ranks. Marshall climbed the steps to his hooch, walked between first and second squads, and stood with Kim in front of their bunk. Marshall said, "What's going on?"

"Soon find out," said Kim.

The front door opened, and Steiner's voice rolled the length of the hut. "Ten-hut."

Heels came together. Behind Steiner were De Groot and Priestly. De Groot said, "As you were."

Then Steiner's voice again. "Listen up, ladies. You will open your foot lockers and wall lockers, but you will otherwise not meddle with them. You will stand in front of your bunk and come to attention when the lieutenant approaches. Is that understood?"

Priestly sauntered to the first bunk of the first squad followed by De Groot. The soldier there came to attention. Priestly pointed to the man's foot locker and said, "Dump it."

Marshall whispered, "Shakedown inspection?"

"That's what it looks like," said Rothman.

The shakedown moved up the aisle. Two cans of Budweiser rolled out of a foot locker. Priestly said, "Is that allowed in barracks, soldier?"

"No, Sergeant."

"Do you know why I'm not putting you on report?"

"No, Sergeant."

"Because you're pathetic. Two cans of warm beer. Dump them outside."

"Yes, Sergeant."

Priestly, Steiner, and De Groot stood in front of Marshall. He came to attention. He dumped his foot locker and resumed the position of attention. Priestly pushed against a deck of cards with the toe of his boot. "Is that a marked deck, Private?"

Marshall felt the blood rush to his head. Priestly put a hand on his shoulder. "I'm joking." Marshall heard a shuffle of laughter around him. Under other circumstances, he might have laughed himself.

The entourage stepped in front of Rothman. "Dump it." They stepped in front of DiMaggio and Ivan. They stepped in front of Hendrick. "Dump it." From the end of the hut, Boyle craned his neck.

Priestly reached among the objects on the floor and picked up an oblong piece of metal. He squeezed and bounced it around in his right hand and handed it to Steiner. Steiner showed it to De Groot, then held it in front of Hendrick's face. Hendrick tilted forward and back. His lips and shoulders shook. Steiner stepped up to him so their faces were inches apart. "What's this, Private Hendrick?"

"First Sergeant, I believe it's a pistol clip, empty."

"And where's the pistol?"

"It wasn't with a pistol, First Sergeant. It was lying around in the arms room a couple of months ago."

"It was lying around? And you just picked it up? Pray tell, what for?"

"A souvenir."

"Get your ass down to the command post."

Hendrick performed a left face and marched to the front door, trailed by De Groot. Marshall's gaze followed them, then returned to find Priestly pulling clothes from Hendrick's wall locker.

"Anything?" said Steiner.

Priestly shook his head.

Steiner pointed a finger at Boyle, "You," he said. He pointed the finger at Marshall. "And you. Don't go anywhere."

Steiner and Priestly left. The platoon restored order to the foot and wall lockers, and the hut emptied except for Marshall and Boyle. Marshall sat on Kim's bottom bunk. Boyle stood next to his bunk. Marshall said, "What do you think, Sergeant Boyle?"

"I wished we'd found the forty-five."

"He must have grabbed the extra clip without realizing it," said Marshall. "But how'd he get rid of the pistol?"

"Down a piss tube. Who knows?"

Marshall contemplated his change of status. He'd still lost the gun, but losing it to internal theft made him less culpable. Didn't it?

"What was he gonna do with it?" said Marshall. "Just getting back at me?"

"Who knows what goes through his head?" said Boyle. "Marshall, when you talked to the lieutenant, did you mention anything about fucking that josan or talking to the mamasan?"

The good feelings about Hendrick taking the fall drained away. Marshall shook his head. "I just said I saw them early on."

"Good," said Boyle. "Just the two of us know about that little episode. Does that suit you?"

"Yeah," said Marshall. "I mean, Sergeant Boyle—"

"Enough said."

Priestly appeared at the front door of the hut. "Sergeant Boyle," he called. "You're wanted down the command post."

· · · ·

THIRTY MINUTES LATER, Boyle returned and jerked his head. Marshall put on his parka and walked the length of the hut. Boyle put a hand against his chest. "When we get down there, leave your parka in the orderly room. Make sure your shirt's tucked in and your gig line's straight."

Marshall nodded.

"When you go in, report to the captain real sharp like. Just stand at attention and take whatever he hands out. Okay?"

Not okay.

"If he offers you a fifteen, accept it."

A fifteen meant nonjudicial punishment under Article 15 of the Universal Code of Military Justice. He'd admit his guilt and the captain would render punishment. Loss of pay, restriction to quarters. He could be busted from private first class E-3 back to private E-2.

"You could demand a court martial, but that would be stupid. Okay?"

Not okay.

"Pull yourself together, Marshall." Boyle had both hands on Marshall's shoulders. "C'mon, it'll be over before you know it."

Marshall and Boyle walked down the hill and entered the command post. Marshall removed his parka and hung it alongside the company clerk's. Boyle looked through the door into the inner sanctum, then turned his head and nodded.

Marshall had the sensation of being outside his body as it crossed the threshold. On the opposite side of the room stood Steiner, Priestly, and De Groot. Boyle joined them. Marshall's body made an oblique left toward the captain's desk, marched two steps, stopped at attention, and saluted. "Sir, Private Jones reports."

Hirschfeld returned the salute but did not put Marshall at ease.

"Private," he said, "didn't you learn at basic—at advanced infantry—that your weapon was like your wife or girlfriend? You took care of it and protected it at all costs?"

Marshall didn't think a mouth could be so dry, like it was filled with gauze.

"Well, didn't you, Private?" said Hirschfeld.

"Yessir."

"This is serious business, losing a weapon. It affects everyone up and down the line. It's the one thing that should never happen. Lose your life, maybe, that's tolerable; lose a limb, that's allowed—but not your weapon."

"Yessir."

"However," said Hirschfeld, leaning back, "due to extenuating circumstances ..." The captain looked left toward De Groot and the sergeants.

Marshall felt his spirit rejoining his body. *Extenuating circumstances.*

The captain restarted the sentence. "Due to extenuating circumstances, I'm letting you off with a verbal reprimand."

Praise Jesus, I'm not getting a fifteen. No fifteen and no court martial, just an ass-chewing, God bless him. Marshall imagined himself in the presence of King Solomon, a fair man, a wise decision, the baby not sliced in two. Hirschfeld continued talking. Marshall lost track of the captain's remarks until he realized a question was at hand. The captain had raised his voice. "Is that understood, Private?"

"Yessir."

"Dismissed. Stay out of trouble."

"Yessir."

A salute, an about-face, a countermarch of two steps, a right face, and freedom. Marshall leaned against the coat rack, his heart racing. Behind him, Boyle said, "One more thing." But Steiner interrupted them, pointing his right forefinger at Marshall. Marshall pulled his heels together and threw back his shoulders.

"You can't afford another fuckup, Private Jones."

"I understand, First Sergeant."

Steiner shifted his eyes to Boyle. "Remember what I told you."

"First Sergeant," said Boyle.

Outside, Marshall zipped his parka and shook off a shiver. Boyle said, "I need to talk to you. Let's go out back of the supply hut."

"Out back?"

Marshall couldn't decipher Boyle's smile. Boyle said, "Just follow me."

Behind the supply hut, Marshall looked around—just the two of them—the main gate a hundred meters north, the motor pool a hundred meters west, but in the immediate vicinity just Marshall and his squad leader.

"I was out of line," said Boyle. "Punching you last night."

Marshall nodded. He didn't care. It was over.

"I just lose it sometimes and was sure it was because of the josan that gun was gone."

Marshall nodded.

"You still shouldn't have had that josan in your bag, you realize that?"

"Right, Sergeant."

"So I feel I owe you one." Boyle cocked his face to one side.

Marshall didn't catch his meaning. Boyle pointed to the side of his face. "I owe you a shot."

Marshall stepped back. "I couldn't do that, Sergeant."

"You sure? I got it coming."

Marshall shook his head.

"We're square then?"

Marshall saw that Boyle had extended his hand. He extended his own hand. "Okay. Yeah, we're square."

They walked back, passing the supply room, passing the command post.

Marshall said, "What's happening with Hendrick?"

"Transferred to headquarters company. Transportation section."

"Jesus," said Marshall.

Boyle laughed.

"But they got him cold," said Marshall.

"They didn't get him cold," said Boyle. "They got a clip that may or may not have come from that forty-five. They don't have the forty-five." Boyle stopped walking and turned to Marshall. "The captain laid it out for us. Not only do we not have sufficient evidence, he said, but we really and truly don't know what happened. Whether it was him or the mamasan or something else. And he's right."

Boyle took a step, then turned again to Marshall. "But that's what saved your ass, Hendrick not getting nailed. That and the first sergeant."

"Don't understand," said Marshall.

"After the captain told us it was impossible to nail Hendrick, he wanted to know what to do with you. That's when the first sergeant told him we couldn't let the man who stole the gun go free and hang the man it was stolen from."

As they resumed walking, Boyle said, "That's what saved you. I wasn't sure how it would really go down, but the captain went along with the first sergeant. Oh, and the other thing the first sergeant told me."

"What's that, Sergeant Boyle?"

"If we see Hendrick around, at the EM club or anywhere, stay away from him. Don't get into it with him. It'll cause more trouble for us than him."

Good advice, thought Marshall.

Chapter Fourteen: December 1967, Unit 124 Training Camp

Jun-seok squatted in a circle with Captain Ho and their new team member, Lieutenant Yoon Moo-hak, passing a cigarette, blowing out smoke mixed with the vapor of warm breath in frigid air. He looked around at the other lieutenants squatting with their captains, ten teams in all. Something sure is up, thought Jun-seok, as he heard the grinding motors and creaking springs of two approaching ZIL-130s.

The teams boarded the trucks, drove for hours, and unloaded in an area of elegant buildings, lawns, and gardens. Jun-seok had never seen anything like this traditional architecture except in pictures. The men formed three ranks in front of a building distinguished by columns and a roof of blue tiles. This must be what Pyongyang looks like, thought Jun-seok. The first rank comprised the team captains and the next two comprised the lieutenants.

A senior officer, a major, faced the three ranks. Jun-seok had seen him before, giving directions and talking to his captain. The major said, "Welcome to the palace of Pak Chung-hee."

Jun-seok did not know what to make of this announcement. Pak Chung-hee was the puppet president installed by the Americans in the southern half of Korea. His residence was in Seoul.

"Of course," said the major, "this is not his actual residence, but an identical mock-up. In the days to come, you will memorize these grounds. You will receive and practice assignments for your conduct on these grounds. In case you're wondering, I'll tell you now: our mission is to attack the Blue House in Seoul and decapitate the puppet government."

The thirty hand-picked men of Unit 124 stood at attention, staring straight ahead.

Next morning, the teams gathered a kilometer north of the palace mock-up. As the captains conferred with the major, Yoon said, "Can you imagine?"

Jun-seok looked around. "They're putting a lot into this mission."

"There must be a bigger plan," said Yoon.

"I'm sure, little brother."

"Do you think this is it?" said Yoon. "Do you think we're the spearhead to drive the Yankees out of Korea?"

"It's best not to think, little brother. Concentrate on your piece."

The parlay broke up, and Jun-seok's captain returned. He said, "Our team's mission is to secure the rear entrance of the palace. To eliminate anyone there and prevent anyone from escaping that way."

The major called the teams to attention. "This is the north gate," he said, "where we'll come in. We may have to fight our way in, so we'll practice that."

Yoon took a step, and Ho put a hand across his chest. "Where are you going?"

"To force the gate."

Ho threw back his head with a laugh. "I like your spirit, but that's not our job. Get down and wait for the forward teams to take out the gate security."

A fourth man had joined the team. "I'm your referee," he said. He had the rough manners of a long-time enlisted man but bore no markings of rank. For the exercise, he was their superior, having the know-how and authority to grade the team's performance.

Ahead, submachine guns and rifles sounded, weapons loaded with blanks. Grenade simulators exploded. Referees called out, telling players they had died. A whistle blew, and the major's voice bellowed. "Let's try that again."

Again, submachine guns and rifles sounded, then faded.

"Let's go," said Ho. "Comrade Pak, take the point."

Jun-seok loped through the north gate, passing two opposition players lying "dead" on the ground, and ran toward the rear entrance of the palace. Forty paces along, he twisted his body toward rifle fire from his left, and let go a burst from his submachine gun. Behind him, the team's referee yelled, "Stop, stop. You're dead."

A whistle blew, and the major ran up. "Try it over," he said.

As the team regrouped, Yoon said, "Let me run alone while you stay back and cover."

"But they'll still get you," said Jun-seok.

"I'm very fast," said Yoon.

"Let's try it," said Ho.

Yoon sprinted across the lawn while Jun-seok and the captain aimed their submachine guns towards the woods to the left.

"Look at him go," said Ho.

When the first rifle shot sounded, Jun-seok and the captain pulled their triggers in bursts of two and three. Yoon gained the woods on the other side of the opposition players without being stopped by the referee and threw a grenade simulator toward the rifle fire.

A whistle blew.

"Much better," said the major.

Two days later, Jun-seok's team sat on the rear steps of the presidential palace. They had just eliminated two opposition players attempting to escape from the "Blue House," and the major had called a break.

Yoon said, "This is more fun than running through the hills with rocks in our packs."

"We'll be doing more of that," said Ho. "We have to keep in shape."

"We'll be ready for anything," said Yoon.

Ho lowered his voice and said, "I hope so."

Jun-seok didn't know what to make of Ho's remark. The two lieutenants looked at their captain, who said, "This is just between us, okay?"

"Okay, Comrade Captain," said Jun-seok.

Ho leaned forward. "Sure, we're tough and we know our team's job, but what else? We don't really know the other teams. There's no cohesion. What if something goes wrong before we get to the north gate?"

Jun-seok didn't like this discussion. He had started to feel invincible: well trained and part of a thought-out plan. But what Ho said about cohesion was true. Jun-seok knew the other lieutenants only in passing and never spoke to the other captains. And here they were embarking on a mission into occupied Korea, where the people would welcome their appearance, but the Americans and Pak Chung-hee's mercenaries would kill them on sight. Jun-seok's thoughts turned to Chong's parents and his own. He pushed the thoughts away: why was he indulging in morose fantasies? He was a warrior, among the best.

Next day, the running-with-rocks regimen began anew, with nights reserved for attacking the palace.

• • • •

ONE EARLY JANUARY MORNING, the teams stood at attention in three ranks in the main hall of the mock palace as a contingent of officers filed in. A lieutenant general, a brigadier, senior colonels, colonels, and lieutenant colonels. Jun-seok had never seen such an array of senior officers. The general walked behind a podium and raised his voice. "Are you ready to perform your mission, Comrades?"

The commandos' major, standing in the first rank, raised his right fist. As instructed, Jun-seok raised his fist along with the other commandos and called out, "We are ready, Comrade General."

"Comrades," said the general. He donned eyeglasses and looked at a paper on the podium. "Comrades, for too many years our brothers to the south have strained against the chains of oppression. But those chains are at the breaking point. Our brothers to the south need only a spark to rise against the imperialist bastards. You"—the general lifted his right arm and pointed—"You are the spark."

The major raised a fist and yelled, "We will not fail, Comrade General."

The commandos raised their fists and yelled, "We will not fail."

The general remained stone-faced, looking at his notes. "By now, you know what that spark is, to attack the oppressor's den and cut off his head."

"We will cut off the head of the oppressor!" shouted the major.

"We will cut off the head of the oppressor!" shouted the commandos.

The general smiled and looked up from his notes. He removed his glasses and lowered his voice. "I'll speak candidly. This mission has been debated at the highest levels, and naturally there were contrary views. That's the nature of dialectics. But Seoul is only a three-day march. You will take them by surprise. And each of you is equivalent to a platoon."

As Jun-seok's chest swelled, the general closed his left hand about his right fist. "In the dead of winter, it will be like a battalion appearing out of the sky. They won't know what hit them."

The major gave no signal, and the commandos remained quiet, attentive.

"When you have removed the traitor's head, the people will flock to you, and the puppet government will collapse. Now when I say remove his head, I'm not speaking in figures of speech." The general extended his left arm and hand, and closed his fingers. "Imagine I'm holding the traitor Pak Chung-hee by his pompadour."

The senior officers snorted, and the commandos took that cue for a laugh.

"Now imagine in my right hand a honed dagger. I slash once. I slash again. A third time." The general accompanied these words by sweeping slashes of his right hand. "And the traitor's body drops away."

The general raised his left hand as if holding a head by the hair. Still the major gave no signal. Jun-seok tensed his shoulders and tightened his fingers. The senior officers on either side of the general remained at attention.

"Are you ready," said the general, "to cut off the head of Pak Chung-hee?"

The major raised a fist, and a roar filled the hall.

"Then do it. Let me see it."

Jun-seok extended his left hand and clasped the pompadour of the traitor. In three slashes of the right hand, the traitor's body fell away, and Jun-seok held high the head. He opened his mouth to the ceiling of the great hall of the mock-up Blue House.

· · · ·

TWO DAYS LATER, IN barracks, Captain Ho opened a map onto a small table and placed his forefinger on it. Jun-seok and Yoon bent forward to follow Ho's finger and words, their exhalations forming clouds above the topographical swirls of the map.

"Here," said Ho. "We'll enter the DMZ here." He looked at Jun-seok. "Where we went in before." Ho dragged his finger south. "We'll breach the Yankee fence here." His finger moved to the southeast. "Here, north of the village of Changpa-ri, we'll cross the Imjin River and head east and south. We'll guide ourselves on these mountains." Ho poked the map three times. "Papyeong Mountain, near Nullo-ri. Sambong Mountain, near Pobwon-ni. And finally the Bukhan Mountains and Bukak Mountain."

"The imperial palace," said Jun-seok, "is on the other side of Bukak Mountain."

"Correct," said Ho. "We'll come down the west side of Bukak Mountain and force the north gate."

Captain Ho blew warm air on his right hand and replaced his wool mitten. Yoon said, "They're saying this is the coldest winter in memory."

Ho smiled. "All the better."

Next morning, the teams packed themselves into two southbound trucks. Hours later, they disembarked by the high fence that formed the northern border of the DMZ. They passed through a small gate and double-timed south, carrying packs, grenades, PPS-43 submachine guns, pistols, and daggers. The packs contained rice balls, dried fish, kimchi, sesame candy sticks, extra socks, sneakers, overcoats, and ammunition. The men wore thick underwear, boots, trooper hats, and South Korean uniforms with the markings of the twenty-sixth infantry division.

A senior lieutenant and three enlisted men from the 17th Foot led the way. Fifteen hundred meters later, in a copse of bare hardwoods and frosty pines, the commandos stopped and dropped their packs.

"Relax if you can," said Ho. "Have something to eat." He sat on the ground and leaned back against his pack. Jun-seok and Yoon followed suit. Ho pointed at the dipping sun's rays filtering through the trees. "We'll be off soon enough."

The edge of the abyss, thought Jun-seok. All the training, the adventure of preparation, now the abyss. Jun-seok felt less certain than at the meeting with the general in the mock-up palace.

"What's the matter, Comrade Pak?" said Ho. "You look pensive. Ah, I know. You're upset that our job is the rear door. You want to be with the entry team." Ho lifted his left hand and made a slashing motion with his right. "You want to be the one to cut off the traitor's head." Ho laughed. Yoon raised his eyebrows.

Jun-seok glanced around, but the other teams were paying attention to themselves. He decided to play along and said, "Comrade Captain, I'll accept whatever role the Great Leader demands of me, no matter how humble."

"That's the spirit," said the captain. He closed his eyes.

A few minutes later, the officer from the 17th Foot walked over and squatted. Jun-seok recognized him as the same senior lieutenant from the patrol that had cost Chong his life.

"How are you guys doing?" he said.

Ho lifted his eyelids. "As well as can be expected."

The reconnaissance lieutenant turned his gaze on Yoon. "Why are you taking a child on this operation? Is this an infiltration strategy?"

"I'm twenty-four," said Yoon.

Ho chuckled. "Don't be fooled by his baby face. He's as tough as any of us."

A hum sounded from several teams over, picked up by the next team, followed by soft words. "*Arirang, arirang, arariyo.*"

"Not a good time for sentimental songs," said Ho.

"Crossing over Arirang Pass," sang the other teams in somber voices.

"I agree," said the reconnaissance lieutenant. "I'd like to see more resolve and less mush."

Easy for him to say, thought Jun-seok. He's not going with us.

• • • •

THE LAST RAYS OF SUN faded and the commandos huddled for warmth. The moon rose and the commandos stirred. Packs to their backs, submachine guns at the ready, the men entered the cleared area to their front and dropped into the north-south ditch that

Jun-seok had traversed his last time in the DMZ. Minutes later they crossed the MDL into the American sector. Thirty-one commandos from Unit 124—one major, ten captains, and twenty lieutenants—guided by a senior lieutenant and three enlisted men from the 17th Foot.

The contingent crossed the two kilometers of American DMZ without incident and squatted on the back side of the ridge above the American barrier, looking down on a minefield, a chain-link fence, entrenchments, and Yankee soldiers, all but invisible in the dark. Jun-seok wasn't privy to the details of the pioneer efforts—marking the minefield and breaching the fence—he just knew they were finished or in progress. His job, at this point, was to bring up the team's rear and make sure Yoon stayed on course.

Ho stood up. Yoon and Jun-seok did the same. They followed their captain over the ridge at a crouch, down the short treeless slope, and queued up at the start of the minefield. Jun-seok saw his hazy, moonlit shadow as he wriggled between strands of barbed wire held open by one of the enlisted men. He looked ahead to the chain-link fence and considered his visibility from the other side. Most essential at night, he knew, were slow movements and silence.

Jun-seok padded two meters behind Yoon, looking for stones on the frozen ground, making sure he steered clear of them, making sure Yoon steered clear. Each set of stones marked an anti-personnel mine.

The extreme cold was their friend. There being no snow, the frozen ground left no footprints. Streams, marshes, and the river would be frozen, making for easy travel. But it was also impossible to dig into the ground. Jun-seok wondered how the mines had been found. The 17th Foot, he decided, must have mapped out the minefield earlier, before the ground froze, prodding their way through with trench knives at night.

Jun-seok brought his mind back to the business at hand. Ho and Yoon had stopped, held up by the men in front of them. When Ho reached the Yankee fence, Jun-seok saw the hold-up. Three sides of a one-meter square had been cut into the chain-link at ground level, and the square had been bent up like a flap. When his turn came, Jun-seok knelt, removed his pack, pushed it through the hole, then crawled through himself. On the other side, he stood up and put on his pack. Captain Ho stepped close to Jun-seok and Yoon, and nodded. The three men turned, crouched, and moved south with half steps.

A meter to his right, Jun-seok saw sandbags and a trench, but no soldiers. Thirty meters to his left, he noticed a vertical slit of dull light. As the slit grew larger and the outline of a soldier appeared, Jun-seok recognized the slit as the doorway to a bunker. The soldier took several steps toward them, and Jun-seok's team stopped, making themselves part of the night. Jun-seok placed a finger alongside the trigger of his submachine gun but knew shooting would abort the mission.

Jun-seok heard a drizzle—the man was urinating. A few seconds later, the soldier turned, the slit to the bunker opened, he stepped inside, and the slit closed.

Jun-seok's team continued its slow-motion journey. Fifteen paces later they stepped onto a dirt road running parallel to the barrier fence. They crossed the road and walked in old, frozen rice paddies, long unused. Ho stopped, turned, and put his head close to Jun-seok and Yoon. "That was the worst of it," he said.

An hour later, the team stopped in a wooded area and dropped their packs. Ho moved ahead and returned a few minutes later. "That's it until tomorrow night," he said.

At dawn, Jun-seok saw several other teams nearby. The area felt secure, but everyone spoke in whispers. Ho gathered with the major and other captains. When he returned, he motioned for Jun-seok and Yoon to follow him to the edge of the wooded area, where they looked down an embankment to a wide expanse of ice.

"The Imjin River," said Ho. "Let's watch for a while."

Jun-seok noticed movement on the far bank and tapped the captain. The captain nodded and drew close. "American stationary patrols," he said. "They're all along the river, but spread out."

Forty minutes later Jun-seok heard a motor, and a truck stopped a short distance from the embankment on the other side of the river. Seven soldiers carrying rifles and ammo tins walked from the truck toward the river. From the embankment, seven soldiers rose and walked to the truck. "They change every two hours, like clockwork," said the captain.

Ho, Yoon, and Jun-seok moved back to their camp. Ho said, "We'll cross at dark between two of their positions while they're making one of their changes."

At dark, Jun-seok's team moved to the edge of the near embankment. They waited for the sound of a motor on the far side and the clanking of rifles and helmets and ammo cans. Jun-seok moved down the embankment with short steps and skidded onto the ice. The surface, after a few steps, proved easy to maneuver; he slipped along at a good pace. On the embankment ahead, Jun-seok could hear the Americans settling in on either side of the team's destination point. Ho signaled his men to keep moving. The team climbed the far embankment, crossed frozen rice paddies, a dirt road, and more rice paddies. An hour later, they passed into wooded hills, keeping a rapid pace, eight kilometers per hour.

• • • •

AT DAWN, THE COMMANDOS camped on the side of Papyeong Mountain, near Nullo-ri. At dusk, they continued south and east, arriving on Sambong Mountain, near Pobwon-ni, the next day. The teams huddled against the face of a large south-side ledge, taking in whatever warmth they could. At noon, Jun-seok awakened to the shaking of his shoulder. "Our turn for guard duty," said Captain Ho. Jun-seok, Yoon, and Ho descended fifteen meters of the steep terrain. On occasion, a voice, a dog, or a motor caught their ears, letting them know they were near a village.

A half hour later, Jun-seok heard a voice and the snapping of twigs. Another team, he thought—they should be more quiet—but it wasn't. Below Jun-seok, no more than ten meters away, appeared a man of nineteen or twenty. He wore shabby work clothes and held a sickle in his right hand. Another man, early twenties, A-frame on his back, followed. Jun-seok caught a third movement and noticed two more young men angling off to the left.

The man with the sickle looked at Jun-seok, Yoon, and Ho, then looked away. He sidestepped left as though he hadn't seen anything. He flicked a hand at the second man, who was setting down his A-frame.

"Hey there," said Ho, contorting his voice to a southern accent.

Both young men looked up.

"Hey there," said the one with the sickle.

"As you can see," said Ho, "we're soldiers. We're with the twenty-sixth division. We're investigating suspicious activity in this area."

The sickle man said, "So that's it. We thought you were choppers too, horning in on our territory." He gave a chuckle that came out flat.

Jun-seok examined the threads of his captain's phony uniform, bare and seedy in the daylight filtering through the leafless trees. He listened to his captain's tinny rendition of a southern dialect. He didn't sound at all like the man with the sickle.

Ho edged down the slope as the two young men stiffened. Jun-seok stiffened too. If the men ran, they would have to be chased down with daggers. Firing a submachine gun or pistol was out of the question.

"What's your name?" said Ho.

"Woo," said the first man. "We're both Woo. We're cousins."

"There are two more. Where did they go?"

"Not far. We're chopping in this area."

Ho had approached to within three meters of the woodcutters, trailed by Yoon. Jun-seok dropped down the slope to the other side of the two young men and felt relieved. The wood cutters were trapped.

"Listen," said Ho, "we have to take you up the hill to our command post."

"That's not possible," said Woo. "We have to get on with our work."

"It's a matter of security," said Ho, his southern accent slipping away. "You can't refuse."

Woo opened his arms. "We're simple peasants. We're cutting grass and twigs to buy rice to feed our parents. We'll forget we saw you."

"Drop that sickle and come with me."

"I need it for my trade."

"Then put it on your A-frame and come with me. Before I lose my patience."

The Woo cousins climbed the hill to the south-side ledge. There they stared at the lounging commandos, their packs, their weapons. The commandos stared back. One of the captains, whom Jun-seok had never cared for, thrust his dagger into a nearby sapling, all the while smiling at the captives. Several other commandos took his cue and thrust their daggers in the air or into trees. A few minutes later, the remaining two Woo cousins entered the camp encircled by another team.

The major descended from the top of the ledge. He glared, and the daggers were put away. He turned to the woodcutters and addressed them in a polite manner, not attempting to disguise his accent. "By now," he said, "you must realize we're not Hanguk soldiers, but Choson warriors on a special mission, which we've accomplished. Now we're on our way back."

So they would think the commandos were heading north. Clever, but what did a ruse matter if the woodcutters were taken prisoner or eliminated?

"Here," said the major. "We have some sweets for you." He handed sesame sticks to the Woo cousins. The cousins held the sticks but made no attempt to eat.

"What's the matter?" said the captain who had first thrust his dagger. "Where's your appetite?"

The commandos laughed.

"Enough," said the major.

The youngest cousin, the one who'd had the sickle, said, "Please understand, we're peasants, scraping by the best we can. We're not part of the Hanguk government, we're under it."

"What about the Americans?" said the major.

"What can we do? We have sickles, they have guns. They beat us and rape our women, but what can we do?"

Several commandos murmured in sympathy. The young man spoke further of the depredations of the Hanguk government and the American soldiers. Jun-seok thought Woo was laying it on a bit thick. He felt a tug at his sleeve—his captain. Jun-seok and Yoon followed Ho around the side of the ledge, where they squatted in a circle in the frigid air.

"What should we do with them?" said Ho.

When no response came, Ho said, "Here's what I think. We can't release them alive. It risks the mission."

"I agree," said Jun-seok.

Jun-seok and Ho looked at Yoon. Ho said, "Tell us what you feel, Comrade. We want an honest vote."

"I think we'd betray the revolution by killing them. They're proletariat."

Jun-seok felt Yoon's argument was nonsense. He just didn't have the stomach for killing them. But Ho said, "Then that's the vote for our team. Two to eliminate, one to release."

Jun-seok's team returned to the front of the ledge. Other teams had been leaving and returning. The daylight grew weaker as Ho reported to the major, who nodded.

As the votes were being collected, shouts wove their way through the trees from the base of the mountain.

"Our parents," said the youngest Woo cousin. "They're wondering why we haven't come home."

The major squatted and opened a sheet of paper on a flat rock. He sharpened a pencil against the rock, removed a mitten, and wrote. He motioned to the Woo cousins to come close.

"This paper," said the major, "inducts you into the Democratic People's Workers Party. You will affix your names and addresses."

The younger Woo cousin took the pencil and wrote his name in the scant light. As his cousins followed suit, the major said, "In half a year, Korea will be united under Choson rule. If you violate the terms of this agreement, if you go to the Hanguk government, we'll hunt you down like dogs."

The woods darkened, visibility down to a few meters. The major extended his hand. "Take this." He handed the youngest cousin a watch, a Shanghai knock-off even the commandos considered inferior. "To compensate for the firewood you did not cut today."

The cousin bowed.

"We'll be listening," said the major. "Once you go inside your compound, if your gate squeaks again, we'll know you've betrayed us."

Another bow, and in seconds, only snapping twigs remained of the Woo cousins. Then nothing. Jun-seok whispered to his captain. "I thought we voted to eliminate them."

"We did, but not all the teams. The final tally was sixteen to release and fifteen to eliminate."

"Our commander could have overridden the vote," said Jun-seok.

"Another problem is the frozen ground. Their parents would report them missing, and the bodies would be discovered."

Yoon put his face close to Jun-seok's. "Do you think I made the wrong vote? I didn't want to cut their throats."

"I understand," said Jun-seok. *But what about our throats?*

Chapter Fifteen: December 1967, Changpa-ri

The morning Sally went looking for the stolen pistol, after Jones and Kim had gone back to the jeep, the girl in the next room came out and stood on the veranda. "Hey, Rawn, how you doing?"

Lorne gave her his jagged smile.

"So, Sally tell you?" the girl said.

"Tell me what?"

"Oh, oh." She made a zipper motion across her lips and hopped back into her room.

Sally returned and handed the pistol money back to Lorne. "Gun no in ville."

"What else?" said Lorne.

Sally looked down and circled her right rubber shoe on the ground with her toe. She looked up. "Good news, yobo. Move to Nullo-ri."

"You?" said Lorne.

"Yeah, move to Nullo-ri." She placed the fingers of her right hand on the front of Lorne's parka. "Now can come all a time. No have to take truck."

Very convenient, thought Lorne, except he'd started to think more of disengagement than its opposite.

• • • •

THREE EVENINGS LATER, instead of hopping the truck to Changpa-ri, Lorne walked to the compound gate. He knew the soldier standing outside the guard shack.

"Hey, Dan."

Dan stepped out of the guard shack, crossed the road, and pointed toward the ville. "When you come back in, be sure to stay in the paddies. Stay out of the road in case the commanding general is paying a visit."

Lorne laughed.

"Seriously," said Dan. "Sometimes there's an officer on the road. You never know. Sometimes the MPs. So when you come back in, stay off the road till you hit the gate."

Lorne walked the kilometer to Nullo-ri's main street, turned right toward the center of the ville, and at the first alleyway turned right again. Twenty meters down, just before the alley emptied onto rice paddies, he found a square compound of stone walls and a row of attached hooches. Lorne entered the second from the right, lowered himself onto the linoleum, and looked at the papered walls and ceiling. No bed or wardrobe. Blankets lay across the warm floor with clothes and utensils stacked in one corner. He sat cross-legged, facing Sally.

"Yobo, no more Sally Lee. My name Min-hee. Lee Min-hee."

"If you want Min-hee," said Lorne, "Min-hee it is." *For another month*.

At zero four hundred, Lorne slipped from under the blankets and dressed. He grabbed his boots, which he'd brought in to keep warm, bent over, and kissed Min-hee. Minutes later, he stopped at the edge of the rice paddies for a piss, then walked toward the camp atop a dike that paralleled the road. At the camp fence, Lorne turned right, dropped down to the road, and entered the circle of light thrown by the gate lights. A soldier came out of the guard shack, looked at Lorne's stripes, smiled, and went back in.

• • • •

ONE EVENING EARLY IN January, Lorne made the walk into Nullo-ri with Jones, Rothman, DiMaggio, Ivan, and the rest of the squad, except Kim. They turned right, passed Min-hee's alleyway, and continued to the east end of the ville. Their destination: the

Terrace Tea House, the occasion, Rothman's going-away party. More members of the platoon showed up. Girls dribbled in. Priestly and De Groot appeared.

Priestly sat at a table with Lorne. "In two weeks," he said, "this is you. Out of here."

"Yeah," said Lorne, "out of here. You know what I'm doing on my last night? Instead of a party?"

"Don't want to hear."

"I'm finding Hendrick, dragging him into the latrine—"

"That might delay your departure."

"And then I'm finding the first sergeant and—"

"The top likes you," said Priestly. "He just has trouble expressing it."

Lorne laughed. He didn't know what he wanted: to be free of the army, to be free of Korea, just to be free. "Sergeant Priestly, let me ask you a question now that we've had a few beers. How can you stand being a lifer?"

"It's not so bad," said Priestly. He tapped a long, brown finger on the table. "You're from Alabama. You know what it's like on the outside."

"It's changing," said Lorne.

"Maybe."

A hoot went up at the bar. Lorne and Priestly looked over to see De Groot being dragged by the left hand toward the rear door, the girl dragging him, grinning like she'd hit the jackpot. De Groot raised his right hand. "Carry on, men."

Priestly gave a head nod. "Looks like your houseboy's joined the party."

"Yeah," said Lorne, "Cho lives in Nullo-ri." Cho made the platoon's bunks and cleaned their boots for forty dollars a month.

"Damn," said Priestly, "we should've invited our KATUSAs."

Lorne shook his head. "They'd feel funny in the ville."

"But the houseboy—"

"He lives here. He's a civilian. Not the same."

At the bar, Rothman put a bottle of OB beer to his mouth and tipped back his head. Amber fluid flowed down Rothman's bobbing throat to foot stomps and the chant, "Chug, chug, chug."

Rothman dropped the bottle and weaved a few steps toward Lorne, helped by a girl on each arm. Priestly had vanished, and Rothman stood behind his vacated chair across the table from Lorne.

"Sergeant Boyle, Sir," he said, "in honor of my departure I am getting double laid tonight."

Around him, the party-goers cheered and hooted.

Rothman shook off the girls, came to attention, and put up a salute. "Sergeant Boyle, Sir, it's been a great honor serving under you."

"Specialist Rothman," said Lorne, "save that shit for the lieutenant."

As the men laughed, Rothman maintained his position of attention and the salute. Lorne shook his head, straightened his shoulders, and returned the salute, like he was the captain at his desk. This brought more hoots and boot stomps. Rothman dropped his salute, performed a left face, and marched to the rear door, followed by the two girls, who mimicked his military carriage.

Another girl sat on Lorne's right knee and draped an arm over his shoulders. Lorne encircled her with his saluting arm and said, "What's your name, honeybunch?"

"Lucille. You rike?"

"I like a lot," said Lorne.

"You rike all night?"

"I like one time," said Lorne. "Can do?"

"Can do," said Lucille.

As Lorne lay on Lucille's bed smoking an afterglow Marlboro, he thought, these girls are so nice, all of them. Why did I go the yobo route? Why didn't I see what was coming?

Lorne left five and a dollar tip and walked west on Nullo-ri's main street. He turned down the alleyway to Min-hee's compound, gave a light tap on her door, and sat on the portico unlacing his boots. The door slid open revealing another girl next to Min-hee in the yellow candlelight. Inside, Lorne dropped his parka and sat cross-legged looking at Min-hee and her companion.

"Yobo," said Min-hee. "This Soo-jin."

Soo-jin said, "Min-hee and me old friend. I live Dongducheon."

Lorne nodded. "Camp Casey."

"Yeah," said Soo-jin. "Camp Casey."

"Where you tonight?" said Min-hee. "Party time?"

Boyle nodded. "Rothman go home." Boyle inverted his hands over his face to give the appearance of wearing glasses and stretched his torso. "You know Rothman?" Min-hee had run into most of Boyle's squad one time or another.

"Yeah," she said, "know Rothman."

Soo-jin said, "You go home America soon?"

Lorne turned his smile on her. "When army say go, have to go."

"Yeah, have to go. You send money for baby?"

Lorne looked at Min-hee. "Send money for baby."

· · · ·

NEXT MORNING, LORNE sat on his bunk with his short timers' calendar. He filled in a piece of torso and looked to his side as the bunk sagged. Jones had joined him, almost pressing hips.

"How many more, Sergeant Boyle?"

"Ten and a wake-up. What's the problem?"

"You were right."

"About what?"

"About not doing it in the field. I have VD."

"How do you know?"

"Burns when I piss."

"How bad?" said Lorne. "Jaw clenching? Pipe grasping?"

Jones shook his head. "Not that bad, but it burns."

Lorne gave Jones a pat between the shoulder blades. "It's not serious. Just a strain, but you gotta go on sick call."

"What'll they do to me? Will I get a fifteen?"

"Nothing. Won't be reported to the company. This happens all the time."

"If it's not serious, why do I have to go on sick call?"

"You gotta get some terramycin pills. That'll knock it out."

As Jones stood, Lorne said, "Go on, Marshall, now. I'll clear it with Sergeant Priestly."

Lorne watched Jones walk off and thought, I better follow up, make sure he gets those pills. Once again Lorne's bunk sagged as Kim took the place of Jones. Kim pointed to the short timers' calendar. "How long you got, Sergeant Boyle?"

"Ten and a wake-up."

"Sergeant Boyle," said Kim. "How come you call him Marshall and me Kim?"

"What? You want me to call you YS?"

"My name is Yeong-su."

Lorne leaned forward, elbows on knees. Kim leaned forward, elbows on knees. Lorne said, "So what's up, Yeong-su?"

"Do you think I'm a good soldier?"

"Number one," said Lorne.

"Some day, you think I be squad leader?"

"That won't happen. Sorry."

"Why not?"

"Because KATUSAs can't be squad leaders."

"You think that fair, Sergeant Boyle?"

"It doesn't matter what I think. That's the way it is."

Kim remained sitting next to Lorne.

"Look, Yeong-su, put in your time, stay out of trouble."

"That what my uncle say."

· · · ·

FOLLOWING HIS HEART-to-hearts with Jones and Kim, Lorne thought, I wouldn't mind talking to someone myself. He liked Priestly but not the idea of blabbing to him. He needed someone outside the company who could be addressed in confidence, and so, a little before noon, entered the Quonset hut that housed the chaplain's office and chapel. When the chaplain looked up from his desk, Lorne was dismayed to see he was the same Catholic major who had visited Camp Walley some months before. What was he doing down here? Either transferred or working both sides of the river.

"Are you Catholic?" said the chaplain.

"No, Sir."

"The protestant chaplain visits once a week. Can you wait?"

"I just need someone to talk to, Sir."

The chaplain pointed to the chair next to his desk. Lorne eased into it. "It has to do with a girl," he said.

The chaplain gave a half-smile. "A Dear John?" He shook his head. "It's one of those things."

"No, Sir. It's not from back home. It's a girl from the ville."

The chaplain's forehead and cheeks flushed. "I call them harlots," he said. "Stay away from them."

Lorne began to wish he hadn't taken a seat.

"I do not understand the policy of the army on this point," said the chaplain. "We should be cleaning up these dens of iniquity. Instead, we practically encourage them, sticking temptation down the throats of our young men. And you, a non-commissioned officer, you should know better."

The only grace from the chaplain's harangue was that Lorne didn't have to say anything. Ten minutes later, he stood, saluted, and escaped into the midday cold. He traipsed across the camp to the company mess hall and took a tray to a table by himself. When DiMaggio and Ivan attempted to join him, he said, "I'm eating alone."

Minutes later Priestly walked over from the senior NCO table and sat down. "What's going on, Lorne?"

"I've got a yobo in the ville."

Priestly nodded. "Everybody in the company except the captain knows that. Probably the battalion."

"She's pregnant."

"That too." Priestly pushed a hand across the table until his fingertips touched Lorne's forearm. "Lorne, there's nothing you can do about it. Inside a week, you're out of here."

"It just seems like there should be, I don't know, a proper resolution."

"It's different here," said Priestly. "These girls, they take their chances. It's their call."

"Do you think I should send her money?"

"Sure, if it makes you feel better."

"Makes me feel better?"

"Lorne, with all the girls here, and all the pregnancies ..." Priestly's eyes wandered over Lorne's shoulder. "Uh oh." He stood up and Lorne turned to see Steiner just inside the main door. As Priestly approached the first sergeant, Steiner curled a finger at Lorne.

• • • •

LORNE AND PRIESTLY followed Steiner from the mess hall to the command post, passing through the front room into the captain's office. Hirschfeld sat behind his desk. Arrayed against the far wall were the other three platoon sergeants, the supply sergeant, and the mess sergeant. Sitting on the second desk in the room, off to the right, were two lieutenants, but not De Groot. Lorne was the lone squad leader there.

Hirschfeld leaned back in his swivel chair and scanned the room. "As usual," he said, "nobody knows what the fuck is going on, so I don't have answers, just orders." He leaned forward. "The company will assemble"—Hirschfeld looked at his watch—"at fourteen hundred. Cold weather gear, full combat gear, rifles, one hundred rounds per man, four grenades per man."

Around the room, the sergeants wore their game faces, mouths straight, eyes dead. Priestly asked, "Are we heading north, Sir?"

Hirschfeld shook his head. "The one thing we actually do fucking know is it's down here. We'll be moving south, toward Pobwon-ni. Lieutenant De Groot's going on recon to figure out exactly where."

The weapons platoon sergeant said, "That's good, Sir. At least we know the balloon hasn't gone up." The other sergeants gave light laughs.

"How's that?" said one of the lieutenants.

The weapons platoon sergeant said, "If it was war, Sir, we wouldn't be going south. We'd be moving to the MBPs." The main battle positions, along the south side of the Imjin River below Changpa-ri, where the battalion went in the event of an all-out attack from the north.

The supply sergeant said, "Should the men draw rations, Sir?"

Hirschfeld said, "Three apiece. But"—he looked at the mess sergeant—"if we're there tomorrow, let's get some hot food down." Hirschfeld looked around the room. "Well, let's do it."

As the sergeants and lieutenants filed out, Steiner held Lorne back with a hand on his chest. Priestly stayed too. Steiner said to Hirschfeld, "Sergeant Boyle, Sir."

Hirschfeld said, "Ah, yes, Sergeant Boyle. Technically, you don't have to go with us. You can stay here and start out-processing."

"Sir," said Lorne, "I'd rather be in the field with my squad."

"Pleased to hear that," said Hirschfeld.

In the front room, Steiner said, "If it's more than a couple of days, you start out-processing from the field."

"Right, First Sergeant."

Lorne stood in place as Steiner formulated his next words.

"Sergeant Boyle, we appreciate you coming out with us." Lorne nodded. "But don't expect a kiss on the lips."

"Understood, First Sergeant."

Lorne and Priestly walked out of the command post and tightened their parkas. A jeep idled nearby with Jones at the wheel, a helmet perched on the hood of his parka and a loaded rifle leaning across the left door channel.

Priestly said, "What are you doing, Private Jones?"

"Lieutenant De Groot ordered me to meet him here with a jeep, Sergeant."

As De Groot walked towards them from the supply room with combat gear and rifle, Lorne mulled over one last chore he should take care of before going to the field. He said to Priestly, "I need a half hour in Nullo-ri." Priestly looked away. "Half an hour and I'll double-time back across the paddies."

De Groot said, "Sorry to leave you, Sergeant Priestly, but I got pulled off for this recon."

Priestly said, "Could you give Sergeant Boyle a lift into the ville, Sir?"

De Groot raised his eyes. "Into Nullo-ri?"

"A short errand, Sir," said Priestly. "Don't worry, everything will be straight on this end."

Halfway to Nullo-ri, De Groot turned to Lorne, sitting midway in the rear seat. "Are you coming into the field with us, Sergeant Boyle?"

"I am, Sir. I'll be back with my squad in half an hour."

"Technically, you don't have to."

"I know, Sir."

The jeep turned right and stopped at the first alleyway. Lorne jumped out.

"Don't get lost," said De Groot.

"Half an hour, Sir."

Lorne saluted and turned away. Approaching the end of the alley, he hadn't heard the jeep move and turned around. De Groot had lowered his head to his map. From the other side of the lieutenant's profile, Jones looked straight at Lorne, as if for reassurance. Lorne broadened his smile and waved a mitten. Jones nodded and turned forward.

• • • •

LORNE ENTERED MIN-HEE'S compound, sat on the veranda in front of her door, and unlaced his boots. He had been putting off this moment, but there was no more putting off. What was he going to say? It's been fun while it lasted, wish you hadn't got knocked up. Lorne had the address of the translation office across the street. He'd do that much: send a letter, send some money.

The door slid open a trickle, and Min-hee looked out, her lips going to a soft smile. "Yobo," she said.

Inside, Lorne let his parka drop and sat cross-legged, rubbing his hands together. Min-hee leaned over and blew warm air on them. The hooch's floor was warm. Lorne pointed in the direction of Blue Lancer Valley. "Trouble," he said.

Min-hee swept an arm in the direction of the main street. "Yeah, Joe Chink come."

"You hear? Joe Chink?"

"Yeah, everyone say. Joe Chink come."

"Gotta go to field," said Lorne.

Min-hee bobbed her head. Lorne wasn't sure how much she caught. She must have caught "gotta go."

"Then go home America."

Min-hee's head stopped bobbing.

"So I say goodbye," said Lorne.

"Goodbye?"

"Will write," said Lorne. He made circling motions with his right fingers on his left palm. "Write. Send money."

"When you come again?" said Min-hee.

"No come again."

Min-hee's lips rounded without sound. Lorne leaned forward over his crossed legs and kissed her. He rocked back to a sitting position, leaned forward again and placed his arms around her shoulders and his cheek against hers. He held her several seconds and rocked back.

"Gotta go," he said. Lorne pulled on his parka and opened the door.

Min-hee followed Lorne out the door, standing on the veranda as he laced his boots. When Lorne stood up, she stepped into rubber shoes and dropped to the ground.

They faced each other in the courtyard a meter apart, the vapor of their breaths touching. Min-hee no longer looked like a working girl, front-heavy, wrapped in peasant skirt and shawl. Tears tumbled over her cheeks.

"No come again?" she said.

From Blue Lancer Valley, Lorne heard the deuce-and-a-halves firing their big diesels. He stepped forward and placed his arms around Min-hee. He thought of the Korean word for "does not exist" or "there is not," not sure if it fit, but used it anyhow.

"I'm *ubsumnida* from here."

Lorne dropped his arms and backed away. As he continued backing out of the compound, Min-hee stood in the same spot, peasant skirt and shawl, sobs shaking her. Lorne took a deep breath and a last look, then rotated his body toward Blue Lancer Valley. He took one step and then another; Min-hee disappeared. Lorne double-timed over the berms enclosing the frozen rice paddies toward the rising volume of the diesel motors—trucks rolling out of the motor pool. He stretched the double-time to a lope.

Chapter Sixteen: January 1968, Sambong Mountain

Jun-seok and Yoon hefted their packs and followed Ho at a jog, descending Sambong Mountain and crossing a valley. Jun-seok heard distant motors and saw lights.

"Keep up the pace," said Ho, "in case we've been discovered."

The Woo cousins, thought Jun-seok. A big mistake to release them.

To Jun-seok's relief, the teams had soon crossed the lowland and were climbing into the safety of the Bukhan Mountains. An hour before dawn, the major ordered a halt under the overhang of a large rock. He walked among his commandos. "Rest up," he said. "Tonight's the night."

Two other teams took the first watch, and Jun-seok closed his eyes. He opened them in the midst of a dream populated by Chong, Chong's sister, and the cook from his unit's training camp, a stiff penis pushed against the flies of his underwear and pants. As daylight filtered through the trees from the southeast horizon, Jun-seok registered the sounds that woke him: static, a drumbeat, and laughter. Then the major's voice: "Keep it down."

Shaking off his erection, Jun-seok moved toward the knot of men surrounding the major. He found Ho among them and asked, "Comrade Captain, what's going on?"

"Comrade Major turned on his radio, and out came decadent imperialist music."

"We have a radio?"

"Just a small receiver," said Ho. "We're trying to find some news. And we're expecting a message at eight hundred hours."

The major put up a gloved hand. Ho, Jun-seok, and the other men closed their mouths and leaned in. An announcer, in mid-broadcast, said, "—disguised as soldiers of the twenty-sixth infantry division, but their uniforms are poorly made, and their accents are northern. They are believed to be in the area of Sambong Mountain or farther north."

"That's good," said the major. "They don't know where we are."

"But the alarm is up," said one of the captains.

"Yes," said the major. "The alarm is up." He pushed back the cuff of his jacket and looked at his watch. "Let's hear what our superiors have to tell us. Four minutes." He thumbed the tuner on the transistor radio, a Russian Selga. "Let me find the frequency." A hum replaced the newscast, and everyone waited in silence. The major smiled as the radio crackled on the hour. A woman's voice said, "The people sleep at home tomorrow." The radio crackled again and went back to a hum.

"Comrade Major," said a captain, "what does that mean?"

"They're talking in code."

"Right," said the captain, "but what does it mean?"

The major ran his tongue between his lips. "I don't know. I never received any codes." He shook his head. "I thought they'd say something we could understand, like 'go ahead' or 'don't go ahead.'" Under his breath, the major said, "Why do they do these things?"

Jun-seok had the same sinking feeling as when he realized that the probable cause of Chong's parents not being notified was incompetence. In this case, he imagined the bureau of encryption devising an elaborate set of codes but failing to disseminate them. He'd like to get a few of those pointy-heads in the field for a while.

The major turned off the radio. "Okay, I need to meet with the captains."

"Comrade Major," said Yoon. Jun-seok and Ho looked at their junior lieutenant, as did the other commandos. A bit cheeky to give the major a shout-out, even in an egalitarian setting, even with a handsome face that resembled a sixteen-year-old's. The major nodded and Yoon continued: "If you analyze the words and syntax of the message, they are telling us in an indirect manner to return home."

The major blinked. "You want to abort the mission, Comrade Lieutenant?"

"It's not what I want, Comrade Major. It's how I interpret the message by parsing the words and syntax. Don't you see the significance of the words 'home' and 'tomorrow'?"

Jun-seok didn't know how to react. He maintained silence along with the other lieutenants and captains, waiting for an eruption. But the major smiled and said, "Comrade, I appreciate your enthusiasm, but this is not the time or place for a grammar lesson." As laughter rippled through the group, the major added, "Now everyone, if you're not a captain, clear out."

Jun-seok and Yoon retreated to where they'd been sleeping. In a whisper, Yoon said, "Don't you see my point. Look at the placement of the word 'home.'"

"Stop, little brother," said Jun-seok. "On top of everything else, you're giving me a headache."

"But—"

"But nothing," said Jun-seok. "Do you want to be the one to tell the Great Leader we took it upon ourselves to bug out? You think the major wants to do that?"

"Okay, okay," said Yoon. "I get the picture."

Fifteen minutes later, Ho returned and squatted with his team. He delivered a sharp slap to the side of Yoon's head and said, "That's to clear out the cobwebs. Do you need another one?"

"If you wish, Comrade Captain," said Yoon.

Ho reached across but instead of the head, delivered a tap to Yoon's shoulder. "We all have misgivings," said Ho, "but the mission continues and we must pull together."

Ho waited for Yoon's acquiescence by way of a nod. Jun-seok nodded also.

"There are some changes," said Ho. "First, we'll leave our Hanguk uniforms here because that's what they're looking for. We'll change into our overcoats and sneakers. In fact, we'll cache everything here except what we wear and our weapons."

Jun-seok nodded but wasn't happy about leaving his gear. What if they couldn't return to their cache?

Ho pointed west. "Come dark, we'll follow a trail down to the Cheongun neighborhood of north Seoul. From there, we'll march straight down Changuimun Road onto the Blue House grounds."

"March?" said Jun-seok.

"We're posing as the Korean Counterintelligence Corps. That will explain our civilian clothes. Keep your weapons under your coats."

Jun-seok and Yoon stared at their captain. Ho said, "Everyone here's afraid of the CIC."

Jun-seok was incredulous. "The CIC marches down roads in formation?"

"They will tonight."

"Why don't we stick to the woods?" said Yoon.

"Because they'll be looking for us there, and it will take too long. Bluffing our way down the road is our best bet. Anyhow, that's the decision."

"And do you like the plan, Comrade Captain?" Jun-seok asked.

Ho leaned forward and brought his face close to his lieutenants. "I'm not thrilled about it. But marching down the road is better than stumbling through the woods at this point." Ho leaned back. "Get some rest. And eat up—we won't be carrying much with us tonight."

• • • •

DUSK ARRIVED, THEN dark. The teams snaked single file down a path of rocks and roots to a wide gravel road running southwest along the middle contour of Bukak Mountain: Changuimun Road, dark and deserted, pathway to the north gate of the Blue House grounds. The commandos formed up in three ranks facing the mountain, the captains in the front rank. The major ordered a right face, and the formation changed to three columns. Jun-seok occupied the right column, seventh back, Yoon the middle, their captain the left. The major, at the front of the formation, ordered forward march. "Look sharp," he said over his shoulder.

The commandos marched in step, their sneakers scratching the gravel in unison. Jun-seok counted cadence to himself, one, two, three, four. One, two, three, four. As he counted and considered the cohesion of the unit, his misgivings slipped away. Once again, he felt a shield of invincibility, each commando equal to a platoon, their unit the equivalent of a battalion.

Scattered one-story houses appeared on the right, all in deep shadow, the moon not up yet. From the houses, Jun-seok caught glimpses of candle and lantern light. The left side of the road remained steep and wooded.

Twenty minutes into the march, headlights and flashlights appeared ahead. "A checkpoint," said Ho.

The major called back, "Swing your arms. Look like you own this road."

When the checkpoint neared, the major deployed his phony southern accent in a shout. "Get those lights out of my face. CIC. Get out of our way."

The thirty-one men of Unit 124 maintained their quick-step, arms swinging, eyes ahead, skirting the checkpoint, which stood in a cut-out to the left. With sideways darting pupils, Jun-seok took in the nervous faces of uniformed police. Young men, babies, nothing to fear. But behind the uniformed police, Jun-seok noticed two older men in civilian clothes with leaden eyes. They didn't appear in awe of Unit 124 and the major's phony accent.

A moment later, a whisper came down from the ranks behind. "We're being followed. Pass it on."

Jun-seok didn't dare look back but imagined the two sets of leaden eyes trailing their formation.

Minutes later, another whisper came down the ranks. "Trouble back here."

Ho turned his head. "What is it?"

A lieutenant from the rear rank said, "They've grabbed our captain."

"What?" said Ho. "What do you mean?"

"Those two guys grabbed our captain."

Two Hanguks grabbed a captain from Unit 124? How could that be? Ho whispered the information forward. A response came back: continue the mission but watch the rear. *What else could they do?*

The commandos, minus one captain, approached a three-way intersection. Jun-seok knew from the map in his mind that they were within a kilometer of the north gate. He reached through the front fold of his coat and ran a mitten along his submachine gun. He'd feel better once the teams entered the Blue House grounds and assumed their assigned roles. As he worried again about the leaden-eyed police behind, cones of light approached from ahead. Two vehicles—four headlamps—stopped side by side, blocking the road.

The major again deployed his southern accent in a shout. "Turn those lights down."

A third, larger vehicle came up the road, and, in its lights, Jun-seok saw that the first two vehicles were open jeeps. The passenger in the leftmost jeep stood and yelled, "Identify yourself."

The major called for the formation to halt. No, thought Jun-seok, let's keep going, let's keep strutting, let's maintain our invincibility. But the two jeeps and the third vehicle took up the width of the road. Now the third, larger vehicle edged by the jeeps.

"Be ready to shoot," whispered Ho. "I don't like the looks of this."

Up front, the major shouted at the jeeps, "CIC. Stand aside."

The upright passenger in the first jeep shouted back, "Show me your papers."

"Stand aside."

"I am Choi Gyu-sik, the police chief for Jongno District. I demand to see your papers." With his right hand, Choi undid a holster flap and started to extract his pistol. Jun-seok waited for the major's next bluff but instead heard the burp of a submachine gun. Either the major had fired, or another commando had jumped the gun, but either way, the police chief for Jongno District fell sideways from his jeep. Additional submachine gun bursts shattered the windshields of both jeeps.

As the front ranks engaged the jeeps, the larger vehicle continued its advance and came alongside the commandos. Jun-seok brought out his submachine gun then saw that the vehicle wasn't military but a minibus. Civilian faces pressed against the windows—women and men of various ages. The windows shattered under gunfire, and the faces fell away amid cascading screams. To his front, Jun-seok caught the contours of two grenades in the air, bound for the bus, and dropped prone to the road, tucking his face in the crook of his elbow. He listened as the grenades detonated and the screams subsided.

Removing his face from his elbow, Jun-seok saw streaks of yellow overhead. Tracers, he realized, and recognized the staccato thumping of a big fifty-caliber machine gun. There must be a tank or armored truck to their front—or their rear; all was confusion. Jun-seok looked to his left, and Yoon, lying next to him, stared back.

"Are you hit, little brother?"

"I don't think so," said Yoon. "And you?"

"Crawl to the side of the road. Stay down."

Slithering on stretched-out elbows and knees, chests to the ground, Jun-seok and Yoon gained the east side of the road. They pressed their backs against the embankment that rose to Bukak Mountain. One of the jeep lights still burned, and in its mustard beam, Jun-seok surveyed the carnage. Up and down the road, back-dropped by the smoking bus, lay a dozen or more trench coats, sneakers jutting, some toes up, some heels up. So fast, thought Jun-seok. How can this be? One moment invincible, the next shattered.

To Jun-seok's right, a trench coat scrambled up the embankment. Jun-seok grabbed Yoon's sleeve, and they followed, digging in sneakers and pushing through branches until their legs pumped against a rough trail that angled left.

Jun-seok sensed movement ahead and raised his submachine gun.

"No," said a voice. Followed by a loud whisper, "Don't shoot."

It was the team that had marched behind Jun-seok, ensconced among rocks and a tree.

Jun-seok said, "We don't know where our captain is."

The captain of the other team said, "Then you're a team of two."

"What should we do?"

"Go back the way we came."

Rifle fire echoed through the woods to the south. Here and there, Jun-seok detected the rattle of one of their PPS-43 submachine guns, but most of the firing came from rifles.

The captain of the other team said, "It sounds like we're cut off from our cache." He turned away from the gunfire. "Listen, Comrades, guide north by west until you get a glimpse of Papyeong Mountain. Then follow the east side of Papyeong Mountain until you reach the Imjin River."

"What about you?" said Jun-seok.

"We'll cover the withdrawal, then follow. Good luck."

Minutes later, Yoon said, "Stop."

Jun-seok twisted his head around. "What is it?"

"I have to shit."

"This is no time for a shit."

"That's not what my bowels say."

Crazy, thought Jun-seok, of course we can stop for a shit. He loosened his pants. *And I best empty my bladder.* As he pissed, he thought, sure, we've been dealt a setback, but we're elite soldiers. We have to calm down and behave like professionals. Our mission now is to get back north and render a report. Jun-seok thought about the report—don't trust the proletariat in the south, don't try to bluff your way with bad accents and cheap watches, stick to the woods. His thoughts wandered to his parents and his home village.

• • • •

BY DAWN, JUN-SEOK AND Yoon had reached the base of the Bukhan Mountains, crossed a valley, and climbed over and down another ridge. They pressed themselves into a culvert for the daylight hours. On occasion, gunfire grumbled in the distance. Once, footsteps could be heard within a hundred meters. Jun-seok and Yoon pressed themselves closer to the earth.

At dusk, the two men probed their way north by west.

"How are you doing?" said Jun-seok.

"Hungry," said Yoon.

When daylight returned, Jun-seok and Yoon stowed their trench coats in their packs. Jun-seok rummaged about and found loose rice and kimchi, which he shared with Yoon. They advanced at a measured pace through wooded terrain, stopping every ten seconds to listen for ten seconds. Ahead, streaks of sun announced the end of the woods. Moving up behind the last bit of brush that provided cover, Jun-seok let his knees drop, then his body, not rustling a branch, so that he could lie on his stomach looking forward. He pushed ahead, a few centimeters at a time, to the edge of the woods. To his front stretched three hundred meters of open ground. First, a hundred meters of frozen rice paddies, then a north-south road, then another two hundred meters of paddies. A cluster of ramshackle hooches, not quite a village, nestled across the road beyond and left of the far rice paddies, before the terrain rose toward a ridge.

Jun-seok pointed south. "The road from Pobwon-ni." He pointed north. "Papyeong Mountain is up there somewhere. Tonight we'll cross the road and follow that far ridge up."

A motor puttered from the south, and up the dirt road bounced a crowded minibus. "They have a lot of buses," said Yoon.

Yoon pointed to the right, where the rice paddies ended against a treeline that ran down to the road. "We could go now. We could use those trees for cover and cross the road when it's clear."

Jun-seok shook his head. "No, little brother, best to wait for dark and cross through the paddies." Jun-seok pointed at the trees. "We'll make noise in the woods. We won't know who's on the road until we get there." He pointed at the paddies to their front. "We need the cover of dark."

Chapter Seventeen: January 1968, Nullo-ri

Marshall sat with the motor idling and his foot on the clutch, watching the back of Boyle's parka recede down the Nullo-ri alleyway, not sure what was happening with his squad leader. DeGroot, his head lowered to the map in his mittens, said, "Straight out of town, Private Jones."

"Right, Sir." But still Marshall hesitated.

At the end of the alley, Boyle turned and looked back, lifting the corners of his lips and raising his right mitten. His yobo stood to his left, her wraparound dress accentuating her pregnancy. She faded away, and Marshall realized with a start that he'd imagined her. Weird, to see a figment of the imagination standing next to a real person. Or was Boyle a figment too?

"Private Jones," said De Groot, "straight ahead."

"Right, Sir." Marshall released the jeep's clutch. At the east end of Nullo-ri, past the Terrace Tea House, the road turned south, skirting the eminence the soldiers called Easy Queen but the maps called Papyeong Mountain. Forty minutes later, the road passed between two small American artillery camps and entered a large three-way intersection where another gravel road jutted off to the west. On the east side of the intersection, across from the west-jutting road, stood a square, cinder block building, a police checkpoint. A Korean with a padded jacket and trooper hat, flaps up, stood in front of the building, cradling an M2 carbine with a banana clip. On the south side of the intersection, five American jeeps, stripped for combat and fitted with M60 machine guns, idled: the battalion recon platoon.

De Groot and the recon platoon leader stepped from their jeeps and met in the middle of the intersection. Several times the two lieutenants raised their eyes from their maps and looked south.

Another jeep trailed dust from the north and braked in the center of the intersection. It was the battalion commander, his vehicle in full combat mode, no canvas, windshield flat upon the hood. Luppino wore a camouflage helmet and driving goggles, his parka draping his shoulders. Salutes weren't allowed in the field, but bodies tightened to semblances of attention.

"We're nailing a few," Marshall heard the colonel say. The lieutenants answered in the affirmative.

"I want pursuit," Marshall heard. "I want bodies on the ground."

De Groot returned and said, "Straight ahead." Marshall drove south from the police checkpoint, and De Groot said, "This is our sector. For a click or so." Marshall nodded as he surveyed the barren surroundings.

The jeep bounced between thin leafless trees on the east and frozen rice paddies on the west. The rice paddies gave way to trees, and the road dropped at a six percent grade for three hundred meters, with rising woods on both sides. At the bottom of the hill, the road opened to level ground, with rice paddies on either side.

"Stop here," said De Groot.

De Groot stepped from the jeep, and Marshall followed his gaze east across the dull patchwork of paddies, each twenty meters square, sunken, partitioned from its neighbors by berms. The paddies extended a hundred meters from the road before rising to a tree line. "That's where they're coming from," said De Groot.

"Who, Sir?"

"North Koreans. Commando types. There's been some trouble in Seoul, and they're heading back this way. That's all we know."

De Groot turned and looked to the west. More rice paddies. "So we'll set up on this side of the road facing east."

"Our platoon, Sir?"

"The whole company, but our platoon will be taking this area down here." De Groot looked north, back up the road. "The other platoons can take the hill and the section going to the police station." He resumed his seat in the jeep. "Let's head back to the intersection."

• • • •

JUN-SEOK HAD MERGED his body into its surroundings but still felt unnerved when the soldier on the passenger side stepped from the jeep and looked toward him and Yoon. A tall Caucasian with eyeglasses. The driver was a Negroid.

Nothing to do but lie still. After a moment, the tall Caucasian turned and looked toward the other side of the road.

"Americans," said Yoon.

Jun-seok lifted his right hand for silence.

The driver clapped his mittened hands and hunched his shoulders. The tall Caucasian stamped his feet. They're cold, thought Jun-seok, and smiled. For him, the weather felt balmy. His attire without the trench coat comprised padded cotton pants and shirt over wool underwear, a trooper hat, wool socks, and high-top sneakers, and he felt fine. The Yankees should come up north if they want some real cold.

The tall American resumed his place in the passenger seat. The driver worked the steering wheel and gearshift, reversing the direction of the jeep, and drove back north.

Yoon said, "Shouldn't we make a break for it now? Before more come?"

"Too risky." Jun-seok pointed. "Look at the distance. Look at the village. We need the night, little brother."

• • • •

MARSHALL NOSED THE jeep back up the hill, jiggling the steering wheel as he drove—something felt wrong. At the police station, he jumped out, circled the vehicle, and spotted the problem, right rear.

"Sir, we got a tire going flat."

"Okay," said De Groot. "Let me see what's happening with the company." He picked up the handset from the radio mounted on the back of the jeep and pressed the push-to-talk button. "Alpha-niner, this is alpha-four. Can you hear me, over?"

The speaker blasted Steiner's voice as if he were standing next to them. "Alpha-four, this is alpha-niner, roger that, over."

De Groot said, "We've finished scouting. We're at the intersection by the police checkpoint, over."

"We're on the artillery compound just north of you. We've found an empty hut for our command post, over."

As De Groot talked with Steiner, Marshall approached the Korean with the M2 and pointed at the bad tire on the jeep. The Korean pointed down the west-bound road. "Masan-ri," he said, holding up one finger.

De Groot walked over. "They don't know where there's a motor pool. I guess we'll bring the jeep in as is."

"Sir, this guy says we can get it fixed in Masan-ri, a click down the road."

De Groot pondered the idea for a second. "Let's do it."

. . . .

MOON EUN-AE POURED water into the medium-size vat on the diesel-fed stove. She put the water bucket on the floor, crossed to the front door, and stared out. Another winter day clawing its way south from Siberia, across Choson Korea, across the DMZ, across the Imjin River, into the streets and alleyways of Masan-ri, but with a buzz in the air. Last night, her husband, Chang In-soo, heard on his transistor radio warnings to watch for Choson guerrillas disguised as Hanguk soldiers, seen near Pobwon-ni. This morning, when In-soo had brought the water, he'd said, "Now they're telling us the guerrillas are disguised in trench coats, that there was a gun battle in Seoul."

Eun-ae walked back to the stove. From an overhead shelf, she pulled down containers of cocoa powder, powdered milk, and sugar. From outside, In-soo pushed the door open and stepped in, rubbing red hands. Eun-ae wished she could keep off the weight like him, skinny as sixteen, except she thought his face too gaunt. He seldom drank her cocoa, saying, "Save it for your customers." Never ate the chocolate candy. Stuck to kimchi and rice, and cigarettes.

Eun-ae said, "What's the latest?"

In-soo pointed his chin east. "We just talked to some guys who came through the checkpoint. The police there said the guerrillas tried to attack the Blue House."

"Are you serious?"

"The police took one of them alive. He told them their mission."

"Which was?"

In-soo paused with lips parted, his favored posture before an important announcement.

"You won't believe it," he said.

"Well, yobo, I won't know whether to believe it until you tell me."

"It was to cut off the head of Pak Chung-hee."

Eun-ae peered into her vat of water, which was coming to a simmer, giving her time to consider In-soo's news. She looked back and said, "That would be so awful. I couldn't bear it if anything happened to the head of Pak Chung-hee."

In-soo opened his mouth in a raucous laugh. Eun-ae smiled, pleased that she amused her husband. But as she turned back to the counter next to the stove, she thought more on the matter, and her smile faded. She said, "Is this bad? What are they doing south of the river?" Usually the Chosons confined their provocations to the DMZ and the area north of the Imjin.

In-soo placed a cigarette in his lips, flicked open an American Zippo, and thumbed its flint wheel. On the first exhale, he said, "I don't know. There was a big shootout. They killed the police chief of Jongno. They threw grenades into buses."

Eun-ae poured cocoa powder into a mixing bowl. "They killed a police chief?"

"Some of them are still on the loose," said In-soo. "They could be coming this way. To escape back north."

Eun-ae poured powdered milk and sugar into the mixing bowl. "So there were a lot of them?"

"Yeah. A big operation."

"Do you think more are coming down?"

"I think it's just a raid," said In-soo.

"How can you be so sure?"

In-soo cupped his right hand to his ear. "Wait. Are those tanks I hear?"

"Very funny," said Eun-ae.

"They'd be crazy to come down." In-soo flicked ashes from the cigarette. "They'd be destroyed by our airplanes and artillery."

Eun-ae pointed west toward the Imjin River. "Not before they drove us out again."

Eun-ae found it impossible not to recall June 1950 when her family, and all the families of Masan-ri, fled in the face of Hanguk tanks and infantry. As the evacuation moved south, it accumulated mass. Eun-ae, age 13, had looked around in amazement. It appeared that all Hanguk Korea was on the move. The people walked on both sides of the road, making way for motor vehicles—military trucks and jeeps and black limousines—trailing dust down the center. Eun-ae crossed the Han River on a small ferry with an outboard motor. Upriver, against the rising sun, the northernmost span of the steel Han River Bridge dipped into the river. Pieces of carts and vehicles floated toward her. Human bodies floated her way, along with a dead ox.

Eun-ae returned to Masan-ri in November in the wake of victories by the United Nations army. But three months later, in the dead of winter, the people fled again, this time in the face of Chinese tanks and infantry. Eighteen years later, a third evacuation seemed improbable but not impossible.

In-soo turned and walked to the door. "Now what?"

Eun-ae followed and looked past In-soo's shoulder. Outside sat an American jeep with two soldiers, a black one behind the steering wheel and a tall white one unfolding himself from the passenger seat. They had rifles with magazines inserted and wore helmets, an unusual sight. The Americans below the Imjin usually went unarmed. And Masan-ri was not for GIs—no tea houses, no working girls. Eun-ae wasn't sure how it had gotten that way, but it had become the unwritten law: not a camp town. Five young boys, including her son, had gathered around the jeep. One of them pointed to the tall soldier's belt and made pulling and throwing motions. Eun-ae saw that indeed the soldiers carried grenades as well as loaded rifles.

"Just what we need," said In-soo.

Oh oh, thought Eun-ae. In-soo wasn't fond of Americans. Eun-ae remembered a few months ago catching him pissing into the street as an American jeep rolled by. "You think that's funny," she said from the doorway of the store, "sticking your cock in their faces?" He turned with a smile and said, "Do you have a better place for it?"

"Get back to work," she had said with a blush.

"But I see why they're here," said In-soo.

Now Eun-ae saw too. A soft tire on the right rear of the jeep. From outside, Eun-ae's father called, "In-soo, I need your ass out here now."

In-soo opened the door a crack. "Tell them to fuck off."

"Don't be a fool. We can charge them two times over to fix that tire."

In-soo turned to Eun-ae with a smile. "I better fix that tire or there'll be no peace with my father-in-law." He stepped outside.

M arshall thought of a trick he liked to play on his younger brother and friends back in the world. He could turn out his eyelids and lips, displaying intense red against black skin, white teeth, and bulging brown eyes. Marshall pulled off his mittens, tucking them under his armpits, ducked his face away from the gathered boys, reversed his eyelids and lips, and turned back.

The two boys nearest Marshall shrieked. The others laughed as De Groot turned to check out his jeep driver, about to say something but then motioning sideways with his eyes. Marshall followed the lieutenant's pupils to a doorway next to the garage, where a woman stood in peasant dress and shawl, no doubt mother to one or more of the boys. She reminded Marshall of his own mother just before she said, "I love you son, but you're still getting whupped."

The woman crooked a forefinger and said, "*Irriwa*." Marshall took a tentative half-step. For a second time, the woman said, "*Irriwa*." But she was looking past Marshall, crooking her finger at De Groot. Good, thought Marshall, we're in it together.

The woman moved aside and swept an arm toward the interior of the building. Marshall and De Groot stepped past her into a small shop with a dirt floor and several tables, one displaying bars and boxes of candy. At the far end of the shop, a wooden platform stood in front of two sliding doors. In front of the platform, a small stove held a large steaming pot. The woman brushed by Marshall and De Groot and walked to the stove. She ladled from the pot into a tin cup and handed it to Marshall. Hot chocolate. She did the same for De Groot. Marshall held his cup between his mittens and sipped.

"*Komapsumnida*," said De Groot. Thank you.

"Yeah," said Marshall. "*Komapsumnida*."

"*Ye, ye,*" said the woman and motioned with her hands for them to drink.

The room was not warm, forty or fifty degrees, but much better than outside. The stove was small, meant for cooking. The stovepipe ran Korean-style under the platform to heat the floors of the raised rooms behind the sliding doors.

Marshall observed the woman. Like moms everywhere, he thought. She looked to be in her early thirties. Marshall hoped she didn't mind them being in her shop with loaded rifles and hand grenades. But she looked more concerned than annoyed. *Like moms everywhere.*

The woman pointed outside, and Marshall saw the jeep was ready. He and De Groot set down their cups and stepped into the frigid exterior air. De Groot gave the older man a wad of *won* notes. He tried to return some, but De Groot waved him off. The younger man had turned a bicycle upside down and was spinning its front wheel.

Marshall drove back to the police checkpoint, turned left at the intersection, then right into the artillery camp on the east side of the road, and found the captain's jeep in front of a Quonset hut.

Marshall said, "Do you think we'll stay on special assignment, Sir?"

"I seriously doubt it, Private Jones."

• • • •

INSIDE THE QUONSET hut, Steiner and the company clerk stood warming their hands over a stove. Marshall joined them as De Groot walked farther into the hut where the captain sat on a footlocker.

Steiner said to Marshall, "You can leave the jeep here."

"Where's the rest of the company, First Sergeant?"

"They're coming. The whole battalion's coming."

De Groot finished his parley with Hirschfeld, and Marshall followed him back outside. At the camp gate, Marshall and De Groot turned left and walked south to the intersection. As Marshall stamped his boots and clapped his mittens, De Groot looked back up the road toward Easy Queen.

"Damn, Sir," said Marshall, "they got a latrine next door. Did you see that?"

"I did, Private Jones."

"Aren't you freezing, Sir?"

"Officers don't get cold, Private Jones. Ah, here they come."

Marshall looked to the north. Balanced on the frigid horizon, a deuce-and-a-half spat smoke upward from its side pipe. As the truck dropped down from the horizon, trailing trucks appeared. They grew larger and slowed as De Groot waved them down.

De Groot looked into the first truck and yelled at a lieutenant from Bravo company. "Keep going, you're all the way down to Pobwon-ni." Three trucks rumbled by. De Groot yelled at a lieutenant from Charlie company. "Keep going, down the hill after the next set of paddies."

Alpha company rode in on the last set of trucks. Lieutenants and platoon sergeants swung from the cabs. Squad leaders and riflemen poured over tailgates. Marshall found his squad, relieved to see that Boyle had made it back. Priestly called for the platoon to form two ranks.

"You know where we go?" said Kim.

Marshall pointed a mitten south. "That way, down the hill."

Priestly called attention and waited for the soldiers to loosen their slings and hang their rifles from their shoulders.

"Right—face," called Priestly.

The two ranks twisted a quarter-turn, morphing into two south-facing columns.

"Forward—march," called Priestly.

As Marshall marched, he glanced west to see the first platoon taking positions in the rice paddies that ran from the intersection to the hill. In a few minutes, the column reached the end of the paddies and dropped onto the six percent grade between the two wooded slopes. There, third platoon had started scrambling up through the trees on the west side of the road. Marshall's platoon marched to the base of the hill, where the road leveled and the woods opened to rice paddies.

"Platoon—halt," called Priestly.

The men broke ranks as the squad leaders huddled with Priestly and De Groot.

Boyle came out of the huddle and motioned to his squad. They stood where Marshall had turned the jeep around earlier. Boyle pointed across a shallow ditch on the west side of the road. "Our new home," he said.

The squad crossed the ditch and set up, two men per position, except for Boyle, who went solo. Marshall and Kim formed a team to the south of Boyle—on his right. DiMaggio and Ivan set up on Boyle's left, with two more teams farther up.

· · · ·

DURING THE LATE AFTERNOON hours, Jun-seok and Yoon had watched American military vehicles pass on the road in front of them. They'd heard gunfire from the south. They didn't see any more minibuses. A string of jeeps sporting top-mounted machine guns sped south. Ton-and-a-quarter trucks and deuce-and-a-halves lumbered south.

The sun was descending toward the paddies to the southwest when talking and the jangle of gear sounded on the road. From the north, a column of Yankee soldiers appeared on foot. Jun-seok recognized the Negroid soldier who had driven the jeep that morning and the tall Caucasian with eyeglasses. The Yankees deployed on the far side of the road, facing Jun-seok and Yoon.

Jun-seok nudged Yoon, and they withdrew centimeter by centimeter.

"What do we do now?" said Yoon.

"Same as before. Wait for night."

"We can't walk through them," said Yoon. "They're too close together."

"And they're looking for us," said Jun-seok. He contemplated the problem. "But we can run through them."

"Run?"

"When it turns dark." Jun-seok extended an arm. "We can cross the paddies. Slow and steady. They won't see us."

"Then what?"

"When we reach the road, we'll run through their positions. They only have one thin line. We'll be past them before they know it." Jun-seok paused and visualized their actions. "Keep your submachine gun pointed forward, safety off, fingers alongside the trigger. Run as fast as you can."

"What will they say when we get back?" Yoon asked. Jun-seok didn't understand. "What will our commanders say," Yoon said, "because we failed in our mission?"

"Ah, that," said Jun-seok. "Well, we did the best we could. They'll be happy to have our report." Jun-seok smiled, wanting to believe what he was saying. "They'll take us to Pyongyang for medals."

"Ha," said Yoon.

• • • •

BOYLE WALKED TO THE middle of the road and circled his hand in the air. The squad gathered around. Boyle said, "They hope to get the mess truck down here in the morning. For now, it's C rations."

"What about sleeping bags?" said DiMaggio.

"Not tonight."

"We'll freeze to death out here."

"Don't be a pussy," said Ivan.

"Yeah, well I wasn't raised in Siberia, numb nuts."

"Listen," said Boyle, "this is the way the army works. You'll get so cold you'll think you're dying. You'll wish you were dying, but you won't."

The squad stamped their boots and laughed.

"Sergeant," said Ivan, "what are we doing here? What's the mission?"

Boyle pointed south. "This road runs down to Pobwon-ni." He turned to the east and spread his arms. "We're setting up on the west side of the road facing across. Facing east. That's where our commanders figure they're coming from. Our mission is to stop them."

"Who's they?"

"Joe. Apparently a raiding party come down and shot up Seoul. Now they're trying to get back north."

"Jesus," said DiMaggio. "Is there a war starting?"

"Just a dustup," said Boyle. He stamped his feet and clapped his mittens. "So I say again, we won't be sleeping tonight."

Priestly walked over and looked west behind the squad's positions. "Did you notice," he said to Boyle, "there's a little village back there?"

Along with Priestly and Boyle, Marshall peered across the rice paddies to their rear. He made out a cluster of a dozen hooches three hundred meters away that he hadn't noticed earlier on scout with De Groot.

Priestly looked the other way, east, the direction Joe would be coming from. The squad looked too, examining the terrain that formed their front: a ditch on the other side of the road deeper than the one on their side; a hundred meters of rice paddies and berms; the land rising to a tree line.

Ivan said, "If they're coming at us from there, we got clear shooting."

"Not at night," said Priestly.

Priestly turned to the squad. "Look, men, the chance of any of them hitting this exact spot is slim. A hundred to one. But I want eyes and ears open. If you feel drowsy, let your buddy know. Make sure someone's always awake."

De Groot walked over and stood next to his platoon sergeant. "What do you think, Sergeant Priestly?"

"I don't like that tree line, Sir. They could be sitting there watching us."

Static cut through the frosty air followed by Korean chatter. The squad turned to Kim, who had his radio in hand. Kim said, "Try to get news."

Neither De Groot nor Priestly objected as Kim tuned the radio. Everyone stood in silence watching their KATUSA, waiting for his report. Kim's face tightened. He looked up from the radio and said, "They attack Blue House."

"What's that?" said DiMaggio

"Their White House," said De Groot. "Where the president lives."

"Big fight," said Kim. "Many dead in Seoul."

"See if you can get American Armed Forces Radio," said De Groot.

The squad laughed. Priestly said, "Sorry, Sir, that's the last place for reliable information."

Kim thumbed the tuner. Guitars and drums blew out of his transistor, followed by the voices of Paul McCartney and John Lennon wailing about a hard day's night.

"American Armed Forces," said Kim.

DiMaggio threw up an arm and a knee. He threw them down attempting to move to the beat.

Marshall looked upon DiMaggio's gyrations with disgust. Stepping forward, he flexed a shoulder and hip, raised an arm, and twisted on the balls of his boots. *This is how it's done.*

Boyle skipped forward with both elbows out.

"Sergeant Boyle," said Marshall, "what the hell is that?"

"It's a square, the best I can do to this music."

The squad laughed, clapping their mittens.

De Groot entered the dance with stuttered movements, like a giraffe after a night out. On the edge of the dance, Priestly surveyed his combat soldiers with a somber demeanor. *What could he say with the lieutenant in here too?*

• • • •

TINNY MUSIC CROSSED the paddy, decadent imperialist music with the boom-boom beat. Jun-seok and Yoon edged forward and peered. Three soldiers strutted in the road, the Negroid and a Caucasian with fluid motions, and another Caucasian with spasms. The tall Caucasian with eyeglasses joined them with jerky up-and-down movements. Jun-seok and Yoon watched with wide eyes and slack jaws before withdrawing.

Yoon said, "What are they doing?"

Jun-seok gave the matter some thought, and an explanation came to mind, from the forbidden cowboy movies. Far-fetched maybe, but what else? "I think they're doing a war dance," he said.

"They make themselves crazy before battle," said Yoon. "Wait till we tell them back home."

"First we've got to get there." Jun-seok put a hand on Yoon's shoulder. "Look, when we get close to the road, we'll split up. You move off to the right." Jun-seok pointed. "Up toward the woods. We'll cross at two points."

"Then what?" said Yoon.

"We'll join together later on the ridge. One hand to the right of that little village."

"One hand?" said Yoon.

Jun-seok said, "Let's take another look while there's still light."

Jun-seok and Yoon edged forward on their bellies.

"I see the houses," said Yoon.

"Put the left edge of your hand on the side of the village. Now follow the right edge up the ridge. That's where we'll meet."

• • • •

THE EXITING GUITAR chord trailed across the frozen landscape, and the dance stopped. Kim clicked off the radio and pushed it under his parka.

De Groot raised his face to the sky. "Dark soon." He pointed up the west side of the road to where the woods started. "Men, the command post is in there." He and Priestly left.

Boyle said, "Positions."

Marshall and Kim moved behind a small mound of frozen, brown earth. To their rear was the first of a checkerboard of paddies partitioned by berms. In the spring, the paddies would be flooded, and the people would stand up to their knees in the water, planting seedlings. In the fall, the people would stand in the muck and water cutting rice stalks for harvest. But now berms and paddies were as impenetrable as cement.

Marshall and Kim's mound was a meter high and two meters wide, a pile of extra dirt thrown out from the paddies, frozen in place for the winter. Kim slid down with his back to the mound. From Marshall's left, Boyle called out in a high whisper. Marshall walked three meters in the thinning light and stood next to his squad leader in back of another small clump of frozen earth.

"This is where I am," said Boyle. He swept his left arm up the road. "The rest of the squad's to my left. Past them, the rest of the platoon."

Boyle dropped his arm. "You okay these days? You taking care of that little problem?"

"Yeah, I did what you said."

"Make sure you finish the tetracycline. You got it with you?"

Marshall nodded.

Boyle said, "Before I leave Korea, I want to tell you again how I'm sorry about going off on you that night."

Marshall stamped his feet. "I sort of don't blame you, Sergeant Boyle. When I look back on it."

"I don't know what it is. Sometimes I just lose it. It's like shooting standing up."

"How's that?"

"It's another dumb thing I like to do. Prone or kneeling gives a lot more accuracy. And reduces you as a target. But I love to stand when I shoot. Can't help it." Boyle leaned toward Marshall and put a mitten on his shoulder. "Anyhow, didn't want to be leaving with that between us."

As twilight faded to starlight with no moon, Marshall's eyes dilated. He could make out the far side of the road and a few berms in the rice paddies beyond. With some concentration, he made out the tops of the trees on the far side of the paddies, mushrooms against a blue-gray background. Marshall pressed helmet and hood close to Kim and whispered. "How you doing?"

"Cold. Bored."

"Go to sleep," said Marshall. "I'll wake you up when I get tired."

Marshall rolled with his stomach against the mound, rifle pointing over and out. He shifted to his left side, up on one elbow. Then to his right side. No matter the position, the cold crept in. The boredom increased. He sensed movement to his left.

"Easy," said Boyle, "it's me."

Marshall turned his head to see Boyle squatting a meter away. "Just make sure one of you's awake."

He faded from sight.

As the sun dropped, Jun-seok and Yoon watched the far off ridge fade and merge into the dusk. Soon the road and the Americans disappeared. The rice paddies disappeared except for the nearest one. Good, thought Jun-seok, if we can't see, neither can the enemy. Jun-seok and Yoon crept from their cover, moving a half meter at a time. There was sufficient starlight to watch where their steps fell in the paddies and belly over the berms.

• • • •

MARSHALL BLINKED AND looked again. Nothing. Then a flash—no, not a flash, but an adjustment of shadow, a movement, halfway across the paddies on the other side of the road. Marshall scanned from left to right and back. He shivered. Nothing.

Marshall tried to assess his state of awareness regarding the movement to his front. Had he been awake or asleep? Had he just seen it? Had he dozed off and dreamed he saw it? Had he seen it, dozed off, awoken, and remembered it? Real or fantasy? Now or then? He remembered his first night on SCOSI patrol, ready to shoot at anything—but this felt different.

Kim lay on his stomach next to Marshall, rifle pointed ahead. Marshall tapped his shoulder and leaned into his ear. "I think something's out there."

Kim shook his head.

Marshall said, "You didn't see anything?"

Kim shook his head again.

Marshall said, "Wait here."

Marshall moved sideways, crablike, crouching, staying silent. He moved sideways again. And again, left boot, right boot, until he heard Boyle's whisper, "What is it?"

Two more sideways steps and Marshall squatted next to his squad leader. "I think there's something out there."

"I think I saw something, too," said Boyle. "Can you make your way to the CP?"

Marshall looked up the road into the stillness.

"Take your time," said Boyle. "Keep a low profile."

Marshall crouch-walked with measured steps. On the fourth step, DiMaggio said in a hoarse whisper, "Who's there?"

"It's me, goddamnit."

"Jesus Christ, Marshall, you trying to get shot?"

Marshall took two steps and knelt between DiMaggio and Ivan. "You see anything?"

"Sometimes I think I can," said DiMaggio. "Sometimes I think I'm going blind."

"What are the passwords?" said Ivan.

"Lick me," said Marshall.

"Wrong," said Ivan.

"There are no fucking passwords, you jerk," said DiMaggio.

"Right," said Ivan.

"I'm going to the CP," said Marshall.

"There should be a sign and countersign," said Ivan. "For situations like this."

"Goddamn, Ivan," said Marshall. "What, are you taking Rothman's place?"

"Seriously," said DiMaggio. "You're gonna get yourself shot."

"Look," said Marshall, "if Joe's around, he's to our front. Where your rifles should be pointed."

Marshall stood, took a breath, and went back to his crouch-walk. Six steps later, Priestly's whisper reached him. "Jones, what the fuck are you doing?"

Marshall froze mid-step.

Priestly said, "Get your ass over here."

Marshall found Priestly, De Groot, and Gomez, the radio operator, huddled in trees at the edge of the last paddy. "For Chrissake," said Priestly. "We can hear you all over the place."

"Sergeant Boyle sent me. We think there's something out there."

De Groot entered the conversation. "You sure?"

"Sure enough, Sir."

De Groot pushed his helmet against Priestly's; Marshall couldn't hear their conversation. He shifted close to Gomez and patted the radio. "What's happening out there?"

"Nothing," said Gomez. "Hey, do you know your name's Spanish?"

"Yeah, yeah."

"No, really. It's short for Cojones."

"Ha, ha," said Marshall.

Priestly's face appeared between Gomez and Marshall. "Specialist Gomez, could you do me a big favor and call the CP?" Gomez pulled off his mitten shell and lifted the handset. "Tell them," said Priestly, "we've got possible movement to our front. We're checking it out." Priestly looked at Marshall. "Let's go."

Back they went, crouch-walking, Marshall, Priestly, and De Groot, the radio chatter fading. Boyle stood as they approached.

"How sure are you?" said De Groot.

Boyle looked across the road. "Eighty percent, Sir."

Marshall said, "Same, Sir."

De Groot said, "I guess we should take a look."

Marshall studied their front. Still no moon.

"What do you think, Sergeant Priestly?" asked De Groot.

"Better to let them come to us, Sir."

"The battalion commander wants action."

Priestly said, "I understand, Sir. But they got to come through us."

"We don't know," said De Groot. "Maybe they'll back off. Go around."

"Then they'll hit one of the other units."

Marshall held his rifle in the crook of his arm so he could rub his mittens together. He wriggled his toes in wool and leather, Priestly having said no Mickey Mouse boots tonight. *What was the lieutenant talking about? Crossing the road to see if they could stumble into something?*

"We'll take Sergeant Boyle's squad," said De Groot.

Should have kept my mouth shut, thought Marshall.

The squad assembled on the road and formed a skirmish line facing east, Marshall and Kim holding the right flank, DiMaggio and Ivan next to Marshall. Marshall looked down the line and made out Boyle in the center, with De Groot a few steps behind him, Priestly and the others all but invisible.

· · · ·

JUN-SEOK HEARD WHISPERS and scraping from the American line and motioned for Yoon to stop. Minutes later, dark figures emerged on the road, Jun-seok surprised that he could make them out at that distance. He nudged Yoon. With slow steps, they reversed direction and moved back over paddies and berms. As they reached the last paddy, they heard the Americans coming off the road. Jun-seok and Yoon retreated into the trees. Jun-seok motioned with the flat of his hand, and Yoon pushed his body to the ground. Jun-seok squatted and watched.

· · · ·

BOYLE STEPPED FORWARD, and the rest of the line rippled out, crossing the east edge of the road and entering the deep ditch. From the left came the clatter of a helmet bouncing on frozen ground. Farther down, a curse. Marshall felt his left boot skid away on a piece of ice, and he thumped into a seated position, banging the butt of his rifle.

Jesus, he thought, if they didn't know we were coming before, they know now.

The squad climbed out of the ditch, clambered over a berm, and advanced across a frozen rice paddy. Marshall held his rifle pointed forward, trigger finger through the slit of the outer mitten, touching the trigger, safety on. Firing required two finger motions, forward to click off the safety, backward to let off a round. Marshall practiced the sequence in his mind, pushing aside the temptation to click off the safety now, knowing it would count as a major fuckup to let off a round by accident. Marshall scanned the paddy—nothing. He scanned the tops of the berms to his front and right—nothing.

The squad mounted a second berm and dropped into a second paddy. Marshall had no idea if the line was straight. He could see Kim on his right. He could see Ivan on his left. He could hear clatter on his left. He heard DiMaggio say, "Fuck a duck."

De Groot said, "Keep it down."

Marshall counted a third berm. A minute later he looked over the fourth berm into the last paddy. On the far side of that paddy, the ground rose into ebonized trees. Marshall saw nothing in the paddy and nothing on the slope beyond. In the trees—blackness.

De Groot said, "Hold up."

De Groot went into powwow with the two sergeants. Marshall heard Priestly say, "Risky, Sir."

"Then what?" said De Groot.

A minute later, Marshall felt a mitten on his back and Boyle's voice in his ear. "We're gonna check the trees left to right, just four of us." De Groot's tall, skinny parka moved past them. "The lieutenant's leading," said Boyle. "Then you and Kim. Then me."

"Why not Ivan and Di?" said Marshall.

Boyle moved a slanted smile toward Marshall and Kim. "Because you're my best men." He patted the back of Marshall's parka.

Behind them, Priestly said, "Just take a look in the trees. Don't go in."

You bet your ass, I'm not going in, thought Marshall. And take a look? At what? You can't see shit.

"If anything happens," said Priestly, "roll to your right into the paddy. We'll be covering, but you gotta get out of line of fire."

Roll into the paddy? That was the plan? Did any of these idiots know what they were doing?

"From the paddy, you'll be able to throw grenades."

Roll into the paddy? Throw grenades? This is not fucking Fort Benning with dummy grenades and blanks. Has everyone gone mad?

Marshall felt Kim's face near his ear. "This suck."

From behind Kim came Boyle's whisper. "Go."

Marshall followed De Groot's high back, with Kim and Boyle trailing. They went over the berm and crossed the last paddy obliquely from right to left. They climbed the short slope, approached the tree line, and, one by one, turned right.

• • • •

FOUR YANKEE SOLDIERS poked their way toward Jun-seok and Yoon. Jun-seok could only hope he was invisible in the shadows of the trees and brush. Shooting was a last resort—they might take out some of the enemy, but they would be trapped.

The tall soldier with eyeglasses poked so his rifle came within a meter of Jun-seok. He moved on, unseeing. Jun-seok started feeling confident of his invisibility, but the next soldier, the Negroid, stopped, poked, and stared straight at him. Jun-seok brought his mitten over the trigger of his PPS-43. As the Yankee continued staring, Jun-seok tightened his trigger finger.

• • • •

MARSHALL SENSED A FACE looking back at him, an Asian face with a trooper hat. Marshall pointed his rifle, his finger resting between safety and trigger. Push, pull, he thought.

The face disappeared, replaced by the murky outlines of branches and brush. I'm real close to pissing my pants, thought Marshall. He remembered his second day in the army, in-processing at the reception center, prelude to eight weeks of basic training, sitting with a dozen other draftees on folding chairs, still in civilian clothes, their hair yet uncropped. A sergeant first class stood to their front telling them they could sign up for the regular army, extending their service one year but getting to choose their branch. They could sign up for quartermaster, signal corps, whatever they wanted. The draftees smirked. Another year? Get out of town. "Choice, not chance," said the sergeant.

Why didn't I listen to him, thought Marshall. What the fuck was going through my head? Three years of anything else was better than two years of this shit. Three years of anything was better than one second of getting a hole blown through you.

Marshall saw the lieutenant fading and took two quick steps to catch up before going back to poking and looking. Twenty paces later, De Groot turned right and dropped back into the paddy. Marshall dropped into the paddy. Kim and Boyle followed.

Boyle came up to Marshall's left ear and whispered, "Did you see something?"

Marshall turned and whispered, "I thought I did for a second, but it was nothing." He added, "It scared the shit out of me."

"It'll do that," said Boyle.

De Groot and the three enlisted men walked back across the paddy. Priestly said, "Sir, why don't we go into the next set of paddies to sweep back."

"Okay, let's do it," said De Groot. The squad filed south into the next paddy, turned west and swept back toward the road. Halfway back, Marshall heard the tick of jeep motors, raised his eyes, and saw the low cast of blackout lights. Four jeeps facing north and one south.

"Now what the fuck?" said De Groot.

"Looks like everyone wants a piece of the action," said Priestly.

· · · ·

THE SQUAD CROSSED THE last paddy, climbed the last berm, crossed the deep ditch, and came up on the road, Marshall alongside a north-facing jeep. It was from the recon platoon and resembled a raptor in the darkness, with its windshield down and an M60 machine gun jutting forward off a swivel mount. The gunner leaned over the breech of the machine gun, a hundred-round ammo belt locked in place. He wore a parka with the hood pulled over his helmet, goggles draped over the parka hood, hanging around his neck. He smiled down at Marshall. "Having a good time?"

"Wanna trade places?"

The gunner slipped down to the rear seat, pulled his hand from his mitten, and pushed it inside his parka. Two cigarettes and a Zippo appeared. He lit the cigarettes and handed one to Marshall. The driver turned his head and said, "Did somebody say light up?"

The gunner extended his re-mittened hand, cigarette hanging from his lips. "Looks to me like we're taking a break."

Marshall followed the gunner's mitten and saw that the first north-facing jeep belonged to the battalion commander, and the south-facing jeep to Marshall's company commander. Luppino and

Hirschfeld had exited their vehicles and stood facing each other on the road.

The gunner tapped the driver's helmet. "You want one?"

"I don't smoke. Haven't you read the surgeon general's report?"

"The what?" The gunner turned to Marshall. "Do you know what he's talking about?"

"I've heard of it," said Marshall.

"And?"

"And I'm gonna quit once I'm back in the world."

The gunner laughed. "Back in the world. Who wants to go back to the world?"

"You wanna stay here the rest of your life?"

"If I could. Machine guns. Cheap smokes." The gunner sighed. "Pussy."

Marshall said, "What do you guys do? Ride around all night?"

"Fuck no," said the gunner. "We're in a camp a few clicks down the road. Battalion's set up there. In a hooch with a stove."

"Nice."

"When something happens, we jump in our jeeps and come roaring out. The colonel too. He's hot shit."

"Been roaring out a lot?"

"Not enough," said the gunner. "You guys are our only real action. What's the deal here, anyhow?"

Marshall pointed across the paddies toward the trees. "Thought we saw something. The lieutenant took us out for a look."

"Fucking lieutenants," said the gunner. "They'll get us all killed."

"What would you do?"

"Stay here and blast the shit out of that tree line," said the gunner. "Just sit here and let her rip."

"Sounds like fun," said Marshall.

"It is." The gunner stood and swung the M60 toward the tree line. "Bap, bap," he said. "Bap, bap, bap."

The driver leaned his head back and looked up. "Hey, doofus, would you mind not fucking around with that loaded weapon?"

Marshall imagined Hendrick behind the M60, looking down, saying, "Hey, Marshall, how they hanging? Want a cigarette? Sorry I fucked all over you. Sorry I'm such a dickhead." *What was Hendrick doing tonight? Driving a truck? Getting soused? Both?* He'd be less dangerous with an M60. Marshall wondered how Rothman was doing back in the world.

"Bap, bap," said the gunner.

"Knock it off, doofus."

Marshall drifted to the perimeter of the parley between Luppino and Hirschfeld. De Groot and Priestly hung inside the perimeter, the rest of Marshall's squad outside. A surreal scene. On the west side of the road lay a company of American infantry with their rifles pointed east. On the east side of the road, maybe, lay enemy commandos with their weapons pointed west. And between the combatants, in no-man's-land, stood the American commanders having a chat.

Luppino had turned away from Hirschfeld toward De Groot. He said, "And then what, Lieutenant?"

De Groot stumbled for words. "Well, we came back, Sir. We didn't see anything and came back."

"Why didn't you go into the trees?"

De Groot's voice rose in pitch. "We couldn't see anything, Sir. It would have been crazy to walk in there."

Hirschfeld interrupted: "In my opinion, it was a little crazy to walk up to the tree line in the first place."

"Really?" said Luppino.

"From my experience, Sir, as a platoon leader in Vietnam."

"Of course," said Luppino. "And I defer to your combat experience, Captain Hirschfeld. Nevertheless"—Luppino looked across the paddies—"our job is to engage the enemy, to put bodies on the ground."

"We could raise a flare, Sir," said Hirschfeld. He pointed toward the north-facing jeeps with the M60s. "Then send in recon for a more thorough search."

Right, thought Marshall. He could see the colonel's elite reaction force abandoning their jeeps and swivel-mounted machine guns, trudging across open rice paddies, in the face of possible fire. Marshall couldn't tell if the captain's remark was sarcasm. If it was, he did a good job of hiding it.

Luppino turned and walked toward his jeep, reversed himself, and walked back pointing a gloved finger. "I want some bodies on the ground," he said. "If you see them again, I want aggression. I want pursuit."

Hirschfeld stared at Luppino in silence. Luppino switched his gaze to De Groot. "Is that understood, Lieutenant?"

"Yessir," said De Groot.

Luppino returned to the passenger seat of his jeep. The driver backed obliquely, braked, swung the steering wheel, changed gears, and pressed the gas. The recon jeeps backed and turned, and the entourage sped south.

Hirschfeld stood in the road with De Groot and Priestly. He spoke in a low voice, but Marshall picked up the words. "Despite what the colonel says, you have my permission to use your brains."

Hirschfeld walked to his jeep. It turned and sped north. De Groot and Priestly walked back to their command post in the trees.

Boyle said, "Show's over. Back in position, boys."

"What time is it, Sergeant Boyle?" DiMaggio asked. "Past midnight?"

Boyle's smile broadened as he pushed down his mitten and examined his watch. "About twenty-two hundred."

"Jesus," said Marshall. DiMaggio groaned.

Marshall didn't feel like going back into position. He felt like standing in the road and chatting. "Sergeant Boyle," he said, "why did you come out anyhow? You like this shit?"

Boyle set his face as if in contemplation. "It has its allure."

"Sergeant Boyle," said DiMaggio. "Who's taking over the squad when you go?"

Again Boyle set his face in contemplation. "Let's see, Rothman's gone, so—I'm thinking Ivan."

The men laughed.

"What's so funny?" said Ivan.

"No," said Boyle, "Ivan's a good choice, but Gomez is the senior E-4 in the platoon."

"Gomez?" said Ivan. "He don't even speak English."

"You're the one who don't *speaka da* English," said DiMaggio.

More laughter. Marshall stamped his feet and clapped his mittens.

Boyle looked across the eastern paddies toward the tree line. "Look, guys," he said, "we can shoot the shit in the morning. Right now, let's button down."

Marshall sat across from Mr. Morris, the assistant principal, and couldn't believe what Morris was saying: Marshall was failing business math, so he wouldn't graduate. Morris was Black, too—maybe that was why he was so tough on Marshall. No, that couldn't be it: math grades were set in stone. Marshall thought, sure he'd struggled, knew he might not get a B, but failure? A punch in the stomach.

Marshall's world tipped sideways, and he flailed his arms. His eyes fluttered, and his right shoulder shook. He shivered and realized he wasn't falling from a chair in the assistant principal's office in Rochester, New York, but lying against a frozen mound of dirt somewhere north of Pobwon-ni, Korea, looking into the face of Kim Yeong-su. Kim lifted his eyebrows, and Marshall rotated his head. Sergeant Boyle.

Boyle's face came closer until their helmets and hoods touched. He whispered his words, sounding instructive, not angry. "Stay awake. Both of you."

"Sorry, Sergeant."

"Just stay awake." Boyle clapped a mitten against Marshall's shoulder. He smiled with the ends of his mouth up. "In case we get company."

Marshall followed Boyle's silhouette and moonlit shadow past the squad leader's position four meters away. Boyle faded in the direction of DiMaggio and Ivan.

· · · ·

"NOW WHAT?" WHISPERED Yoon.

"Same as before."

"Same as before?"

"We can't stay here, little brother. They'll find us come daylight." Jun-seok saw no other plan. He noticed that although the moon was up, it cast sharp shadows off the paddy berms. He whispered to Yoon, "Stay tight against the berms. Stay in the shadows."

Jun-seok dropped into the nearest paddy, followed by Yoon. They crawled in the shadows of the berms, taking their time, stopping every ten seconds to assess the situation. No soldiers in the road, no jeeps, no commotion from the American line.

One paddy from the road, Jun-seok tapped Yoon and pointed north, up the road. This was where they parted. Yoon turned and crawled parallel to the road. Jun-seok watched him slip over a berm and out of sight without a sound. *Good, the Americans wouldn't hear him either.* Jun-seok waited six minutes, counting off the seconds, then crawled over the last berm into the large ditch on the east side of the road.

Squatting in the ditch, Jun-seok heard nothing from the American line. He placed his mittened fingers alongside the trigger of the PPS-43, took a breath, bent his left leg, cocked his right, and leaped from the ditch. In two steps, head down, he attained full speed and the other side of the road. Lifting his head, he was stunned to see that he was running at a soldier with a leveled rifle. The soldier stood sideways to Jun-seok, left elbow cocked under the fore-end of the stock, and the mouth of the weapon centered on Jun-seok's chest. The distance was less than five meters.

• • • •

MARSHALL TWISTED HIS body toward the road and lifted his eyes to a half-moon. He rested his elbows on the mound to his front and stared across the road and rice paddies to the tree line. He couldn't understand why Mr. Morris kept popping into his dreams. Marshall had, in fact, never been called down to the office, but Morris kept popping up, this recurring nightmare where Marshall didn't graduate, that plus the falling thing. He graduated, and here he was, a private first class in the US infantry, entrusted with an M14 rifle, a hundred rounds of ammo, and four hand grenades. Plus cold weather gear and Mickey Mouse boots, which couldn't be worn tonight for reasons of heightened alertness. So Marshall's feet froze along with the rest of his body.

Marshall couldn't decide whether the moon made seeing easier or harder. Visibility felt sharper, but weird shadows danced everywhere. Marshall pulled his wool-covered trigger finger back into the mitten shell. He curled and flexed his fingers. He wished he could forget about his rifle and stick his hands under his armpits. He exhaled and watched a wisp of breath in the light of the moon and stars.

Marshall sensed a moving shadow near the tree line. He wondered if the movement he'd seen earlier, that had brought out the squad and recon, had been caused by enemy forces or forces of nature, or forces of the mind. He wondered if the movement he saw now was Joe or a limb waving in the wind. But the wind wasn't up. Still as death.

Time passed, a minute feeling like an hour. Marshall imagined he saw the same shadow closer, in the paddies, halfway from the tree line. Here we go again, he thought. He leaned into Kim and whispered, "See anything?"

Kim shook his head.

Marshall scanned his front from left to right, bottom to top, right to left, back down. As much to run the clock and stay awake as to do a grid search. He leaned toward Kim, but before he could pose the question, Kim shook his head.

The cold seeped up from the frozen ground, up his spine to his head; even his thoughts seem to freeze. His mind was returning to Mr. Morris—suddenly, a flicker of movement to his left.

Damn! I'm really starting to hate this job. He resolved to ratchet his head left in tiny increments until whatever was there came into focus. Then he would decide on the next action.

Marshall's third head adjustment revealed Boyle, four meters away, as the source of the flicker. That was a relief, but what was he doing? Marshall rolled onto his right side for a straight-on view. Boyle had risen to a crouch, his profile taking the form of a backwards question mark. What did he have in mind? Was he trying to get a better look? Was he trying to signal the rest of the squad?

A rational conclusion might be that Boyle was reacting to something to his front. With the corollary that Marshall should also be examining their front. But logic had yet to enter the picture, and Marshall's attention stayed with his squad leader. Boyle straightened, raised his rifle, and sent Marshall a tight whisper. A second later, the words registered. "Here comes Joe."

Marshall parsed the sentence. Joe had to mean Joe Chink. And he was coming where? Shit, thought Marshall.

Boyle held the classic stance of a standing rifleman, butt of the rifle pulled into his right shoulder, right hand covering grip and trigger, left hand grasping the small of the stock, muzzle straight out, legs spread. An image for a training demonstration. Mens—drill instructors loved that double plural—mens, observe, this is the standing rifle position; this is how it's done, if you deem to use it.

Boyle's rifle barked, and its muzzle rose an inch in recoil. Marshall caught the glint and arc of the ejected shell. His eyes shifted forward, chasing Boyle's bullet, where they met three flashes that coincided with a rattling sound, a rat-a-tat-tat.

A pair of pumping legs passed Marshall. They bore pants that looked like padded, polished cotton, green or olive. The feet wore high-top sneakers, black and white, basketball, looked like Keds. Marshall couldn't get over that—basketball sneakers. Gray wool jutted out at the ankles—socks or underwear, or both.

. . . .

IN THE MOONLIGHT, JUN-seok caught the glint of the rifle's ejected shell. Pain entered his chest as the report of the weapon reached his ears. Jun-seok pulled the fat trigger of his submachine gun, emitting three rounds. He dropped his head, bent his knees, and pushed his sneakers into the ground. He crossed the rifleman's position, crossed a rice paddy and went over a berm. He crossed a second paddy, and realized he was slowing, that the instructions to his legs no longer achieved the desired result. "Aw," he said.

As Jun-seok came alongside the ramshackle village he'd seen in the daylight, he stopped. Pain encased his chest, the front left and the back under the shoulder blade. He knew he had no hope of making the rendezvous on the ridge and veered toward the houses. A knot of men standing near the edge of the village scattered at his approach. Jun-seok saw a light, a door opening and closing, and rushed that way.

He threw himself on a narrow veranda, pulled the sliding door open, and pushed into a room, lit by a single candle. A woman screamed, cramming herself and two toddlers against the far wall. I'm here for you, thought Jun-seok. And I need help. Another screech from the woman assailed Jun-seok's ears. The children cried.

"Get out," said Jun-seok.

The woman clasped one child and pulled the other. Jun-seok closed the door behind them, doused the candle, and squirmed across the room. *So much for being a fish in the sea.*

Jun-seok raised his body to a half-sitting position against the wall opposite the door. He fumbled in his pack for a compress but gave up the effort. His head felt light and his hands numb. The chest pain came in throbs and his breath in gasps. Jun-seok saw the backs of his father and mother walking to the fields, shoulders bent from years of planting and weeding and harvesting. He saw the father of Chong

Myung-seung sitting across from him, desolate but not surprised at the death of his son. He heard Chong's sister crying.

Get a grip. This is no time for morose reflections. The situation is tough, but I've faced tough situations before. What are my options?

• • • •

THE NIGHT RESUMED ITS stillness. Boyle's rifleman profile had disappeared. The pumping legs had disappeared. A tall figure sprang up beyond Boyle's position and Marshall heard De Groot's inquiring whisper. "Sergeant Boyle?"

De Groot raised the volume of his whisper. "Sergeant Boyle."

"Sir," Marshall said. De Groot looked his way. Marshall rose and approached the lieutenant.

"What happened?" said De Groot.

"One of them got through, Sir, I think."

"Got through? You think? Where's Sergeant Boyle?"

Priestly appeared alongside De Groot.

"Private Jones," said De Groot, "where did you last see Sergeant Boyle?"

"Right here, Sir. He said Joe was coming."

"Who fired those shots?" said De Groot.

"Fuck me," said Priestly.

Marshall and De Groot turned to Priestly. Priestly had taken a step toward the road, toward Boyle's last known position, and dropped to his knees. Marshall took a step and dropped next to Priestly. De Groot bent over them.

Marshall's first thought was, aha, this explains why Sergeant Boyle disappeared and didn't respond to the lieutenant. Marshall struggled for a second thought as he stared down. Boyle lay on his back with half-open eyes and a quarter-smile, arms at his sides.

Priestly lifted his head and shouted. "Gomez, call for an ambulance."

"I'm on it."

"Now, not later."

"I'm on it, Sergeant Priestly."

Marshall, still on his knees, still staring, saw there was no rush on the ambulance. Boyle's body made no motion, no sound, just lay there, impervious to the cold, impervious to everything. Nobody could be that peaceful this side of oblivion.

"Goddamnit," said De Groot. "Goddamnit to hell." The lieutenant straightened his frame and looked away from Boyle, first toward the road, then toward the rice paddies behind them.

"On the way," said Gomez. "Recon too."

Marshall couldn't fathom his reaction to the shooting. He had felt no fear as he had when the squad walked up to the tree line. Had felt more like a neutral observer, watching and recording. But, of course, that was a problem. His MOS wasn't neutral observer, but eleven bravo, rifleman. He should have been standing alongside his squad leader, rifle to his shoulder.

It happened so fast. The pumping legs. Sneakers, can you imagine that?

Marshall rose from Boyle's body. His ears perked to new sounds, a rolling rumble of Korean voices from across the paddies behind the squad's positions. A woman screaming. More rumbling.

Priestly said, "It's coming from that little village back there."

"It must be him," said De Groot. "He must be there." De Groot pointed a mitten at Marshall. "Let's go."

"What are you doing, Sir?" said Priestly.

"Pursuing," said De Groot. "Pursuing, Sergeant Priestly."

"Wait for recon, Sir."

From the opposite direction, halfway up the hill, came a cascade of rifle fire punctuated by two grenade bursts.

"Third platoon," said Priestly.

De Groot looked north toward the new fire then back across the paddies. "Can you take care of things here, Sergeant Priestly?"

"I can, Sir, but—"

With his left mitten, De Groot beckoned to Marshall. He pointed at Kim, still huddled in position. "You two. Follow me."

De Groot turned toward the mini-village across the paddies to their rear and stepped off at a lope.

As Marshall put his rifle at port arms and chased after De Groot, he heard Priestly yell, "You too, DiMaggio."

Ahead, De Groot's hood and helmet bobbed, arching high each time he hurdled a berm. The hooches of the mini-village increased in size. A human figure came into focus and screeched. The apparition and screech seared Marshall from throat to anus, but adrenaline, not panic, coursed through his veins. Still on the run, Marshall leveled his rifle and pushed the safety forward.

"Civilian," yelled De Groot.

Jesus. The screech, Marshall realized, belonged to a woman. He lifted his rifle and reset the safety.

De Groot stopped. Marshall stopped, breathing in gulps, feeling warm for the first time that night. Kim and DiMaggio came alongside. More villagers appeared in front of them.

Kim called out in Korean. Good idea, thought Marshall, bringing a KATUSA. Not planned, but a good idea. Kim stepped toward the villagers and said, "*Miguniyo.*" American soldiers here.

The screeching woman cried and pointed. Several men talked over her, pointing, same as the woman, at a thatch-roofed hooch off to the left, in the direction of the road.

Kim said, "Woman in hooch, Sir, with kids, and Joe Chink come in."

The villagers continued talking as Kim spoke to De Groot. "She cry and say don't kill us. Joe Chink say, go on, get out."

"Is he alone in there?" said De Groot.

Kim spoke to the woman. "*Ye, ye,*" she said. She put her hand on her chest and said a few more words.

"All alone, Sir." Kim put a mitten across his chest. "Hurt bad, Sir."

De Groot looked sideways at Marshall and DiMaggio. He looked back to Kim and said, "Private Kim, get over here." Kim stepped away from the villagers and formed a rank with Marshall and DiMaggio.

De Groot said, "We'll cross the front of the hooch in line formation, me first. Maintain interval. Keep your weapons pointed toward the hooch. Ready?"

DiMaggio said, "Sir, is Sergeant Boyle going to be okay?"

De Groot, who had started to turn toward the hooch, turned back and said, "Private Russo, Sergeant Boyle is dead. Didn't you see him?"

That's a riot, thought Marshall, the lieutenant's the only one in the platoon who calls DiMaggio by his real name.

"Yessir," said DiMaggio.

De Groot's voice rose an octave. "Did he look alive to you?"

"No, Sir."

"Then doesn't it stand to reason if he's not alive, he's dead?"

"Yessir."

Marshall didn't fault the lieutenant for his peevishness. It had been a tough night, and here's DiMaggio retarding their combat operation with a stupid question. De Groot started to turn, stopped midway, and said, "Dammit, Private Russo, keep your mind on your mission."

"Yessir."

De Groot completed his turn and advanced on the hooch. Kim followed at a two-meter interval, trailed by DiMaggio and Marshall. The area in front of the hooch looked like a courtyard, flat and open. De Groot sidestepped along the outer edge of the courtyard, keeping his rifle pointed at the hooch. The enlisted men followed his example, sidestepping, rifles leveled. Marshall slipped his finger inside the trigger guard and pushed the safety forward.

De Groot signaled a halt.

Marshall examined the hooch, a free-standing mud-thatch-wood affair with a narrow veranda, twelve meters away. The wall above the veranda had one sliding door, offset to the right, and no windows. Marshall didn't know the lieutenant's plan but thought, if that door slides the least, I'm emptying a magazine into it.

De Groot whispered. "Move apart. Stay at an angle to the door. Out of the line of fire."

Marshall sidestepped to the right until he was off-center from the door by twenty degrees. To his left, Kim and DiMaggio went into kneeling firing positions. Marshall dropped his right knee to the ground, rested his left elbow on his left knee, and pointed his rifle at the door of the hooch.

De Groot stood mute on the far left, maybe listening, maybe working on his plan. Marshall heard nothing, not from the hooch, not from themselves, not from the civilians. De Groot stepped forward. He took three more steps, looked down, and kicked at the ground. He shifted his rifle to his left hand, bent, and picked up a stone that half filled his right mitten. Marshall pulled the butt of his rifle into his shoulder and leaned his right cheek against the thumb of his right mitten.

De Groot hefted the stone once, letting it bounce in his mitten, then cocked his elbow and let it fly.

As soon as the stone thudded off the door, before it even fell away, bullets splintered the door from inside. They made the same rattling sound Marshall had heard back on the road, different from the thuds of an M14.

"Fire," yelled De Groot. "Return fire."

The butt of Marshall's rifle slammed into his right shoulder as the muzzle jumped and a shell ejected. The rifle roared again and again, semi-automatic, a pull of the trigger, a bark and a recoil, a spent shell flying into the night. Marshall looked over the sights of the rifle, both eyes open, not assessing damage, just putting bullets downrange, his colleagues to the left doing the same.

Marshall failed to feel a recoil. He pulled the trigger again and again. No recoil, no bark. How long had this been going on? Marshall dropped the butt of the rifle from his shoulder and looked into an open breech. He fumbled with his right mitten against the magazine latch, and the empty magazine fell away. He ripped off his mitten with his teeth and pulled a fresh magazine from his ammo pouch.

The night had gone quiet again. Kim and DiMaggio must be reloading too. Marshall looked toward what remained of the door. The lieutenant wasn't shooting. Joe wasn't shooting. Marshall pushed a fresh magazine into the bottom of the breech and released the bolt. He grabbed his mitten and pulled it over his frozen hand.

"Cease fire," De Groot called.

Marshall heard motors. Peering left, he made out the dots of blackout lights, jeeps feeling their way across the paddies by way of a wide berm. Jeeps with pipe-mounted M60 machine guns. Raptors. Recon.

De Groot walked toward the lead jeep, waving his arms. The jeep stopped six meters short of the left side of the hooch.

"We got one cornered," said De Groot.

The gunner centered his M60 on the side wall of the hooch. Marshall couldn't make out the gunner's face, didn't know if it belonged to doofus, but it surrounded the flame of a cigarette. *Hot shit, riding into combat with a smoke hanging from his mouth.*

• • • •

WITH A LULL IN THE shooting, Jun-seok's thoughts wandered to the toothless cook and how subsequent encounters had gone better, and how he loved her. Then the shooting started anew but from the right. Bullets entered through the side wall at a fast, even cadence, a rat-a-tat, bursts of six, with yellow streaks from tracer ammunition. A machine gun, a thirty-caliber or an M60. Jun-seok called out to the Yankees: "You're shooting high. Adjust your elevation." Then laughed as he considered the irony of his utterance: attempting to instruct the enemy in his destruction.

Jun-seok's eyelids slumped. A second later, they flickered open to a terrifying thought, that the Americans would find him passed out and take him alive for torture and exhibition. He pulled off his right mitten, fumbled under his jacket, and extracted a grenade. As he pulled off his left mitten with his teeth, Jun-seok worried about the consequences of the mission's failure for his parents. But the consequences would be far worse if he were taken alive.

Jun-seok hooked his left forefinger through the ring of the grenade pin and yanked. He hoped Yoon had made it through the Yankee line. One of us must get back. He relaxed the fingers of his right hand until the grenade spoon flipped free and the striker clicked over, igniting the four-and-a-half second fuse.

Jun-seok placed the grenade to the side of his face above the right cheekbone, his movements mechanical, knowing this was no time to falter. He parted his lips and widened his mouth, keeping his teeth together. He made the fierce face.

• • • •

MARSHALL WATCHED THE machine gun emit a burst of six bullets, two of them yellow-white tracers. A second burst of five, a third of six. Marshall shifted his eyes to the center of the hooch. Tracers disappeared inside the left wall and streamed out the right. Marshall looked right toward the main part of the village. *Watch out, people, get your asses down.*

A second jeep pulled alongside the first. Two machine guns fired into the hooch.

Chapter Twenty-one: January 1968, Masan-ri

Eun-ae awoke on her back staring at dust motes in the faint light. In-soo had already gone out. Eun-ae slid open the door of their room, stepped into rubber shoes, then stepped down to the rear of the store. She got diesel flowing into the stove and struck a match. Outside, In-soo appeared with two buckets of water on a balancing pole. He squatted and set the buckets on the ground. As Eun-ae placed the medium-sized vat on the stove, In-soo came through the door stamping his feet and clapping his hands. He brought in one bucket, then the other.

"Any news?" said Eun-ae.

"Some guys just came through from the police checkpoint. There was a big fight last night. They got some of the guerrillas."

"Who got them?"

"The Americans. The guerrillas got some of them too. That's what I heard."

Eun-ae pictured the two boys from yesterday with the jeep, the black soldier and the tall soldier with eyeglasses. "Where are the Americans now?"

"They're stretched along the road to Pobwon-ni. From the checkpoint down." In-soo held his hands over the stove. "I hope they're enjoying this fine weather."

Eun-ae hung up the medium-sized vat and pulled down the large one with two side handles and a thirty-liter capacity. She positioned it on the stove and carried over the two buckets of water. As she poured, she said, "In-soo, we need more water."

"How much are you making? Are you feeding an army?"

"Sort of. I'm thinking of taking some cocoa to the Americans. It's not much, but it's something, a hot drink in the morning."

"What? Don't be foolish. They have their own commissary. They have more than we do."

Eun-ae knew that. Still she went to the shelves for chocolate powder, powdered milk, and sugar.

"How are you going to carry that?" said In-soo.

"The children are big enough to help. I'll use the cart to get it down the road."

"I forbid it," said In-soo.

"You what?" Eun-ae turned and put her hands on her hips. "Who died and made you emperor?"

In-soo took a step toward Eun-ae and raised a finger. "So what now? My wife is taking up work as a Yankee whore?"

Eun-ae stepped back, feeling the sting of salt in her eyes. *Why would he say that? Is that what he thought? That she would sell her body to the Americans?*

In-soo picked up the two buckets, turned, and went out. Ten minutes later, Eun-ae saw him lowering the buckets, now slopping with fresh water, in front of the door. By the time she got outside, he had disappeared into the repair shop.

Eun-ae thought about the Americans as she heated the water and stirred in the powdered ingredients. It was true, they had their own commissaries and messes, better than what the Koreans had. But when would their messes provide hot drinks for the soldiers in the field? And true, it was little more than a gesture. A cup of cocoa was not the difference between life and death.

Eun-ae licked the stirring spoon.

As for In-soo's mouth, that was his problem. She knew correctness from indiscretion. How could he say that?

Outside, Eun-ae called for her children. She had formed a plan. She and her son, ten-year-old Jin-ho, would lug the vat. Her daughter, nine-year-old Jung-hee, would carry the dipper and dispense the cocoa.

The two-wheel cart appeared in the street, hauled from the garage by In-soo, who averted his gaze.

"Papa," said Jin-ho, "we're going to see the Americans!"

"This is not a pleasure trip," said Eun-ae. "This is work."

"I can work," said Jin-ho.

"I can work, too," said Jung-hee.

Eun-ae, Jin-ho, and Jung-hee entered the store and walked to the stove. Eun-ae and Jin-ho each grabbed a handle and dragged the vat off the stove. They held it above the floor, catching their breath and strength. Then, with stiff steps, they marched the lidded vat, three quarters full, to the door. Jung-hee, carrying the dipper, opened the door, and out slopped the vat between Eun-ae and Jin-ho.

"Here," said In-soo, "let me help you with that."

He grabbed one handle and, with Eun-ae and Jin-ho on the other, hefted the vat to the body of the cart. As they released the handles, Eun-ae and In-soo stood facing each other.

"So," said In-soo, "I wanted to let you know: I've been thinking it over, and I'm not opposed to this idea."

"And?" said Eun-ae.

In-soo coughed. "And, well, it's a good thing to do. After all is said and done, the Americans are here to help us."

"And?" said Eun-ae.

In-soo waved his arms. "And you know how it goes. Sometimes I get excited and say things I shouldn't." Eun-ae maintained a petulant face and In-soo added, "And so I retract anything I shouldn't have said."

Eun-ae smiled.

• • • •

EUN-AE TOOK THE CART traces and pulled while Jin-ho and Jung-hee pushed. Two kilometers of level road passed, Eun-ae stopping short of the three-corner intersection and the road to

Pobwon-ni. She looked south across the rice paddies at a string of American infantrymen in parkas and helmets, some huddling for warmth, some standing and stretching, some talking, others sleeping, others smoking.

Eun-ae and Jin-ho lifted the vat from the cart and hauled it with half-steps across the uneven, frozen ground of the first paddy, Jung-hee trailing with the dipper. These Americans differed so much from each other in appearance. This first one, eighteen or nineteen years old, had a long white face under his trooper hat, hood, and helmet, with a thin nose and blue eyes. He sat with knees up, back against a berm, watching Eun-ae and the children approach.

Eun-ae pointed at the dipper and made a drinking motion. The soldier didn't catch on for a second, then widened his eyes, pulled off a mitten, and rummaged through a rucksack next to him. He extracted a tin canteen cup, replaced his mitten, and held out the cup, blue eyes fixed on Eun-ae.

Eun-ae lifted the lid from the vat, and Jung-hee dipped.

"Not all the way to the top," said Eun-ae. "That's it. Now pour it into his cup with one motion. That's it."

The soldier pulled the cup toward his body with both mittens. He said the Korean word for thank you. *Komapsumnida.*

"*Ye, ye,*" said Eun-ae. Yes, yes, don't get too excited, I'm not your mother, or your girlfriend.

Eun-ae and Jin-ho lifted the vat and moved toward the next soldier, already scrambling for his canteen cup. The threesome worked their way south along the line of soldiers in the rice paddies. Eun-ae couldn't help feeling bad for them. Everyone was saying this winter was the coldest in memory, and here these boys were living on the frozen ground. Eun-ae wondered if any of them had been involved in the shooting last night.

The paddies ended, and Eun-ae and the children entered sloping woods, tilting down both parallel to the road and toward it. The footing was tricky, with Eun-ae and the children sidestepping on the double-sloping terrain, but the vat was lighter.

Through the thin, leafless trees, Eun-ae noticed a commotion on the road. Soon she and the children were abreast of it. They poured cocoa for a soldier sitting, watching the proceedings below, then turned and watched themselves. Three jeeps sat in the road, two pointing south and one north. Next to the north-facing jeep stood a soldier in jacket, gloves, and helmet, with a pistol on his belt. Important, Eun-ae thought, at least forty years old, no doubt an officer of some substance. Eun-ae wondered how he stayed warm, then noticed a parka in the passenger seat of the jeep.

The officer walked around the front of his jeep and stepped into the shallow ditch that bordered the near side of the road. He went down on his left knee and pointed with his right hand. Eun-ae followed his hand and saw the object of the commotion, a Korean boy on his back in the ditch. He wore a trooper hat with lowered ear flaps, brushed green shirt and pants, and sneakers. Eun-ae couldn't get over his face. No older than Jin-ho, she thought at first, but then decided, no, just a baby face, mid-twenties. Eun-ae could not help thinking of the young man's mother and how she would be missing that baby face.

The American officer in the ditch pointed and smiled, and Eun-ae realized he was posing. On the road, to the north, uphill, another soldier aimed a camera.

"Mama, look," said Jin-ho. "They got one."

"There are better things to look at," said Eun-ae. "Watch your footing."

"I wonder how they got him. Did they shoot him? Maybe a grenade." Jin-ho made the motion of pulling the pin from a grenade.

"We don't know how we got him," said a voice behind them.

Eun-ae turned to see a KATUSA with tin cup in hand. He stepped down through fallen leaves and crackling twigs until he was level with Eun-ae. "Hey," he said, "we appreciate you coming out like this. Bringing us a hot drink."

"It's nothing," said Eun-ae.

"It's something," said the KATUSA. "Everybody's talking about it."

Eun-ae lifted the lid from the vat and said to Jung-hee, "Give this soldier some cocoa."

As Jung-hee poured, the KATUSA said, "I didn't know what was going on. I don't think anybody did. There was yelling, but my English isn't very good."

Eun-ae turned her head toward the KATUSA. Her thoughts took a logical yet illogical turn, considering the venue, but one she couldn't help but pursue. "How," she said, "did you get into the American army without good English?" *Wouldn't it be bad if his sergeant told him to go left and he went right?*

"How does anyone get into the American army? You pull some strings."

"You're Korean," said Eun-ae with fervor. "You should be in the Korean army. That's where my husband did his service."

"Your husband's a noble man, I'm sure," said the KATUSA.

"You're very young to have such a glib mouth," said Eun-ae.

"Hey, I'm not looking to offend you. It's just that I like a softer perch." The KATUSA motioned toward the road with his canteen cup. "It looks like they've got enough pictures."

Eun-ae looked back toward the road. The American officer had returned to his jeep and pulled his parka over his shoulders. As the jeep pulled away, Eun-ae noticed the tall soldier with glasses—who had been in Masan-ri the day before—standing in the road, his rifle slung over his right shoulder, his jaw and cheeks tinted with a light red stubble.

The KATUSA said, "They're letting civilian traffic through."

Indeed, from the south, from the direction of Pobwon-ni, a minibus crawled up the hill. As it neared, the driver downshifted to a kilometer per hour, and the vehicle tilted west as the passengers from the right side crammed left to see the dead Choson. The driver, a cigarette hanging from his mouth, smiled and gave the tall American soldier a thumbs-up sign with his left hand. The American looked at the driver without expression then turned away.

"You didn't tell us what happened," said Jin-ho to the KATUSA.

"It's not much of a story, little brother. I heard shots from down the road, from the next platoon. Then a few minutes later, the guys around me start shooting, so I start shooting."

Eun-ae motioned for Jin-ho to lift the vat. The KATUSA continued talking. "It was crazy. Two grenades went off. Then everything went quiet again. We didn't even know we got him."

"Didn't know?" said Eun-ae.

"Not until daylight. Then one of our guys sees him in the ditch."

Eun-ae, Jin-ho, and Jung-hee moved on, working their way downhill until they came out of the trees onto level ground with rice paddies in front of them and the road two meters to their left. Across the road, more paddies. To the oblique right, this side of the road, at a distance, a cluster of huts, a small village. Eun-ae looked in the vat—a few cupfuls left.

To her immediate front squatted two soldiers, the first Caucasian but with a dark complexion and a flirtatious smile. Eun-ae ignored the smile as Jung-hee dipped and doled. The soldier next to him looked more Russian than American.

Beyond them, two more soldiers lifted their canteen cups. Eun-ae recognized the Negro soldier who had driven the jeep the day before. She was glad to see he was okay. The other soldier was a KATUSA.

Eun-ae and Jin-ho advanced with the vat, trailed by Jung-hee with the dipper. Eun-ae stopped as she realized they were crossing another soldier's position. At her feet, in a neat stack, lay a rucksack, belt, and harness. Across the rucksack lay a rifle with the magazine removed. Eun-ae looked around. Maybe he had gone off for a call of nature. But why stack his gear?

Eun-ae said to the KATUSA, "*Ee saram yeogi ubseoyo?*" Isn't this person here?

The KATUSA looked at the stacked gear then Eun-ae. He shook his head.

"*Ubsumnida.*"

About the Author

Robert Perron is the author of the novel *The Blue House Raid* and the short story collection *Wasteland and Other Stories*. His short stories have appeared in numerous literary journals. His past life includes military service, a career in high tech, marriages, and children. Today he bounces between New Hampshire and New York City, where he stays with his longtime girlfriend.

Read more at https://robertperron.com.

www.ingramcontent.com/pod-product-compliance
Lightning Source LLC
Chambersburg PA
CBHW050719180626
46814CB00002B/517